Blood Kin

Blood Kin

A Novel

Mark Powell

The University of Tennessee Press / Knoxville

TENNESSEE PETER TAYLOR
BOOK AWARD PRIZE FOR THE NOVEL

Co-sponsored by the Knoxville Writers' Guild and the University of Tennessee Press, the Peter Taylor Prize for the Novel is named for one of the South's most celebrated writers—the author of acclaimed short stories, plays, and the novels *A Summons to Memphis* and *In the Tennessee Country.* The prize is designed to bring to light works of high literary quality, thereby honoring Peter Taylor's own practice of assisting other writers who cared about the craft of fine fiction.

Library of Congress Cataloging-in-Publication Data

Powell, Mark, 1976–
Blood kin : a novel / Mark Powell.— 1st ed.
        p. cm.
ISBN 1-57233-546-7 (acid-free paper)
1. Rural families—Fiction. 2. South Carolina—Fiction. I. Title.
PS3616.O88B58 2006
813'.6—dc22   2006004521

For Mamma and Daddy

Think not that I come to send peace on earth: I came not to send peace, but a sword. For I am come to set a man at variance against his father, and the daughter against her mother, and the daughter in law against her mother in law. And a man's foes shall be they of his own household.

Matthew 10: 34–36

Contents

Part One

Absence

From his rocking chair on the porch Bobby Thorton could see the gaunt figure coming down the drive, walking in and out of fans of dust, a frail shadow on the hard earth. He smiled, couldn't help not to, then ran his tongue back and forth across his false teeth, settling them. Damn if they didn't fit poorly. The figure drew closer, and Bobby leaned forward, elbows on knees, thumbs hooked in the galluses of his overalls. The dog stirred. Shitfire, he thought. The dead do walk.

The man stopped with one ragged Keds sneaker on the bottom step, a little flap of duct tape peeling back to reveal a tear in the canvas. A smile creased Bobby's face.

"Well, well, well. I'll be damned if it ain't James Burden," he said. He folded a copy of *Field & Stream* on his chest. "How do, stranger."

Around them migrant workers were unloading off two idling trucks, men helping women, passing down blankets and cardboard suitcases that spilled in their hands. The dog was back asleep in a shallow depression by an apple crib.

"Didn't rightly expect to see you up here again," said Bobby. He licked his lips, stood, eased away from the balustrade. His hands were rivered with pale blue veins, and he seemed not to know what to do with them. "Said, didn't expect to see you again."

"I heard you," said James.

"Well, that was never in question."

"Them your new help, Bobby?" James nodded at the migrant workers.

"Them would be the ones. Now you want to sit and explain things to me or just stand there like some damn question-asking fool?"

They sat on the front porch while the now-empty trucks turned slowly—forward, reverse, forward again—then ground back up the road, a scrim of dust rising behind them. The last of the migrants filed down the path past the shed where an International Harvester tractor sat, on down toward the bunkhouses.

"Great war hero returns. What? On a bus? A train? By Southern Rail. Lazarus done went and climbed outta the grave. I don't think it took him but four days but hell, you made it. Shall I count thy blessings?" Bobby laughed. "First in, last out. Do let me count thy blessings, stranger." He looked at James and shook his head. "God Almighty, Sharon ain't gonna believe seeing you. I'll tell you that right now."

"She in there?"

"No. She's out. Be back directly though."

They both nodded. Bobby's tongue took a last swipe across his teeth.

"Shit if you don't look skinny, James."

"Got bout half a stomach is all."

"That ain't what I heard. I heard you got bout one-fucking-third."

And he kept laughing there on the porch while the sun burst like a giant heart against the plumb line of the horizon, while the last of the evening sung itself to sleep.

That night, but just that night, James slept inside, on the couch in the front room, sweating beneath a blanket that smelled of mothballs and machine oil. In the morning he lay still while sunlight painted the thinly veiled window, watched the silhouette of a spider climb the glass. Bobby had passed through hours ago, leaving before first light, all sharp, radiant edges, crisp and angry in the milky dark.

Sharon had not come home.

James had not dreamed.

Now he lay flat on his back studying the low drop ceiling, the head of an oscillating fan tilted toward him, feeling tremors run through the house— the tractor outside. He waited, shook his body, writhed for a moment beneath the thin blanket. The springs groaned but the couch was steady, did not shift, and that was better, he felt better. So he laid there, waiting, listening to the diesel coughs and grinding of gears.

When it grew distant, he rose, dressed, walked into the back room, where a jelly jar sat atop a dusty RCA TV, and lapped his belt just below his left bicep. He was careful with the syringe, pumping his fist until the vein swelled ink-blue, probed for the soft skin then slipped it in like a lover, washed his face, walked outside.

From the porch he could see the migrant workers down among the trees, color flung amid the dung and green so that the world seemed bright and somehow foreign. The tractor moved along the narrow rows, lifting with its hydraulic tongue a wooden crib they'd filled with apples. It climbed the hill to the shed, emptied the crib, and repeated the trip. Black loam fell from the cleats of the tires. James waited. It was after eleven and already the sun had burned away the morning mist, leaving behind a film of humidity. Across the yard, a pattern of grackles came and went, restless and impulsive, moving now and then as a flock, finned against the metallic sky and chattering in a foreign tongue. All the while the morphine moved gently. A light sweat broke across his shoulders.

Around twelve Bobby climbed off the tractor and walked onto the porch, mopping his head with a rag, a plastic grocery bag full of okra in one hand.

"My daddy had a thing to say about people that laid around in bed all day while the sun was up shining," he said.

"Did he now."

"Sure did. Said them people ain't got but one thing on their minds."

"This conversation don't interest me none, Bobby."

"Never said what that one thing was though. Went off and died before he could ever explain himself. So here I am asking you."

"Honestly, it don't."

"I wouldn't allow that it did, partner."

"Can you take me on to work?"

"I'm asking you what it is you laid around all morning thinking about."

"I'm being serious here, Bobby."

"Hell, me too."

Bobby sat, dropped the bag of okra between his feet. He took a little frosted cake wrapped in cellophane from his pocket and tore the plastic with one eyetooth.

"You hungry?"

"Not really," said James.

Down below, the migrant workers sat cross-legged in the shade of the bunkhouses.

"They eat two-handed," said Bobby. "You ever notice that?"

"I'll come on for whatever it is you pay them."

"Ah, hell, James. This ain't work for no white man. You better off flipping burgers or something, my opinion."

"Work's work."

Bobby dug at something in his ear. "Yeah, well, my daddy said that too. And Lord knows it's tough to find work these days." He wiped his finger along his pant leg, studied the six-sided cake. "Why don't you go and do something with your brothers, why don't you? Ain't one of them working with your daddy up on the Whitewater or something?"

James shrugged.

"You don't know?"

"I been gone a long time, Bobby."

"And you don't know that your own brother Enis is working up on the river for some timber outfit, your daddy too?"

"That's exactly what I'm telling you."

"You have been gone awhile. Consider yourself enlightened. You don't have to say thanks." He bit the cake. "What about Roy then, know anything about Roy?"

James shook his head.

"They God Almighty. Clearly we are having some difficulty communicating here, my friend. You sure you didn't come back with one-third a eardrum too?"

"I could drive that tractor for you, Bobby."

He seemed to consider this.

"I know you could," he said. "I know you could."

"I don't think she knows you're back, if that's what's worrying you, James."

"Who?"

"Shit. Who do you think, partner? Your wife or ex, or whatever you call her. Eleanor I'm talking about. She ain't coming up. Not Sharon neither, I fear." Bobby stood jostling the change in his pocket, stepped from the door frame onto the shadowed porch, pulled the screen door shut behind him. "Bugs getting in," he said.

James nodded, though there was no way Bobby could see this. Night had fallen and it was full dark, no breeze. Heat lightning broke along the eastern rim of the mountains, and now and then it lit the yard. Otherwise darkness.

"She said some things leaving. Sharon did. It don't hardly bear repeating."

James looked at the sky. "It's gonna storm."

Bobby sat in the rocker beside him. "You see this?" he asked. In his right hand he held a porcelain dolphin arcing above what appeared to be a sea of blue quartz. "She left this. Forgot just this one."

"How's your girl Sue Ellen, Bobby?"

"Married," Bobby said. "I don't never see her."

James looked away. They sat for a while, the dolphin resting in Bobby's lap.

"I heard in Hawaii they had a train station full of caskets you had to go to and sign off whether or not they had the right fella in the box."

James shook his head. "Where's that TV of yours? You take it inside?"

"In a train station or a airport or something," said Bobby. "A train station, I believe I heard."

"I've never been to Hawaii, Bobby, so I wouldn't know. But I'll say with some confidence it wasn't a train station, not in Hawaii, at least."

"Well, I reckon an airport then."

"Ain't there nothing to drink in there?"

"Let me tell you, James, a couple of years back old Mary Bowhite's—I don't know if you remember her—but her boy had to go up to Camp Lejeune in North Carolina. Get a look at his nephew. Got all shot up in Hue City or somewhere. That whole Tet thing they had on the TV."

"Ain't you got nothing to drink, Bobby?"

"Said it was a pure T mess up there. Said there was women crying the like he'd never seen. He said it set him to studying—war, dying, things like that. Said he wound up back at church for a couple of weeks then went back to drinking, and here he'd dried out for years."

"Seriously. Ain't you even a little thirsty?"

Lightning flared. The breeze was beginning to stir, to ride over out over the fields.

"Likely there's something inside," said Bobby.

The screen door cawed then slapped shut. James went barefoot down the footpath toward what would soon be a bonfire. He paused, looked back at the house, which from a distance seemed nothing more than a cobble of boards, block and copper pipes, a string of wire running from a pole to the roof. Slashes of paint were knocked from the side as if by whip or animal, and the house lurched like a shanty boat moored along the banks of some dark river. Old Gus followed him down past the shed, but turned away to find sleep atop a piece of aluminum that radiated the day's heat. James, too, paused there, the warmth seeping through him, then went on past a spill of rotten vegetables that had drawn a whirlpool of orbiting yellow jackets and blowflies.

The screen door opened. He could see Bobby peering out over the yard, his left hand held level above his eyes, a pint of J&B in his right.

"James," he hissed. "James?"

"Down here."

"Oh, for shit's sake, partner. What are you doing?"

"I'll be back in a second."

"Why we whispering?"

"I ain't."

James walked on. So far the bonfire was only a small heap of broken pal-
lets, a single tendril of gray smoke rising like kite string. When he drew near,
the migrants were quiet for a moment then went on talking, ignoring him,
perhaps thirty of them, men and women and children of all ages. He could
smell that they had been cooking something, could smell the flowery scent
of citronella. A man came up and laid his hand on James's forearm.

"Hello," said James. "Hola."

"Hola, amigo. Hablas español?"

James shook his head no.

The man nodded, held up one finger in the universal gesture of patience,
waved forward a small girl, whispered something in her ear. She blushed, and
turned her glossy black eyes away from him. The man eased her forward, one
hand in the small of her back, the other brushing wings of hair from her face.

"My father asks that you eat with us," she said.

She spoke with no accent, in the flat tones of someone from Utah or
Nevada.

"Oh, no, tell him gracias, but no. I've eaten already, thank you. No tengo
hambre."

"No tengo hambre," said the man, nodding. He smoothed his mustache.
The girl whispered something else to the man, who nodded.

"Thank you though," said James. "Muchas gracias."

"De nada. De nada."

"He says you are welcome," said the girl.

James spread his bedroll just beyond the reach of the arc light suspended between the screen doors of the two bunkhouses, rubbed Deet along his arms
and throat, in the canals of his ears. The cicadas started up, the whippoorwills. Sheets of heat lightning continued to break, though there was no thunder, only an absent pause in which the world seemed to hold her breath. He
slept with his boots on, the ground beneath him solid and unmoving, and
that night, in the arms of morphine and sleep, they took him again. His lips
grew cold. Someone crawled forward and whispered: "Looks like shit out
there. They're coming. Motherfucker, they're coming." He knew the voice,
remembered. "It looks bad. It looks real bad." James peered over the ridge to
see columns of men advancing black on white like words across a page. A

moment later they heard the cold, steady popping of automatic weapons, and then the shrill of 120mm mortar shells. They fell back then, leaving the reservoir behind them, crossing from ridge to ridge, trying like animals to claw their way into the frozen ground. Spits of snow falling slant, the hills patched with bare rock outcroppings.

"I think we all die here," someone said. "I think we do."

They walked backward, a hasty rearguard action, staring into the face of something barely namable, beyond grammar, beyond the word. You could hear nothing in the snow, everything in the wind. Time crept. Morning. Day. The sun rose without heat and somehow James felt safe, feeling that nothing could happen there in the bright, cold daylight. Afternoon they stopped in a shallow ravine and studied the compass, maybe twenty of them, the rest of the platoon with the main body, limping toward Hungnam and the Sea of Japan some seventy miles away. One-twenties continued to fall, though with no accuracy. A man slipped around back and was dropped almost immediately. A single muffled pop, a pink mist, and his helmet cracked like the shell of a turtle, all metal and brain. Then another pop, the echo like the call and response of remembered sermons. They sat and waited, and James thought, well, here is what I wanted. Here is what I came for. A lieutenant stood and was shot in the mouth, and they found his broken teeth in the frozen sand. Well. After that they gave up and that night were whisked across the 38th Parallel, prisoners of war, eleven of them, with twenty-one collective legs, twenty arms. Two bled to death before dawn, another froze, and in the morning the eight survivors were loaded on a train headed north and bound for the Yalu River.

Well, James thought.

Now he had come back home to Oconee County to die among his people, to feel as if he had people—the fantasy he kept locked away from reason, the intrusion of his dream life: he knew all along he had no one, though it wasn't that he had forfeited his birthright with years of absence. He had always been a stranger here, as much a stranger with others as with himself. He thought of the pale, blue-eyed Jesus who hung above his father's bed. Another barefoot wanderer, alone among kin.

After the war, after his convalescence up north, James had come south and spent three days in town tracking both his wife, Eleanor, and his mother. He had felt like a bandit, waiting all day across the street from the Five and Dime. Eleanor had never showed, and he'd crept into their backyard and watched her lying in bed. All day she lay there. She would lick her lips, blink.

Nothing else. He watched a fly circle. He stood blowing ghosts of breath on the window, crouched in the backyard, his feet sinking into the soft earth beneath where the spigot dripped. The grass had been cut recently and blades clung to his shoes. Physical things, touch, pain, but no emotion, no thought. That lodestone—what it is to be human—he had lost it somewhere that day south of Chosin.

He walked away and caught a ride up the mountain. The dogs had greeted him, no one else. Probably his father was out visiting shut-ins or making rounds at the hospital, Roy at school. But his mother—she should have been there. It was a cold, overcast day, a bone-gray sky hazy with mist, and she should have been inside with little Enis. But only the dogs. James stood on the steps scratching behind their ears, then walked inside and crept on cats feet from room to room.

In his old bedroom he found his .410 wrapped in a quilt and buried in a chest. His father would not allow guns in the house, but James knew his mother had hid this, a single last thing, a single memory in the harsh glare of absence.

In the bathroom he undressed and drew a bath. There was no alcohol in the house, so he settled for a cup of coffee he balanced on the lowered toilet seat. He soaked for maybe an hour, waiting. He wanted her to come home, his mother, to catch him there, to force him back into the life he was abandoning. But the only voice was the wind that came guttering through the stove flue like a trapped animal. The water drained and he sat naked and shriveled. A few stray hairs ringed the grate. I am no longer a boy, he thought, then stood and dressed. He left the coffee cup in the sink. If she could read signs, his mother, she would sense something, she would feel his presence, the dark grounds in the cup, the smell of his hands, his thumbprint worn in a nub of soap.

When he came back out onto the porch, the dogs loped over, and James put one finger to his lips to signal quiet. "Make it our secret," he told one. "Good boy. Don't tell nobody now. Good boy."

The next day, his last in town, he watched Eleanor leave the house then followed her. It was like a game to him, but desperate, if there can be such a thing. He couldn't get too close, but he wanted to be close enough to her that their paths might intersect, that their lives blunder back into the chaos of the everyday, the simple routines that hew like muscle to bone, the little burdens that give meaning.

Up Main Street, his storefront reflection following hers like two twinned spirits, he'd come as close as fifteen or so feet before she turned into a diner. He waited on a bench three stores down, knowing she would continue on her way past him, find him. Everything would change and then there would be no change. He heard the bell on the door sound and put his head down. After a moment he looked up to see her striding in the opposite direction, growing smaller down the walk. There should have been a voice then: *go,* go after her, talk to her, start over, but there wasn't. Only the wind, the idling cars. Maybe if he'd strained hard enough he might have heard the tick of the timers in the traffic lights, maybe the sound of her shoes on the sidewalk, but no voice.

That was a little death, he realized later, that silence where there should have been noise. I am no longer a boy, he thought. But neither am I a man.

He thumbed a ride to Clemson and bought a bus ticket for Birmingham, as far as his money would take him. In Alabama he posted a change of address form: his disability pay would now go to Eleanor. He wanted her to have it, he told himself. It was the least he could do. But the money was an abstraction. He wanted her to see his name, to think of him at least once a month, to know a part of him went on living among kin.

After that, there were not so much years as seasons, hot and cold, summer and winter, following jobs and the weather up and down the central valley of California, up to Alaskan canneries, down to Guatemala to pick bananas. He worked on a road crew in Texas, spent a week in jail in Arizona when he couldn't make bail for vagrancy, cut timber through the Pacific Northwest. Twice made it as far east as Atlanta before turning back. Every time he had more than a few dollars he gave them away, walking that tightrope—to have or have not. His only need was morphine or some derivative. The gospel of poverty, the ascetic, the nomadic saint willing to lose his life in order to find it. Except I wasn't looking for anything, he thought. Only age and infirmity finally sent him home. A long winter bout with the flu had lingered on into the summer, until he was certain he would die.

Lying in a flophouse bed, a slim stream of blood dancing down his forearm, he'd hacked up whitish clumps he figured to be lung tissue and thought, You were only thirty-three. I'm so much older. I can't do this forever. I can't keep on. He wanted either to die there at that moment or go home. He injected enough heroin into his arm to kill two men, and reclined back. Crucify me, he prayed. Three days later he came to in a hospital, drifted back from the ether-dreams, and woke emaciated and thirsty in a detox center, a plasma bag dripping into one arm. He chewed off his plastic wristband, found some clothes, work boots and coveralls in a closet marked JANITOR, and crept out.

Several men were huddled against the building smoking. He asked one what city this was.

"Portland," said the man.

The last place he remembered was Denver. He decided to go home. If he was going to die, he wanted to die with his illusions, among his blood kin, to give them, if not his life, at least the memory of who he'd once been. The husk of his body—that would be his offering.

James woke sweat-soaked, shivering again, a thimble of warm urine dampening his pants. He looked into the darkness: no movement, only the tree frogs calling, the evening throbbing, moist and sexual. Dark thunderheads had stacked up one behind the other, but there was no rain. A pear tree leaned against the house, sweeping a single limb back and forth against the tin roof. He sniffed the air. Now and then, odd moments, still moments, he would smell Chosin again, something tender in that pain. But not tonight. In the darkness he fumbled for a syringe, found instead a single morphine ampoule, and popped it into his thigh. In the morning he showered and drove Bobby's truck into town.

Eleven A.M. The Seneca café was empty. He bought an *Anderson Independent* and sat in the rear with his back to the door trying to read. Fifty or so hostages were still being held in the Jordanian desert after a hijacking. Someone had caught a nine-pound brown trout in the Chattooga. The football team had lost twelve to nothing to Oakway. That was about the extent of things. He folded the paper and waited. After a while a man came out of the back and said the place didn't open till noon.

"I'll just wait if that's all right."

The man walked his eyes over James. "Wait a second here. I'll be dog. Is that James Burden?"

"Hey, Marlon."

"Damn if I didn't think for sure you were dead by now, son. I'll be dog. I swear to the Lord Almighty I figured you for gone. Hey, you want me to cook you up something? I was fixin to light the grill."

"No. I appreciate it though."

"I ain't seen you in how long? Lord God, it's been years. You sure you don't want nothing to eat?"

"I'm all right."

"Oh," said Marlon, nodding, fingering a little silvery fishhook of a scar by the corner of his mouth. "No, I guess you don't. Didn't come by for the food, I don't reckon."

James shook his head.

"Well, she ain't here, son. I reckon somebody told you she was working here but she's off today. Now how bout a big hamburger steak, mushroom gravy? A Pepsi-Cola maybe?"

"That's all right. You don't know where she might be, do you?"

"Hell, I don't know, son. Home most likely."

James stood. Marlon stepped back.

"You going over there then?"

James nodded.

"Well, come back if you get hungry. Tell your daddy to stop by."

He was outside the restaurant squinting into the late morning sun before he thought to say good-bye.

He rang the bell at 152 Oak Avenue and waited. The screen door was shut but the front door open, so that he could see into the dim house. A single band of sunlight lay across the hardwood floor. Dervishes of dust stirred, settled, stirred and rose again.

"If that's the delivery man, the door's open," a voice called from the back. James opened the door and walked inside, let it slap shut loudly behind him. Little inside had changed, new curtains, maybe, green and cut from terry cloth bath towels. The couch was still against the far wall, the bookshelves empty of books. A TV sat beneath the window. He couldn't find himself in any of the pictures along the mantle.

"Gimme two minutes," she called. "Sorry."

He walked back into the bedroom and stood for a moment watching her clasp her bra, her back to him. She wore a white bra, a dark skirt, no shoes. Her arms bent behind her like frail wings, the straps of her bra cutting into the flesh of her shoulders. She reached for a blouse, and coat hangers grated across the metal closet bar. He cleared his throat.

"Christ," she said grabbing a towel off the bed to cover herself. "I told you—"

She stopped speaking upon seeing him.

"Hello, Ellie."

"It's you."

"Yeah."

"I thought—"

"I thought I'd surprise you."

"Well, you did."

James nodded.

She dropped the towel on the bed. "Go sit in the den. Let me dress."

In the kitchen he fixed a gin and water, stirring it with a spoon he found in the sink. Most of the cabinets were empty. Bunnies of dust clumped along the baseboards. A mustard-colored mold grew in the grout between wall tiles. He went and sat in the living room, waiting for her, thinking for a moment he heard tiny footsteps above him, a child's steps troubling the attic boards.

"Marlon said you weren't in today," he said when she came in. Her hair was up, and she was wearing a white blouse, fastening earrings. "You're dressed awful nice, Ellie. You look awful nice. Got your Sunday clothes on."

"You didn't come over here to give me some grief about you dying did you? I heard you were dying. That's the first thing people was talking about."

He shook his head. "We're all of us dying."

"You know what I mean."

"I ain't dying," he said after a moment. "I just look poor." He looked away. "Maybe we ought to sit and talk about little things, Ellie."

She fingered a button on her blouse. "I think I might want a drink, too," she said.

He listened to her in the kitchen fixing the drink—the knock of the cabinet, slush of tap water, the spoon dropped back into the sink.

"I have to be somewhere in just a little bit," she said when she returned.

"I could give you a ride. I got Bobby's truck. Where you going?"

"Just somewhere. I got a life, you know."

She sat on the window seat, her knees together, and sipped. "I didn't expect to see you, Jimmy."

"People keep saying that to me."

"Maybe that should tell you something." She drank. "Thinking you can just waltz in and everything be the same, nobody say a word about it. You think I ain't known for a while now you were back? You think people don't talk? Just like before, when you didn't come back. You think I didn't hear it then? 'That James,' they'd all say, 'done went and got above his raising. Got all uppity and can't be living round here.' Or, 'Oh, she couldn't give him a baby, couldn't satisfy him.' That was their favorite. That was the one that stuck. You think I couldn't read their faces? Hear what they were whispering? You think I didn't see it every time I walked out that door?" She looked down into her drink. "I was in the getting-over-it stage for a long time, Jimmy. I'm past that now."

They sat for a while drinking, occasionally rattling their glasses, the ice fast melting. The ceiling fan spun lazily, passing jagged shadows across their faces.

"I'm staying up at Bobby Thorton's place," he said after a while.

"Ain't that something. Two old men drinking away the day. Nothing sadder. Nothing in the world sadder. I heard Sharon quit him."

James nodded.

"You blame her?" She looked back into her drink. "You could still come back here, Jimmy."

He didn't answer.

"Remember that trip up to Gatlinburg?" she said. "I was thinking for some reason of that just the other day. Remember the alternator in the truck caught afire and my Uncle Bill had to come pick us up."

"That was years ago."

"I know. I think about it a lot, though." She sipped her drink, looked from it to the window, back to her drink. "You could, Jimmy. Come back, I mean. But I ain't gonna beg you. Not after all these years, I'm way past that."

"I know you are."

"I mean is that why you came back? You musta had a reason, and I know it wasn't to see your folks. I know they ain't seen you or your mamma woulda let me know. Just what is it you want here, Jimmy? You come in looking so sick, so skinny and—"

"I'm all right."

"I know you think you are, Jimmy, but—"

"I'm fine, Eleanor," he said standing. "I think you said you had to be somewhere."

"Don't go like this, Jimmy."

"Thanks for the drink. It was good to see you."

"Not like this don't."

"Like what?"

"I still wear this," she said pointing at her left ring finger. He could see now that she was near crying. "I still wear it," she said.

"I better get on."

"Jimmy—"

He pulled the door shut behind him and from the street considered the measured beating of his own heart, its quartered chambers and dense muscularity. The trip to Gatlinburg, that had been their honeymoon. And he remembered a moment, standing in the kitchenette of their room at the Rocky Top Inn, how bare the countertops had seemed, the opal white of the sink. They were dressed for a night out, a dinner of steaks, he in his father's hand-me-down suit, a blue jacket trimmed with white stitching, she in a dress of sea-green, nylons that swished when she walked, and while he was digging out the keys to his truck, she had leaned him against the empty counter and said, "Not so fast, Mr. Burden," then pushed him back, his hands behind him for balance and the late evening sun, all violet and soft, falling through the part in the curtains along the right side of her face, her hand down at his fly and then the soft weight of his penis in her hand and she was kissing his neck. He kissed her, her hand slowly waking him. The small Frigidaire in the corner had suddenly shuddered to life, sending a shiver through him. "Mrs. Burden says not so fast. There's something she wants first. Mrs. Burden says Frank's Chophouse isn't going anywhere."

They had made love there against the wall, slow, fast, the eye of him opening inside her, spilling, then missed dinner, drank rum and Cokes past midnight, sitting out on the balcony overlooking the lights of the strip, a citronella candle burning to keep away the mosquitoes. "I'd like to stay like this," she had said. He thought of that moment every day, every hour. But it was years and lifetimes ago, lost now, buried beneath strata of guilt and absence.

The street was quiet, and through the mesh of the door he could see her still sitting on the window seat, drink in hand. Her eyes were dry.

He walked through the orchard, the apples wearing bunched faces and his hands trailing behind touching them, feeling their shrunken teeth and silken hair. They wore faces of bloated disbelief, faces of guilt, outrage, fat and sagging the branches. And he knew them all.

Birds called. Overhead the sun had risen godlike but now was beginning its slow westerly slide. A jet contrail broke to wispy cottoned pieces. The clouds all silk, and James floating through a medium state, registering the seismic bursts of sound, the garbled Spanish, the tractor, walking, and then running, the limbs flaying him, down toward the glassy ribbon of the Chauga River, where he sank to his knees and the world shifted and colors met and ran and embraced and separated like late summer lovers. Apples falling behind him like rain. The water parting around him, sounding broken half words, a plaintive forgotten tongue. The river speaks, touches. The deep morphine kiss. His skin warm with light and the sudden dislocation of place. Thinking all the while: the river, again.

They'd taken him to the river twice, first as a boy, then just before he'd left, Ellie and his family trailing behind him like a dress's train. A silly, sentimental gesture: barefoot in a still cold pool of the Chauga. Looking back at his brother Roy, sneering on the bank. *Oh, Father, we pray that you will hear us now,* the voice of his father speaking into the silences, his hand sealing James's nose and lips, shifting sand beneath his feet, *hear us, we pray.* . . . He rose from his knees and waded out again, older, clothed, messy with sin and crossing not Jordan but a mountain river narrowed by late summer drought. And what was he now that he hadn't always been? A vagrant scarecrow haunting back-alley trash cans? Once, maybe. Maybe still. But welcome home. We missed you. Welcome home, soldier. And God bless the red-white-and-fucking-blue.

Evening. He dripped onto the porch where Bobby sat waiting on him, turning the mother-of-pearl handle of an antique Case knife in one hand. The TV sat on the floor, mute, the picture rolling, a bent coat hanger for rabbit ears. From the waist down James was a different color, the denim of his pants a darker blue, the eyelets of his boots gleaming.

"Your brother come by here looking for you. Enis did. Said he'd come back later. Maybe you ought and go change. Dry off some. I mean if it matters to you."

"It don't," James said. "Not really."

Bobby nodded. "You might could go see your mamma, James. I'd take that as a favor. Or least just send her word. I mean I don't know where that matters to you or not."

James shook his head. "I might wish it some other way, Bobby," he said. "Might wish that it mattered." He stood there for a moment. "We both know it don't," he said.

Madison Burden had dressed and prayed and was cooking breakfast before anyone had even considered waking. Sleep had come slowly, fitfully, and when she woke around four there was a sense of finality to the night, of morning having dawned, even though the room was cast in indigo darkness. She rose, pulled on her housecoat, and walked into the living room, where she sat before the cold hearth. The dogs knocked against the front wall, stirring, restless in the languorous heat, and she leaned back in her rocking chair trying to remember what it was that woke her. There was something there, the figure of something that wouldn't come into focus, the outline of a memory just beyond sight. It was as if she were a little girl again, barefoot down in the cotton field or corn patch, evening time with darkness just coming upon the earth, the ridged shape of the tree line becoming a single, serrated line. Everything blurred, memory and shape, meshed in color and form, and she toed that knife blade of knowing. Then she had it. It had been years ago. James was already gone, and Roy must have been fifteen, which would have made Enis nine or ten.

"Roy found it, Mamma," Enis had told her later, his voice strangled out through tears. "It was Roy's idea and I just went along with it cause he said."

Enis had been sitting in her lap, sprawled like a gangly puppet, too large, too old for such foolishness, Will was always saying, Enis's feet dragging the floor.

"I had to, Mamma."

"Hush now. It's all right."

Past the creek and up through the woods sat a house, forgotten in an abandoned pasture where the field grasses grew waist-high and locust-choked in the summer. Inside were reams of junk, clothes and scraps of newspapers pushed against the baseboards, boxes holding old candles and cooking pots. Weeds and vetch grew through gaps in the floorboards. Wasps, dirt-daubers, and hornets nested in the high corners, in bureau drawers, beneath what had once been the bathroom vanity. The house tilted with the wind, creaking like a leaky ship, a ramshackle collection of boards and sheets of silver insulation sutured with staples and roofing nails, two-by-fours, and old rotting railroad ties—all leaning as hopefully with the wind.

Enis—she was to learn later—would lie in the canyons he shaped in the grasses, marooned and sun-struck and watching the clouds drift, imagining his shape like a spindly footprint, while Roy plowed through the junk.

It was in a box hidden beneath musty quilts that he found three ancient sticks of dynamite bound in electrical tape. He found the old shrimp net in the attic. There was no question what was next.

"It'll take two sets of hands," Roy said.

Enis shook his head. "I don't want nothing to do with it. Seriously."

"Don't you do me like this, brother. You're going."

In the end, Enis—because he was Enis, because he was the youngest, her softest, because he was always and forever to agree—in the end, he had gone.

They had waited until nightfall, the sky iridescent, the woods still and filling with a silvery light that made poplars and birch trees the stark, cleansed white of bone. Beneath the moon the creek appeared still, encased in a skim of glass, flash-frozen, it seemed, so that twigs and leaves and flotsam were encysted in an imagined skin.

The net was dropped into the waters of Cane Creek, attached along the opposite bank to a poplar tree so that it served as a sort of downstream filter. Enis waited on the other bank, sucking his teeth and near crying while Roy attached a brick to the dynamite. He lit the fuse, waited—timing was everything—then dropped it and stepped away, covering his ears.

There was no great geyser of water, as Enis had expected, only a white flash, muted and deep in the bowels of the fishing hole, only the concussion he felt in his gut. Then there were fish, stunned or dead, rising to float on their sides.

"I'll be damned," said Roy. Then he had thought, And you could a been, you lucky son of a gun.

The fish appeared prismatic—a greenish-blue one moment, a silvery red the next, their feathery gills blacked with blood, still or barely flexing, eyes obsidian and bulging from their round heads. When they lifted the net, the fish were beyond counting. Creek chub. Bream. Crowned horny head like sleek muscles cut from a dark body.

"Like in the Bible," said Enis.

"It might make a man religious," said Roy. He laughed. "Shit. We get em to town it might make a man rich."

The next morning while Roy made to haul the fish wrapped in quilts in the bed of a wheelbarrow the nine miles down the mountain, Enis—because he was always and forever Enis—had confessed. An hour later their father had picked Roy up, three miles from the house and huddled on the side of the road with sixty pounds of rotting fish and ruined blankets, clots of flies and gnats circling, Roy vomiting into the gully grass and the stench of flesh hanging in the squat heat.

Punishment was swift. There seemed more than the danger of explosives here, thought Will Burden. Their father had judged this a great evil, an incipient sin that might somehow grow to unseat the natural order of things—insouciant man fashioning a new hierarchy, a new device for the taking of lives—and had quoted long passages from Leviticus before taking his strop to Roy.

I will make thine enemies my footstool, thought Maddy.

She had sat on the porch that morning listening to Will whip the boy, wondering all the while who her husband had become. He was such a gentle man, but something had risen in his eyes that morning, fear or dread, something dredged from the sink of memory and shaking him with some nameless terror. But it wasn't terror, no. It was grief. She'd sat on the porch, rocking and talking to the beagles, trying not to listen to what was happening inside, realizing slowly that what her husband feared most was the slow accumulation of sin, the grain-sized misstep that led to other, greater, missteps. He feared for his straying, because he feared becoming his own father. She felt a great sadness at the thought. She'd sat on the porch knowing that Will realized his own blood was poisoned.

So why the memory? It was something Maddy had not thought of in years, yet as she thought further, its focus drew narrow and tight. Was it that it was the last time she could remember Roy as a boy, as vulnerable and needing something beyond himself? Surely there were other times, but she could not recall them now. She let the memory fade: another vanity, another useless recollection.

Around the time the biscuits came out of the oven, her husband, William Jennings, walked in. He sat at the table, silent, and she picked up the plate of biscuits only to pause: he was praying.

"Amen," he said.

"Amen." She put the plate before him. "Catheads," she said. "Be careful, they're hot." He sat with his hands in his lap staring down at something, some spot or empty space, some orphaned memory, and Maddy thought of how many mornings he had sat like this, silent, still—God is silence, she remembered him saying that once—she thought of him sitting there, mornings, years, how the days knotted on one long cord—heart's time, more of his words—she thought of it and it comforted her. She had never realized, maybe, how much.

"I heard him stirring about. Heard him coming in last night, too. Late," he said. "And you know good and well who it was he was with."

"Now, Will."

"That girl is fifteen if she's a day, Maddy, and that boy is still living under my roof."

"She's a senior in high school, Will. She's eighteen years old, Lord. Enis told you that already."

She set out the butter and a can of King's syrup. He began to eat, pouring out the syrup then smearing a pat of butter into it, swirling it then dipping his biscuit.

"Well, however old she is, he doesn't need to be out at all hours. He needs to get up."

"I thought you said you heard him up?"

"I did," he admitted. He finished his biscuit, took two more, and wrapped them in a cloth napkin. "You've got a talent for keeping a man straight, don't you?"

"Finish your breakfast, Will."

"I'd better go."

"Well, take the thermos," she said. "What time can I look for you?"

"By six." He kissed her. "No use waiting on Enis, I reckon."

"He'll have a fit, Will. You know how he feels about you running on."

"Then he needs to start getting up. I love you."

"Love you, too."

Twenty or so minutes later Enis lurched into the kitchen, his hair on end, shirt half-tucked, and began eating as if he had no bottom.

"Don't founder yourself," said his mother. "Sitting there like a horse out to pasture. The service teach you to eat like that? No manners to speak of."

"I'm a growing boy."

He cleaned his plate, sopping up syrup with a rind of biscuit, then rose to refill it.

"Your father seems mighty worried you've been out running around with that young Abernathy girl."

"Her name is Millie, Mamma."

"Millie, then. He's worried about you and Millie."

"Why's he worried?"

"He just is, Enis. He is because that's his way. He worries. The man loves you to death but you know good and well he's a worrier."

"About what exactly is he worrying about?" Enis asked, chewing a biscuit.

"The man's your father—he's set on worrying about anything and everything that comes to mind. Things get to him, Enis. Real bad. You know as much."

"Well, you're my mother, why aren't you worried?"

"Who's to say I'm not?"

He looked at her and rolled his eyes.

"Well, let's just say I credit you with a lot more sense than your father does."

"Thanks. Or is that not a compliment?"

So much of her life was wrapped up in her sons. She watched the pickup disappear up the drive, thinking of each. Enis was her baby. If I'd lost him like I lost James, I wouldn't have lived, she thought. I wouldn't have made it. She still remembered the morning they came for her. At least once a day she thought of it, felt it flash through her like light off a polished stone: bright and sudden, but broken too. She hadn't heard the car drive up that morning, had been out back taking down the wash when the dogs had started up. It was May and the days were still cool. The clothesline beaded with dew. She'd given it a little pluck and watched the raindrops shiver away, and walked in through the house and out onto the porch to hush the dogs. Then, just the sight of the man—the very sight of him there in his khaki shirt and blue pants, the same uniform James had left in—just seeing him there in the door had crumpled her. At the mere sight, something had come loose inside her, some wild, buried grief.

"Good morning, ma'am." He had taken his hat off and held it beneath his arm, pressed against his side. "Are you Madison Burden? Mother of Private First Class James Burden?"

That was all. Down on her knees then, she drained like a sink, wept, studied the red stripe of the man's pants. She could see her face, warped and swelling, in the polished curve of his shoe. He tried to touch her. There was a chaplain with him, and he tried to touch her as well.

She crawled into the front room and locked the door, praying *Please, Jesus . . . please, Jesus, I need you now. . . . I need you to come to me now, Jesus. . . . I need for it to be somebody else. Please, Jesus. I need for it not to be my James.* The moment the prayer passed her lips she meant to recant but couldn't. She meant it; she meant it more than anything she had ever thought.

A week later word came that James wasn't dead: he was being held at a POW camp north of the 38th Parallel. The Marines meant this as good news. No one could understand why it hurt her so deeply. She feared for what might happen to him, of course, feared for what *was* happening to him. But what she realized—and what scared her most—was that her prayer had been answered: it was someone else. She knew then she'd lose him, that in whatever form he returned to her, he would not be her James, the James she had known.

She was only eighteen when he was born. Will was ten years older than her, already a widower when they'd met, and in many ways Will was a father to her, raising her up as he raised his firstborn son. Maddy and James—we were children together, she thought. She had taught James to fish, first with a cane pole along the creek, then with his first Zebco rod and flies they tied themselves. On the days Will was out visiting or locked away in his study preparing a sermon, Maddy and James would slip away. They would sit on the mossy banks and do nothing but listen, lines drifting in the water, no sound except the soft rippling, the now and then trill of a bird. She felt herself reflected in her son: he was more her than she was. They knew each other intuitively and spoke in gestures and motions. Little blond-haired boy, the skinniest baby she'd ever seen. How many hours she'd spent poking oatmeal into his closed lips or rubbing wrinkles from his closed palms, staring into his sleeping face.

She'd hear the women at the church: *Just look at him. That child is puny. Don't you feed your baby, Mrs. Burden?* He wanted no one but her and would cry in the arms of other women. *He's particular,* one would say. *He's queer.* But he was hers. She had no other. The women thought her silly and vain, though she was neither. She was once beautiful, that was true, but she was a serious woman, not the trivial, fussy thing the old Wesleyan women wanted to believe her to be.

She lived an entire lifetime with James, she felt. Something she would never be able to wholly repeat: she had been so young then, and never again would she be able to love like that, so reckless with her affection. Her love for Roy and Enis was just as deep, just as real, but never again had she imagined love tumbling physically from her breast.

She hadn't wanted another child. Lord forgive me that, too, she prayed. James was nine and badly wanted a brother. Will had wanted another son. For weeks she avoided him, then, losing conviction, gave herself over to him, and he shuddered and sighed and rolled away into sudden sleep, his hand drifting back to touch hers. She hugged her knees to her chest, feeling the wetness run along her skin to dampen the bedsheet, and then she'd cried silently. She felt it the ultimate betrayal.

Roy nursed for eight months, then quit her—that was the only real way she could understand it: the boy had quit her. Will left his position at the church and went into long fits of depression, sealing himself away in the attic. Maddy went to work at the garment mill down the mountain. Will's retreat—until his later retreat in the sixties—was the hardest time of her life, harder even than losing James, and had she not met Sharon Thorton, she would have left. Maybe. She had thought Will was losing his mind. One day, she knew, she would climb the attic stairs and find him dead, his wrists slit and dangling. She had already lost James and felt she couldn't bear anything more. Had I the courage, she thought, had I the courage, I would've packed up and left.

Sharon had saved her.

Maddy met her in the women's prayer group, the only woman near her in age, and they became inseparable, Sharon with her girl, Sue Ellen, on her hip, Maddy with James and Roy trailing behind. It was then that James and Roy took up with Sharon's husband, Bobby. He needs a son, Sharon would say. Maddy would glance at her boys: How about two? He took them hunting and camping, taught them to skin a deer and track a turkey—all of the things neither she nor Will were able to impart.

By the time Enis was born—a complete surprise to Maddy—fatherhood seemed split neatly between Will and Bobby, one handling discipline, matters of spirit and manners, the other teaching them to build rabbit gums. Sunday afternoons, Bobby would take Sharon and Sue Ellen, Maddy, Roy and Enis riding in his dune buggy. They climbed the side of Tamassee Knob once, forded the Chauga on countless occasions—pleasures denied now by government regulation. The children would play in the river while they sat on a blanket on the bank, Bobby sipping from his flask or popping cans of Pearl with the church key he kept chained to his belt, a picnic of fried chicken and tomato slices and egg salad spread at their feet. She and Sharon would tie their hair up in handkerchiefs and wear sunglasses and imagine themselves beautiful. Then the children would come up, and when he was drunk enough, Bobby would tell them about the war—Anzio, then Rome up into Germany where he'd won a Silver Star—calling himself a hero but never meaning it, a certain jaded quality it took her months to understand: he was mocking himself. But he was a man who'd done things, a husband. Still, not once did Maddy miss her own husband. Not once. She missed James, and she might have pined for a man more like Bobby, young and knotted with muscle, although already something of a drunk, but not once did she miss Will.

There was the feeling of having two families, of living two lives. There was her life with Will, and her life without. There was life with James and Roy and then, after Korea, life with Roy and Enis. Two lives, but each so violent and terror-filled, so warped with hope.

Pray—that had become her answer. Pray and let God worry.

Remembering what she'd said to Roy as he left: God's will, child. Not my own. Remembering Will's belief in the Sabbath: there is faith enough to go on, Sabbath morn.

When things started falling apart between Sharon and Bobby, the visits grew less frequent. Sue Ellen left for college and never came back. Sharon began to hate Bobby for his unwillingness to do anything with his money besides drink it away.

"Something. Anything. Just *do* something with it, you know?"

Sharon wanted things. A decent house. A color TV. She started reading magazines and picked out the design of her "dream home." "Which is exactly what it'll remain: a dream," she said. Maddy had lost a son, and nearly lost a husband. There was no pride left. She could understand such desires, but she could no longer sympathize with them.

Maddy hadn't seen her in years now. In passing here and there, a brief *Hello, how are the boys? Fine. How's Sue Ellen?* Nothing more. Sharon took up collecting dolphins: porcelain, ceramic, prints of dolphins, dolphins brocaded on pillow slips. She lined the mantle with dolphins, filled curio cabinets. Their friendship waned, and by the time Maddy realized it, she was past caring. It was just another life, something for the shelf, neat and dustless behind the glass.

Now there were only her sons, and Will, the men in her life, nothing else. Her world felt calm and ruined.

The dust had settled on the driveway without her even realizing it. The sun, mammoth and red, was halfway up the sky. Enis was probably halfway to work by now. She didn't know where Roy might be. James—well, James, she told herself. I've put James on my shelf.

On the table between them sat a gilt frame, within it a sepia print of the girl, her cheeks rose, her hair the color of baked bread and braided in soft plaits. Her hands, one folded primly over the other, appeared porcelain, as did her powder-white forehead. Roy Burden slid the picture toward the glass, the café dim but for the scattershot sunlight that lay like coins across the concrete floor.

"You get this from Millie?" he asked.

His brother laughed. The lunch crowd was gone, the place near empty now. His voice seemed to carry into the far reaches of the diner.

"She don't know you got it? Enis?"

"It fell out the damn sky, Roy. What do you think? Hell no, she don't know I've got it. You see me sitting here? You think I'd be sitting here if she knew?"

"All right."

"She'd kill my ass. Seriously. She would."

"I not gonna argue the point." Roy looked up. "I thought you was working today."

"Took a half day. I had to show you this. How old you think she is there?"

"I don't know," said Roy. "Maybe twelve, thirteen."

"Pubescent."

"Is that the word for it?"

"Yeah, buddy, it is. What the man on the TV said at least."

"Ugly word for such a pretty thing."

"Well, it's an ugly world, brother."

"So I keep hearing."

Through the glass they watched the woman step out into the two o'clock sunshine then turn to study her reflection for a moment in the storefront glass. She tugged at the hem of her skirt. Her hair lay in soft folds, waves not unlike those in the photograph, her eyes pinched by the afternoon glare. She turned to face them, unseeing, a pendant disappearing in the hollow of her breasts. A wasp circled, glittering and trembling on transparent wings. She waved it away.

"Now you got your pros and you got your cons here," said Enis, touching the tips of his index fingers. "Pro one is this, well, look at her. Good God. That's pro one. Fine. Now cons. Cons is this: engaged. Engaged to be married, Roy. That's con one."

"That's the one I'm most aware of."

"It pretty much goes downhill from there."

"So don't worry about it. Besides, it's too late to worry about it anyhow."

Roy finished his Coke. Enis slapped him on the back, harder than he intended.

"You are one cocky son of a bitch, ain't you," he said.

"It ain't bragging if you can do it, brother. You know who said that?"

Enis shook his head, both of them transfixed on the girl across the street who stood by the meter seemingly waiting for something, for some portent or sign.

"Louis Armstrong. The trumpet player."

"The colored fella?"

"Yeah, the colored fella." Roy stood, tucked in his shirt, shoved a pack of Camels in his pocket. "I saw him once in New York and again in Chicago."

"Well, la-di-da, Mr. Big Shot."

"I'm just saying, is all."

"You going over there?" asked Enis.

"What if I am?"

"Cause I can go ahead and give you a road map straight up shit creek if you'd rather. It's pretty much a straight shot."

"I've swam it a time or two."

"I'll be damned if you don't beat it. You're one to talk, that's for sure. Sit for one more Co-Cola, Mr. Big Shot."

"I better not, brother. Better not. But get this back to Millie," he said. He slid over the frame, his eyes never leaving the girl, the living girl, across the street. "I don't want her mad at me right off," he said. "Can't turn the future in-laws off on me too early."

"Well, if you don't think you're the shit," said Enis. "Hope nothing don't run you over."

Roy moved toward the door.

"Hey, Roy." Enis stood, took a hesitant step, undid it. "I meant to say something before. You know somebody said they seen James headed up to the Thorton place a few days back."

"I heard."

"Did you know he was back?"

"I've heard things is all."

"He ain't even been by to see Mamma and Daddy. I aim to ride up there tonight and find him out. If he really is up there, I mean. Thought you might want to ride along."

Roy shook his head. "That ain't my job, brother. It ain't yours either. He's a grown man."

"You're right. But still, I thought I might. Ain't seen him so long and all. Cain't even really remember what he looks like. Feel like I've never met him."

"You do what you think is right." Roy winked and pushed open the door. The bell tinkled.

"Hey, Roy," called Enis. "You keep this, why don't you."

"You don't think she'll miss it?"

"I ain't worried about it."

"All right, then. Thanks. Let me know about James."

"I'll do it."

Enis sat back down and began to loop figure-eights on the checked table-top with the sweat off his Coke. He watched his brother pause then skip across the street to where Faith Abernathy stood on the walk. He knew the continuing list of cons like a verse memorized in Sunday school: Faith Abernathy was educated at Agnes Scott College near Atlanta, which was exactly where she was headed as soon as she married Peyton Fowles, lieutenant in the U.S. Navy, Furman class of '66. He knew it because he was dating, if that was what you called it, Faith's sister, Millie, from whom he had five-fingered the photograph. Same old story, he thought, studying the grooves in the wood-paneled walls. Same old tired worn-out story, so worn-out they wouldn't even bother to sing about it in Nashville, wouldn't even run it in L.A.—sighing this as Roy hustled Faith up the street from sight.

Somehow Enis's own life felt less complicated, though emptier, too. Missed chances, broken promises, and the way he saw it, Vietnam had been the biggest broken promise of all. Rumors of war had been slow to creep up the mountain, but once he heard, after the initial surge of bloodlust had subsided, Enis, like virtually every other boy his age living on the mountain, had begun to worry that the war would end before he could get to it, thus leaving him forever trapped by the inertia of poverty and absent of man's defining experience—combat. At least it was the defining experience of virtually all the men he knew.

He graduated high school in June of 1965, but was seventeen and needed the permission of a parent to join. "You can get to your killing soon enough without my blessing," his father had said, just before locking himself in the attic with a gas lantern, a transistor radio, and a King James Bible. A few weeks later, his father gave up his position as pastor of the Mountain Rest Wesleyan Church—the same position he had lost years earlier after locking himself in the attic during the Second World War. On August 3 of that year, his birthday, Enis had waited outside the recruiting depot in Seneca then followed the recruiting sergeant in as he unlocked the door.

"Early riser, are you?" the man had said.

"Yessir."

The man had motioned toward the chevrons on his sleeve.

"Not sir, son. I work for a living."

"Sorry."

"Well, the U.S. Marine Corps might be the place for a young buck like yourself."

"Yessir, then."

Instead, he walked through the wrong door and joined the army.

Before he left, Enis had tried to go up and talk to his father. Each evening around seven his mother would take up a plate of food and a thermos of coffee, and his father would open the door to take the fresh plate and pass out the old. "I cannot abide this war," he said to his wife. "I cannot abide war in any form. I cannot abide to know another of God's chosen people are dying." The man was time-warped, caught in the solemn and joyful death throes of the 1940s, and no one tried to convince him otherwise. Most of his congregation was sympathetic—though they believed in nothing so much as a war they weren't fighting—thinking that one son flying off the deck of an aircraft carrier and another on his way there were sufficient grounds for a nervous breakdown. Though there were other considerations, too, other factors left largely unspoken. W. J. Burden was a remarkably learned man, a Doctor of Divinity from Sewanee, and the very inclinations that allowed such bookishness seemed to presage some germ of insanity. Then there were the stories of W.J.'s own father, "The Monster of the Dark Corner."

The night Enis went up to see his father, he waited for some time at the attic door, hearing the drone of the nightly news that came on the TV Will had recently lugged up the steps. The attic was filled with boxes of dried flowers the church used for funerals. Enis thought the place smelled like death. He knocked tentatively, waited. When the door opened, he barely recognized him, so emaciated was his father's body, so white was his hair.

"Yes?" his father said.

"Can I come in?" Enis asked.

"And you are?"

Enis had a date later that night and was wearing his best corduroy slacks and a blue button-down shirt. His hair was slicked with brilliantine so that it appeared at all times as if he had just surfaced from a pool of water.

"It's me, Daddy. Enis. Your son."

What he thought was a flicker of recognition caught deep in the flat black eyes: "Oh, yes, son. Come in. Sit. Please stay a minute."

Enis sat on an old sagging trunk.

"I'm going away in a few days, Daddy. I wanted to come up and talk to you."

His father nodded. "Leaving so soon?"

"Yessir. I've got to."

"Well, you only just got back didn't you? Just this afternoon."

"No, Daddy—"

"From flying, I mean."

"Sir?"

"From flying off your ship, of course. Now, Roy, I'm—"

"*Enis,* Daddy."

"Roy, I'm very concerned. Very concerned," he said leaning forward. "Roy," he whispered, "they have His people."

"Which ones, Daddy?"

"Why, His *only* people, my son, His chosen people. The Jews. Hitler has them."

"Hitler's been dead since before I was born."

His father stared blankly into the distance. He sat like an idol, a glass god. He sat like stone. "His people," he said. "Their blood, hers, it's on my hands."

Enis nodded. "I know, Daddy. I aim to do something about it."

"There are none of us without guilt, my son, but I cannot bear to know that another has died. It's a blight upon His world. I wish it could be some other way."

His mother was waiting for him on the stairs.

"How is he?" she had asked.

"He's fine," said Enis. "He's better than ever. Mind's as sharp as a tack. He wished me luck."

His date that night had been with a girl he had met the week before at a party at a place everyone called the Four Corners, which was actually nothing more than a large birch wood hut sitting at the intersection of two abandoned logging roads a half mile off Highway 183. Her name was Millicent though everyone kept calling her Mill or Millie. They had talked briefly, Enis's eyes bright with alcohol, his tongue loose, before the crowd surged, separating them. Everyone was talking about who was leaving and when. It seemed everyone was going somewhere. All the poor kids had all been drafted or had volunteered for the hell of it. The middle-class kids were headed for colleges or jobs all over the South. "Monday. Fort Jackson. The U.S. Army," Enis told anyone who would listen. Walking away she threw a wad of paper at him that ricocheted off his cheek. He flattened it to reveal a phone number. The next day he had caught a ride to town and used the pay phone outside the Foothills Diner to call. They made a date for the next night, Saturday, the night he climbed the steps to visit his father.

He took his father's truck down the mountain into town, parking three houses down from the Abernathys' two-story colonial. In the front room Enis had sat making small talk about Roy's flying with Millie's brother, who was a flat-footed college junior set to become vice-president to his father's president of the local branch of the First SC Bank and Trust. When she finally came down the steps, he was stunned beyond speech. Luckily, she had given him no time to speak, hustling him out of the house and onto the sidewalk.

"Don't tell me you walked all the way down the mountain."

"You look beautiful," he said.

"Is that it?" she asked, pointing down the street at the truck.

The best he could manage was a nod.

"Why, Enis Burden," she asked. "Why exactly, pray tell, did you park three houses down?"

They drove to the movie theater, and he bought two vanilla Cokes and a tub of popcorn and they watched the coming attractions, then sat through John Wayne in *True Grit,* Enis's left arm tingling, resting lightly on the armrest. Finally, just before the credits, he put his arm around her. She looked at him, lips pursed, then looked back to the front, hands on her knees. After a moment, she faced him and held her open palm in front of his face.

"I've got a paper cut there," she said.

"Whisper."

"I've got a cut there and the salt's burning it."

"I'm sorry."

"So kiss it."

"Your hand?"

"The cut. Haven't you ever heard that a kiss will make it better?"

He kissed her buttery hand.

They barely spoke in the truck on the way home, up empty Church Street past the cool, sleeping automobiles, the lights out in the houses. Two streets up from her house she reached across the seat and flicked down the turn signal, the most subtle, the most delicate of moves. He loved her.

"My parents are out of town. My brother thinks I'm sleeping over with Ashley Bonner," she said.

"All right."

"Don't be so thick-headed, Enis. Turn right up here."

He knew it then: he loved her.

They parked and sat on a dock that reared into newly dammed Lake Keowee. Millie took her shoes off and dangled her legs over the edge. The water was a flat and glossy mirror, a mercury sheen to its surface.

"I should probably tell you something," she said. "I'm really hesitating to tell you this, but I think it's only fair that you know."

He looked at her.

"Do you want to know or not?" she asked. "Well, I don't see as how it matters but just so you know: I'm only fourteen. I know you probably thought I was a little older than that. If my parents had been home they never would have let me leave the house. I had to pay my brother ten bucks to shut him up."

Enis sat.

"You thought I was older, didn't you?"

"Substantially."

"Do you care?" she asked, but before he could answer she had leaned forward and was kissing him, her tongue warm and viscous in his mouth. "Do you?"

She pushed him back flat on the dock and threw one leg across his waist. By starlight he could just see the white expanse of her thigh, the snow-light down. He put his fingers in her hair and kissed. She held his face in her hands, and each time she began to pull away his lips followed her up.

"Yes or no?" she said, looking down at him.

"I forgot the question."

"Fourteen."

"What is that? A number?"

"Silly."

"Well, the way I figure it, by the time I get back from overseas you'll be just about marrying age."

The bed of the truck was filled with dirt and dust, a series of rusty chains, a set of posthole diggers, a bucket of three-penny and roofing nails. They drove back up the mountain and Enis slipped inside to grab a couple of blankets. His mother was asleep on the couch in the front room, the TV a field of fuzzy snow, and it hurt him to slip out like that, knowing that she was sitting up waiting for his return, but it hurt him only for a moment. Some strange new electricity was moving through his body.

They drove into a hollow just down Highway 28 and slept there stretched on a tarpaulin and wrapped in blankets, his heart hammering out his back into the hard earth. They kissed again at sunrise then he drove her home, and there she kissed him again. Two days later he was at the Greyhound station in Clemson with his mother when he spotted her in the crowd.

"I'll be right back, Mamma."

"The bus will be here any second, Enis."

"Right back."

They crammed themselves into a closet-sized bathroom and his hands ran along the side of her body, up her sharp pelvic bones, along the swell of her stomach up to her breasts. He undid the top three buttons to her sundress and slipped the strap of her bra down until one soft breast puddled in his hand. He put it in his mouth, and she moaned. He kept kissing her, but when his hand slipped beneath her dress and up her thighs she pulled back.

"I'd rather not associate this with a clogged toilet for the rest of my life, thank you very much," she said.

"We could get us a room," he said.

"Don't you have a bus to catch?"

"I'll catch another."

"Boy, are you in love or in heat?" she said buttoning her dress. "Get out there and kiss your mamma good-bye."

He did, and the next morning he found himself in the late August sun of Columbia, South Carolina. There was no place hotter, he decided, no place more bug-infested. His legs ached. His skin was patchy with the bites of mosquitoes and sand fleas. She wrote him three times a week, and he wrote back, sleep-drunk and dreaming what a wonderful, romantic thing this was, that it might even be worth it to die somewhere in the mountains of Vietnam. One of his favorite fantasies was imagining her weeping over his flag-draped casket while a bugle choked out "Taps."

In November he finished boot camp and was given ten days leave. He spent his mornings working around the house, fixing the gatepost, nailing down roof shingles, fixing all the things that had fallen into disrepair, before driving down at three to pick Millie up from school. Each afternoon he would have another spot picked: a hollow, a meadow, a spot along the Chauga or the Chattooga, and they would wrap themselves in a quilt and make love then stare up at the stark winter trees that raked like fingers at the bone-colored sky.

Enis would spend whole hours beneath the quilt studying the topography of her body, his mouth against her stomach, her throat, the tiny ridges that rimmed her nipples, his mouth down between her legs. For ten days the air was clear and cold, so quiet there almost seemed a buzz to the world, not unlike static on a phone line.

His father was still living in the attic, though his mother said now and then he would come down and they would walk in the evenings along the fence line and pray for the delivery of their sons and of God's chosen people. Enis knew he should feel greater sympathy for his mother and he did, if sympathy was the right word. He should do more for her, worry more. But he was carried by that bullet of love, drunk on sensation, by the flutter in Millie's voice when she spoke, the look of her when she slept, the soft network of veins that spidered her hands. At the end of ten days he boarded a bus headed for Fort Benning, Georgia, managing to strangle his tears until he was seated.

He flew from Benning to San Diego to Hawaii to Okinawa before landing on the airstrip at Long Binh, and there it was all bicycles and dirty streets, outgoing artillery and bottles of Coke. A vegetable rot and trash everywhere. He worked in the rear, behind the wire, while the slow bleeding gained momentum. I've listened to more battles than most men will ever even know about, he thought.

He ached to fight. Even after months assigned to a Graves Registration unit, loading the rubber bags like packages, the shattered men laid side by side down the long bays, even after the spilled blood soaking the shredded wheat of jungle fatigues. Even more so after seeing all this, he wanted to fight so badly that sometimes something clamped inside him. "I want to die in this god-forsaken, motherfucking country," he mumbled. But he was a Dial Soaper, white-washing rocks and toe-shining his boots with lighter fluid. Another REMF bitch: a rear-echelon motherfucker. He had won some cosmic lottery: he took his R&R at China Beach in Danang, and all he ever saw of Vietnam was from inside the camp's wire, that and the view flying in: distant, velvet hills shrouded in blue mist. His war was bodies, outgoing fire, and secondhand Dexedrine, Sam the Sham and Herman's Hermits on Armed Forces Radio Network, stub-nosed C-130s, and helicopters, always helicopters, Hueys and Loaches and twin-bladed Chinooks, all with the milk-rot air spraying from their rotors, then gone chasing their spindly shadows over the land.

In the base beer halls he met Green Berets, spooks, Australian commandos, Lurps and SEALS, empty-eyed men defined by acronym and their lonely trade, and these men told of entire NVA divisions sleeping in the hills north of Khe Sahn, of a battalion of sappers biding their time in Saigon, a true guerrilla war in the Mekong Delta, and already it was clear this was a war that would never be won, but that meant nothing to him. Around him the war pulsed, flexing up beneath the skin of the country, and all he wanted was a taste, a chance, just something outside the wire. But he never asked for a combat assignment. Eleven months in-country and he just liked to think about it. Tomorrow, maybe. Or the day after that.

Millie wrote, "I'm almost marrying age, lover."

Then one day he woke to realize he was thirty days short and he vacillated between the joy of going home to live with Millie and the clawing disappointment of having missed something, of having missed that defining moment of manhood: how would I have acted? The question was acid. Would I have run? He remembered Fleming in *The Red Badge of Courage*. Would I have fought? The war was escalating, and he knew if he reenlisted he would get his chance. Soldiers were fighting and dying in droves. Millie settled things. If you don't come home to me now, she wrote, don't ever bother. So instead of fighting he spent three weeks at Subic Bay in the Philippines and was in San Diego by late June of 1967, two years after leaving. He was discharged and home by the Fourth. His father came out of the attic sometime in August.

Now he drummed his nails on the table, turning over the image of Roy and Faith in his mind. Why is me and Mamma the only two in this family with any damn sense? he wanted to know.

Enis left the Foothills Diner and headed up Highway 28 past Deadman's Curve and the turnoff for Isaqueena Falls, before veering onto 107. The evening sky was hazy with heat shimmering up off the blacktop, the road lined and sometimes hooded with mountain laurel and oak. Here and there twin gutted tracks disappeared from the road at right angles: loggers cutting their way through Sumter National Forest. A car passed. The driver raised his hand. Enis raised a single finger. Everything slow, weighted.

Rearing from a cut bank the block letters of a sign read

BURRELL'S PLACE

AMUSEMENT GAS WINE USED CARS

COLD BEER ICE BREAD MILK

PICNIC & FISHING SUPPLIES

He looked down to see a dog sleeping in the road, all slatted ribs and hide, and laid down on the horn, cursing the mutt. "Looking to get killed," he called after it. The dog paid him no mind, walking away to settle onto the shoulder.

"Damn mutt."

He stopped by the house for dinner. No one was home, but he found collards on the stovetop before finding a plate of salmon patties, creamed corn and mashed potatoes and gravy covered with tinfoil in the still-warm oven. He sat at the table eating methodically then left out again headed for Long Creek.

The light was just beginning to wane by the time he turned off the main road for Bobby Thorton's place. The clay of the drive was baked to a sour mouse-gray, dust as fine as sifted flour rising behind him, cattails and weeds crowding forward—it was Indian summer now, Enis realized. When he drove up, Bobby was sitting on the porch, his TV playing low, a fan canted toward him. An extension cord ran through a slit in the screen door to power both.

"Who is that?" Bobby called from his rocker.

"Enis Burden, Mr. Thorton. W. J. Burden's youngest."

"How do, young Burden. Come on up. I cain't say as I'm surprised to see you."

"No, sir. I reckon you're not."

"You want to sit a minute? The war's on."

"I'm obliged to you, but I'm really just up here looking for James."

"I figured as much. Go on and sit a minute. He's as like to come along in a week as he is in a minute."

"He's up here then?"

"He is. Sit on down. Let me see if anything else is on."

"I ain't particular, sir."

Enis sat. The TV droned static before a detergent commercial came on. Across the yard fireflies winked, made pale by the ambient light of the screen. Clouds lay like lace over the mountains. Through a break shone the Dog Star.

"When'd you get electricity up here, Mr. Thorton? I didn't think they would run it up this far less you paid for it."

"Hell, they run it up here twenty years ago, son. Rural electrification program. Just after the war. The Second, I mean. I got it up this far being what they call a producer of staples—apples and all. I know your daddy's place has got it now."

"Yessir. Had it long as I can remember, actually. Still no phone, though."

Bobby nodded then bent forward studying the boards between his socked feet. Curls of old paint and the tops of eight-penny nails, a single ant crawling from sight.

"You eat yet? I might have something in the Frigidaire there."

"Yessir, I did," said Enis. "Thank you though."

"Well, don't never say I didn't ask."

They sat listening to the whippoorwills. Bobby packed Prince Albert in his pipe.

"Sharon ain't in there," he said after a moment.

"Sir?"

"Sharon. My wife. She's done gone and quit me looks like. For good, I fear."

"Well, I'm sorry to hear that," said Enis, standing.

"I fear for good. I do. She always talked like she would but I never believed it. We had our ups and downs I just never took em to heart."

"No, sir."

"Here I sit, fifty-two years old. Just never did believe it."

Enis walked to the edge of the porch.

"You got a girlfriend, don't you, son? Pretty young thing, I'll bet."

Enis didn't answer. The night collapsed at the edges, and he shivered though the air was warm. Down below the shed he could see the migrant workers erecting something. He motioned toward them. "What's that?" he asked.

"Them migrants down there. They're building something is all."

"Oh, yeah?"

"A bonfire." Bobby made a motion of dismissal with the pipe. "I ain't got a mind to stop em if that's what they set on doing. Seasonal work is all. I try not to trouble with em too much. Sharon mostly took an interest in em."

An old hound dog limped onto the porch and collapsed at Enis's feet. He bent to touch it.

"Why, if it ain't old Gus," said Bobby. "Rub his ears there. Old Gus loves to get his ears rubbed."

The dog yawned and rolled onto its side, showing patches of bare skin.

Enis walked down the steps, pulled his hat from his back pocket, and dusted it along the leg of his pants.

"I don't want to keep you, Mr. Thorton."

"Well, I wish you wouldn't run off. I could find something else on the TV if war don't suit you. Or we might could go looking around for that brother of yourn. He's here somewhere."

"That's all right. I suspect if he wants to be found he'll come around."

"I suspect you're right."

"Waited this long to see him I reckon I can wait a little longer. Tell him I come by, if you would."

"I'll do it. You tell your mamma and daddy I said hello."

"I will."

"Roy, too. He's something, ain't he. Local boy makes good and all."

"He likes to live hard."

"Hell, they ain't no other way to do it. Hard is all mountain folk know. If you living soft you must be town-raised."

Enis nodded. "Well, goodnight, Mr. Thorton."

"Goodnight, son."

They were both sweating, damp in every fold of skin, along the ridges of hairline, under arms, wherever flesh met flesh. Roy climbed from the bed, slipping off the opaque skin of a condom. Faith rolled over onto her back, sighed, pulled the bedsheet up to cover her breasts, the down along her arms backlit by the lamp.

"This is what someone might call complicated," she said.

Roy nodded. Out the open window he studied the cloudy bands, the sky star-smeared, bruised and wounded. Below was the street, the town square centered on a granite obelisk erected as a memorial to Confederate dead. It was near empty now, the square, a single couple walking hand in hand through the laced shadows of a tulip poplar, together but alone. A black Chevy, its alloy Cragar mags gleaming, went jetting from sight. Faith took the near-empty bottle of peach Boone's Farm wine off the nightstand and drank.

"Complicated," she said.

"Doesn't necessarily have to be."

When he looked at her again, her eyes were closed, the burned nub of a joint in the tin ashtray, the sheet rising and falling along the contours of her body. She seemed distant but content. Far from God. He sat on the edge of the bed smiling, the room lacquered blue with lamplight.

"Well, complicated or not, I like it."

She smiled, eyes still shut, offered him the bottle. "Finish it."

"You take it."

"Put a quarter in the bed, lover."

She drank, and when he kissed her she tasted like overripe fruit.

He spread atop her like a flood, the sheet between them and then nothing between them.

"Easy, Mr. Pilot Man," she said. "I've only got tonight."

"Don't know easy," he said. "Never met him."

She laughed with her mouth against his ear.

"What time is it?" she asked.

He kissed her neck. "Who cares?"

"The desk clerk for one."

"Oh, him."

"Yeah, him. Besides, you know the Fowles are expecting me tonight."

"Really."

She clasped his head, looked at him. "You know they say really is *really* a polite way of actually saying fuck off."

"Really?"

"Oh, you're a quick one, aren't you?"

But they were moving again now, tangling like vines, neither listening.

Later, driving, the slim highway running beneath them like a line on a map, she leaned her face against his shoulder and shut her eyes. Roy hung his arm out the window, feeling the car give back the day's heat. Faith purred in her sleep.

He drove blindly into the mountains, having no real destination, desiring only the solace of movement. They neared an overlook, and he slowed, pulled onto the shoulder. The guardrail was stenciled with graffiti. Candy wrappers and beer cans lay scattered among the weeds. To the west lay the last sulfur remnants of dusk, below it the poison glow of artificial light. To the north, six-thousand-square-foot summer homes clung to the mountains like polyps, lit now against the dark of the forest. The rich and the famous, he thought. Like the quick and the dead.

It was almost nine. Faith stroked his arm in her half-sleep, and Roy imagined himself moving on gauzy wings over the Blue Ridge, then over the Appalachians. These mountains were old, riddled with hard, stone-eyed trilobites, older than the Rockies, older than anything Europe had to offer, and like all things old they were slouching, heaving forward, tired, no different from the men and women who grew old trying to beat or scratch a living out of them.

There at the overlook it wasn't difficult to imagine the world as sea, to imagine the world before the oceans receded turning submarine ridges to mountain ranges, deep slit trenches to rivers. He imagined wavelines plowed like furrows in sand twenty million years old, curling reefs and blind prehistoric fish lost and hapless and bumbling like old men. Fossils. The relics of some antediluvian graveyard, a cradle for wrecked lives. He saw it all as beneath water: a gentle slope shelfed with fluted things; shells and the spiraling arms of creatures never recorded. When the wind shifted, he smelled gas: the petroleum reserves his million-year-old body would someday regenerate. It was the sense of something very old in the world, as if this were a holding ground, a place of last things, a sense of something here that would outlast him, and though he did not know its name, it comforted him.

He watched a hawk ride a thermal, arcing upward into the chasm before being negated by darkness, and he thought of his long-ago illusions of certainty, of his well-laid plans made false as hope. A wall of night sounds rose around them, and he felt lonely despite Faith's presence. She was transient. The night was not. The night would go on.

In Long Creek he stopped at a gas station with a soot-blown Coca-Cola banner heaving like a sail and filled the tank. An old woman stood behind the counter.

"Seven-fifty, and two of them little Cokes," Roy said.

"Purty car you got," said an old man seated in the far corner, his ladder-back chair tipped against the wall. "Real purty thing."

"Seven-fifty, you say?"

"Gas is high as a cat's back," said the old man.

"And two Cokes, please."

"Them Cokes is free," said the woman. "Some promotional thing."

"Giving em away, are they?" He turned to the old man. "That's a '65 Fastback, old-timer. Midnight blue."

"Purty, purty thing," said the old man. "Bet she'll scoot."

"Better damn believe she will."

"How fast will she go?"

"Don't know myself."

He took the two Cokes, mixing drinks from his flask in a couple of waxed paper cups marked DQ, but Faith never woke. A mile down the road he turned the radio on low, drove on, watched her eyelids flutter. She was dreaming. Her smell caught in the streaming air—peaches and sex and Tigress perfume. He rolled up the window to keep the wind out of her face. A voice on the radio said Jimi Hendrix had overdosed in London, then Don Williams started singing.

Roy drained the Jack and Coke and dropped the bottle down onto the floorboard to roll between Faith's feet. He threw the empty cup out the window and started on the second.

All his life Roy believed he had been born to greatness, or at least that greatness would eventually be thrust upon him. But it hadn't been greatness, it had been Faith. He had taken up with her years ago, and theirs had been a decade-long affair. Like two satellites orbiting a common sun, they were bound to collide, separate, collide again, gravitating toward each other in the way that those who know themselves to be physically superior to others always will. But the truth was, he was afraid of her. She was two years younger than him, and by virtue of this he felt he should hold some sway over her. But he didn't, never had. She had always scared him.

Their first formal date had been Roy's junior year, the Walhalla High Junior/Senior Prom. That Friday he had knocked at the Abernathys' front door, and when Faith answered it wearing a bathrobe, Roy had bent forward, kissed her cheek, and said, "Good evening. I'm Roy."

"Good evening. I'm not ready," she answered, and shut the door.

A moment later a mortified Mrs. Abernathy had let him in, leading him toward the kitchen before asking what he would like to drink. He asked for a glass of water. Mrs. Abernathy brought him a bourbon, a "gentleman caller's drink."

Shortly, Faith had come down the stairs to tell him she would be ready in precisely one hour. "Finish your drink and go wait in the car."

He had. Five minutes later she had slid in beside him.

"In twenty minutes I've got to go cut the bath water off and turn on the hair dryer," she said.

"You left the tub filling?"

"I climbed out the window. I'll climb back in. Besides, Mother thinks it 'proper and fitting' that a young lady take a long, steaming bath. Good for the complexion, she thinks." Faith lit a cigarette. "Oh, also she hopes you're driving something 'fun and sporty.'"

"Oh, go easy on old Amanda Wingfield," said Roy. "She's just nostalgic for the mint juleps she never had."

"That's funny, it is. But why should I go easy on her? You're not."

"I haven't said a word."

"You're thinking them though. Don't tell me you're not thinking them. Or are you just so horny seeing me you can't think straight?"

Then they climbed into the backseat for exactly twenty minutes. Then left. Roy wound up paying for and installing new bathroom linoleum himself.

He drove on through a copse of loblolly pines, past a deserted roadside stand where a hand-lettered sign read HONEY–APPLES–FIREWOOD, thinking of their early days together, all the evenings after that first rushed date, late nights at high school parties after football games or school dances. Fifty, maybe forty, people packed into some abandoned cabin someone had talked an uncle into letting them use. Couples making out in closets filled with plastic-bagged overcoats, on bare mattresses in dim back rooms, on front porches leaning against abandoned drink boxes marked RC COLA. Then the attrition of night and drink, the sleeping sprawled in bathtubs and on the porch, passed out in the backseats of their cars, and there would be perhaps twenty, then ten, eight of them awake and packed into some girl's new coupé her father had bought her just the week before, the girl herself asleep in the back, chin shiny with drool, Roy at the wheel, a fifth of Wild Turkey passing among them while one by one the riders gave in to sleep, so that only he and Faith were left to greet the dawn, parked in some faraway hollow, eyes red-rimmed, mouths cottoned, clothes littered with beggar lice and flecks of gravel.

"You tired?" she would want to know.

"No," he'd lie. "You?"

"Not in this life."

Sex seemed to steam from her, a musky, fragrant scent strong enough to undo logic and good sense, and he was fascinated in an almost empirical way. On those long high school Friday nights, he would study her by the pale dome light that flashed when the car door swung open. She wore the promise of sex like an old shirt—that comfortable, that casual. The prospect of pleasure beyond scope. The type of woman one simply desired not just to have but to be had *by*. Something in the curve of her hips, the way she would leaf her fingers through her hair. The way her tongue slipped from her teeth when she laughed. She seemed the embodiment of health and good fortune. Everywhere she went, men followed her full of the biblical fear and trembling.

The weekend she lost her virginity, she had sex with two different boys, both in the crowded back room of a houseboat moored on Lake Jemike, the pontoons beating out a rhythm against the dock. Afterward, she had felt no less full, not thinned or broken as perhaps other girls might. Instead she recognized a certain strength, a well that when tapped had the power to change things, to bring things about. "The only thing they can't resist," she told other girls, "is temptation itself." Had she led the two boys up the dock, her fingers in their nostrils, leading them like nose-ringed bulls, it would have been no less fitting.

She was two years behind him at Clemson, and Roy gave up first baseball and then studying to keep up with her. Had it not been for Navy ROTC and, more importantly, Faith's parents forcing her to transfer to Agnes Scott after her freshman year, he would never have graduated. He spent his nights at the Esso Club, a converted gas station cum honky-tonk where he drank Pabst tallboys and followed her into the shadows of the next-door laundromat. He was not, however, a jealous man, and that had served him well. There had been other girls, diversions, some better than others, but in the end, he found himself driving to Georgia to howl on the steps of the ZTA house, cursing her never being there, crying as he drove home.

Now she was set to marry another man. He thought back. There was only once she had spoke of why Fowles and not Roy. Years ago it must have been. She had been drunk, or slipping across the frontiers of sobriety. The radio playing low. They had sat in Roy's Fastback, just up the street from the Abernathys, rain plunking against the vinyl top. Hank Williams, so mournful and world-weary: *You'll walk the floors the way I do.* On the seat between them sat a white paper bag of French fries, four little cardboard sleeves' worth they'd bought then dumped together. Little salt packets, torn and empty, lay scattered on the floorboard. The fries were just beginning to bleed through the paper. She kissed him, her mouth salty and spreading over his face, and he'd felt slick with lust. *Your cheating heart will tell on you.*

"It's not what you think," she said. She'd pulled back from him, and when he leaned forward, she stopped him, a single finger to his lips. Then she was laughing. "Not at all what you think. You don't have any idea."

"Then why don't you tell me?"

She studied the smear of lipstick along her Styrofoam cup. She reached for a fry but stopped. "It's not what you think."

"You keep saying that, Faith, and honestly I'm not even sure what the hell it is you think we're talking about."

"I feel like it's raining," she said.

"You're drunk."

He offered the flask, and she took two quick pulls from it then poured a finger's worth in her cup. The heat from the bag was just beginning to fog the glass. He cracked his window, and little drops began to accumulate along the upholstery.

"Is this about him?"

"You don't understand, Roy. It's not about him, it's not even about me, really. My parents. I want—"

"Bullshit."

"What they want—"

"You never gave two shits what your parents wanted, Faith. Don't sit there and lie to me."

She traced one finger along the cool glass. "No. No, I haven't." He watched her finger sliding back and forth while she spoke. "It's just . . . I don't know. Have you ever felt like we might burn each other up or something?"

"Well. Wouldn't you rather be ashes than dust?"

"I need a refill. I am drunk. And I'm sorry, too. I can't explain it, Roy. It's just, it's just this feeling I get with you, it's like I'll wind up doing something. I don't know. Hurting myself. Or you. Bad." She looked at him. He looked out at the street with its antebellum homes and felt his eyes filling. "I don't know," she said. "I'm drunk. We're both drunk. I can't explain it. I need a refill."

"Faith."

"Please. I need a refill, Roy."

After that it lay between them, buried in silence and guilt, hardening, but shifting now and then, the tectonics of hurt, and neither willing to dredge the implications.

What's easier, Roy thought, was the silence, the pretend.

At the dead-end bulb of an old CCC logging road they made love a third time that day on the dry, packed ground scrubbed clean decades before. She rode him, rolling her hips in quick manic thrusts, a sort of bird's cry stillborn in her throat, her thighs coarse, unshaven in three or four days. Afterward they dressed quickly and sat in the car, a sharp burning sensation in Roy's groin.

"Look here," he said, taking the sepia print from the glove box.

She held it with two hands, inches from her face in the full dark.

"Oh my God," she cried. "Oh. My. God. Where did you get this?" She laughed. "Look at that hair. Oh my God. Someone should burn this."

"I like it."

"Oh, God. Where did you. . . . God, where did you get this thing?"

"I think Millie must have give it to Enis. Or something like that."

"Oh, God, look at me. This was probably twelve or thirteen years ago at least. Didn't I look so young then? I was so young. God, Roy, look at me. Didn't I?"

"I wish I had known you then," he said.

She slept that night at Roy's, after calling Dr. and Mrs. Fowles to explain that she would be staying with her friend Amy, who had taken with the flu. Mrs. Fowles thought it might be awful early in the year—or awful late, depending on how you looked at it—for someone to be taken with the flu.

"That's why I'm staying," lied Faith. "I'm worried about her."

"Maybe I should send Abner over?"

"Oh, no, not this late. No need waking him. I'll call back if I need him. Goodnight, Mrs. Fowles."

"Oh, Faith, darling. I got a phone call from Peyton today. He was disappointed you weren't here."

"Oh."

She could hear the Fowleses' TV blaring in the background.

"Yes. He asked about you. He was talking all about Okinawa and Hawaii, about the house he lives in and the garden and—"

"Oh, Mrs. Fowles, I'm sorry, I can hear Amy calling me. I'd better go. Sorry. Goodnight."

"Faith, darling—"

"Coming, Amy."

They slept in the next morning until light filtered through the curtains, then stood at the stovetop frying eggs and bacon, Crisco crackling out of the pan, until Roy sat her on the counter and slipped the spatula under her thighs and she doubled over laughing.

"Mrs. Abernathy, Mrs. Abernathy," he called over and over.

"Why do you always think that's so funny?"

"Isn't it?" he wanted to know. "I mean you are laughing."

Then the laughing stopped. They ate quietly, dutifully, only the scrape of utensils for accompaniment, sullen at the thought of departure, faces puffy with lack of sleep, the fringe of a pillow imprinted like a seam down one of Faith's cheeks.

"In three months I intend to marry Peyton Fowles," she said.

"I know you do," he smiled.

"Well, you're a smug one."

He agreed that he was.

"And you know you shouldn't eat this stuff every day either," she said. "All this bacon. You were an athlete once. You should know as much. Gonna wind up a fat old man."

He nodded. They listened as the garbage truck came up the street, heard the whine of its brakes, the muffled voices. It moved on.

"And don't say a thing about love," she said.

"Never said a word," he pointed out through a mouthful of egg.

"I know you didn't. But I'm still intending."

Roy laid his fork flat on the table, wiped his mouth, a formal gesture, arranged his hands in his lap.

"*Intend,* my dear. Intend being the operative word."

"Your mamma's trying to talk to you there, Scruff."

Bryan Ellcott, the county's high sheriff, leaned across the seat to motion at the woman on the steps. He gave her a little wave. It was not yet light out, and she stood just to the left of the porch light, batting away moths and mouthing words. Then she took a single step; the light took her; he made to smile.

"Ah, I'll see her in Sunday church, Sheriff. Let's ride on."

His deputy, Scruff, pulled the shut the door, and the sheriff eased into the dark street. A few minutes later, they sat in the back booth of the Dairy Queen, sipping coffee, the morning's newspaper spread before them.

"They all crazy for cocaine this year," said Scruff.

"You reckon."

"What they said. The white-collar affliction, it's called. Some criminologist from Atlanta. FBI or something."

"Money well spent," said the sheriff, and sipped his coffee. Scruff had just returned from a three-day conference up in Memphis.

"What we've done is moved past the counterculture stage, past what they call the 'mind-enhancing' drugs—you got your LSD and your acid and whatnot, on to the harder stuff: heroin, speed. Cocaine, that's your big one there."

The sheriff began straightening the sections of the paper. Scruff sat sideways in the booth, right boot poking into the aisle, right arm along the seatback, reading "Peanuts" and smiling. He had the gelled pompadour of a fifty-year-old TV evangelist, though he couldn't have been more than nineteen. His application had listed him as twenty-one, but the sheriff had figured he was lying, had hired him anyway, remembered his daddy, an old tobacco farmer who had come up hard then gave out one day walking down the front steps of the church. Boom. Heart attack. Walking one second, dead the next. The trip was sort of a charity thing. He figured the boy had never been out of the county, let alone the state.

"How's the wife?" asked Scruff.

"She's good. You not seeing that Alder girl no more?"

Scruff twisted in his seat, lowered his leg. "I'm all knotted up from setting here too long," he said.

"That a no?"

"You a hard man, Sheriff."

"I'm just asking is all."

He shook his head. "Nah, I ain't seeing her. Not no more I ain't. And that's pretty much the lay of the land, Sheriff."

"I reckon so." He swirled his coffee, swirled it. Out the front glass he could see cars going by, beat-up pickups and family cars, American-made mostly, hurrying to work or school, lights cutting the blush of early dark.

"Hey, I bout forgot." Scruff reached into the bag down between his feet and came out with a guitar-shaped ashtray that read GRACELAND in beaded letters. "You ever seen the beat?"

"Well, ain't that something. I'll be, Scruff, that is real nice."

"It's a find. I'll say that of it." Scruff scooted it toward the sheriff. "I got to thinking of you and Jeanne and your girls."

"How bout that."

"As a present."

"You don't say. You gonna make up with the Alder girl after all?"

"Nah, this is for you, Sheriff."

"You're kidding me."

"Serious as heart attack. Now go on and take it. Don't argue with me none. My mind's done set on it."

"Well, I'm flattered, Scruff. I really appreciate that."

"For sending me and all."

"Thank you. I mean that. I hope it didn't cost much."

"Ah, it wasn't nothing. Just some little thing."

"Well, I appreciate it. I know Jeanne and the girls will too."

"Just some little thing is all."

They sat for a while, the sheriff sipping his coffee and glancing from the ashtray out the window then back again. The clock out front was ticking, barely audible.

"I don't reckon you'd know James Burden, would you?"

The sheriff took another sip. "Rings a bell."

"James Burden. Preacher's son. One that went crazy for a while."

"The preacher or the son?"

"The preacher. Lives on the mountain. Locked himself up and all that."

"W. J. Burden. Yeah. My daddy knew him well. What about him?"

"Well, his oldest, James, he just strolled back into town. Fifteen years he's been gone. More maybe. Never come back after Korea."

The sheriff nodded.

"You must've known his brother, Roy Burden?" said Scruff. "Flew planes."

"He was a few years behind me in school. Joined the Navy. He was buck wild back when I knew him. Played baseball."

"You reckon we ought to check up on him?"

"James or Roy?"

"Whichever one. Hell, both. We could."

"You got any reason to? I mean, other than just wanting to stick your nose out where it might not belong?"

Scruff made a little motion, his hand like a bird, delicate and tender. There for a second, the sheriff thought of a tiny bird taking wing. Then he had to pull his mind back, found it wandering to other things, his girls, Jeanne. He tried to think of James Burden's homecoming but couldn't. He saw a man in ill-fitting clothes, worn-out dungarees and empty eyes, more shape and narrow shadow than flesh and blood. But who can say what a man has seen, he reminded himself. Who can say what it does to you, you get shipped off, get yourself in a fix, head down in the sand and begging to God. Bargaining. He'd known plenty of old boys like that in the service, the one's who'd fought and froze their way across Europe, the ones who'd caught malaria and trench foot in the South Pacific. Who could say, really. Let no man judge—it was best to remember scripture: do not judge, lest you be judged yourself. Or something like that.

"We best just stick to the white-collar afflictions," he said.

Scruff sat up a little higher in the booth. "I'm serious about that."

"I'm kidding you. I know you're serious." He sipped his coffee. "Don't the youngest Burden do his firefighting with all y'all?"

"He did. Quit though. Hey, you never did say how your two girls were."

"You never did ask. You never did say what happened with you and the Alder girl, either."

"Hell, Sheriff. Women. Born to flit from one to the next. I don't know."

The woman behind the counter came out to top off their cups. She wore too much makeup and had her ponytail clipped with a rubber band.

"Now who is this you got with you, Sheriff?" she asked.

"This is Terry Wilbanks, Lorie."

"Wilbanks. Kin to the Wilbanks out on Flat Shoals Road?"

"Yes, ma'am. That was on my daddy's side."

"I declare. I know all your daddy's people. Your mamma's side, too. You ain't married yet, are you?"

"No, ma'am, I ain't."

She shook her head. "Say now. Well that just ain't right." She stood shaking her head and sloshing coffee. "Reckon I made him blush, Sheriff. Holler if y'all need anything."

They watched her walk back behind the counter. He had missed both the wars, Ellcott, coming of age after Korea and before Vietnam was really stirring. U.S. Army. Spent some time in Germany and England. Probably should've stayed in, would be near retirement by now, drinking beer in Hei-delberg, sleeves full of stripes, listening to war stories and driving his girls to the base school. Instead he was serving his second term, and so long as they kept electing him, he figured he'd sheriff on for another twenty years. Some-times, though, nights mostly, he felt those years looming, slow but creeping, coming steadily for him. Nights were the time.

"Flit, flit, flit," said Scruff.

"Well, you're young yet. Don't take it to heart."

Scruff sighed. "Nothing much ever happens, does it, Sheriff?"

Don't take it to heart, he wanted to say, and thought again of James Burden, thought of all the bargaining and hurting of those old boys talking about Bastogne and the Philippines, of Okinawa and all those mama-sans holding their babies and jumping off rocks into the ocean. All that pain like bedrock, foundation: you wind up building a life on it. Love the quiet times, he wanted to say, be thankful. Love the quiet and hate the loud.

That night a boy named Eddie Gathers rode his bike from his parents' house on the mill hill on South Street in downtown Walhalla over to Chickapee ball field. It was early evening, and by the time he arrived, the game was already in the middle of the third inning. He bought a grape Sno-Cone and wheeled his bicycle one-handed back up the road, where he left it leaning against a telephone pole, then took a seat on the grassy bank along the first-base line. Two men sat just below him on the bank, one perhaps sixty, wearing a black frock coat despite the late summer heat. The other was younger, not too much older than himself, Eddie figured, maybe eighteen, twenty, dipping a finger into a can of Vienna sausages then licking it clean. The pitcher for the Toccoa Yellowjackets was warming up. The Chickapee Mill batter, a fellow he knew named Berg something, stood off in the dust swinging three bats, spitting chew, and knocking mosquitoes away from his face.

"Hey, old-timer," Eddie called down to the man in front of him. "Hey, old-timer."

Eddie plucked a strand of grass, threading it for a moment between his fingers.

"Say, old-timer," he called. "You deaf?"

He plucked the head off a daisy and threw it at the man, hitting him square between the ears. The man put one hand back to smooth the gray mane that hung just below his shoulders.

"Hey, old-timer," he yelled again. "You hard of hearing?"

"We heard you the first time," said the boy beside the man, half turning.

"So you ain't deaf then?"

"No, we ain't deaf. Just ain't paying you no mind."

"Well, I just wanted to ask the score is all," said Eddie.

"It's 4 to 2. Home team."

"Fair enough."

The man turned.

By the time they had thrown on the new sodium lamps that sat shuddering on lean power poles, the Toccoa pitcher had found his groove and struck out seven consecutive batters then forced an eighth to fly out. The score was 7 to 4 Toccoa, top of the eighth, and Eddie was bored. He plucked the heads off several daisies, lining them along his outstretched leg, and one by one tossed them at the old man in front of him. The first stuck, a tiny face caught in a waterfall of gray. The next hit the old man's shoulder. The third and fourth found his right ear and neck. The boy turned.

"You got no call to do that," he said.

"Ah, I'm just shitting with ya is all," laughed Eddie.

"You got no call for that language either. This is a reverend you're fun-
ning with."

"A reverend?"

"That's right."

A lone bat dipped from one bank of haloed lights down toward second
base and rose, gliding upward to disappear in the distant trees. Eddie watched
it, studied for a moment the vacuum into which it had disappeared.

"A reverend," he said after a moment.

"What I said," said the man who had turned back to the field.

"Well, he must be from the Holy church of the tone deaf and stone blind
then, cause he's about as lifelike as a damn rock."

He threw another daisy, hitting the younger man this time. What the hell.
He was bored. Another bat took wing, shifting through the haze.

The man brushed wildly at his neck as if stung.

"I tell you what, I got a mind to come up there and whip that young
ass," said the man.

Eddie shushed him. "Mind your talk now," he whispered. "Didn't you just
say we in the presence of something holy here? We in the presence of the
granddaddy of the Vatican his own self. I swear to God if that ain't the truth."

"Why you little shit," said the man.

"Shut it, holy roller. Trying to watch a ball game here."

With that the reverend, who Eddie at this point was half-convinced was
actually a clothed stone, stood, unfolding himself, and turned.

"I think my associate has already made clear we find this behavior rather
childish, to say nothing of irritating."

Eddie stared at him. The man looked like a pilgrim, a buckle on his hat,
his belt, one on each shoe, two starched kneesocks that climbed impossibly
long legs. The man was every inch of six foot five.

"Do we have an understanding here, young man?" asked the reverend.

"You some sorta hippie-Pilgrim guru or something?"

"I'll take that as a yes," said the man.

Eddie gave a half bow, and the man nodded, then began the slow process
of sitting back down on the grass. Just as he did so, Eddie nailed him with
the last of his daisies and sprung upwards toward his bike, calling, "Better
believe we do, you foot-washin son of a bitch."

A half step up the bank his feet went out from under him and his face
was down in the grass, the hard copper taste of blood in his mouth, the ground
suddenly sharp, scarring his face. The man had his left leg and was dragging

him back down the hill. Eddie kicked and screamed, fingernails digging. Around them the stands turned to watch—even the umpire seemed temporarily amused, nodding behind the cage of his mask as if this suited him.

"Wait, now," cried Eddie. "Wait. We got us a misunderstanding here."

The old man dragged him down the bank to the dugout entrance. Halfway down, he dropped Eddie into a mud hole, dipping his face and lathering his hair in the muck for a good twenty seconds.

"I asked the lad," said the reverend, "I don't know how many times."

The players smiled. Someone in the stands began to cheer the reverend on through cupped hands.

"Lather him," a voice called.

"My patience grew thin," said the reverend. "My patience grew naught."

"Lather that redneck sumbitch, Rev. Lather him good."

"'And if any mischief follow," cried the reverend, "then thou shalt give life for life, eye for eye, tooth for tooth, hand for hand, foot for foot,' so saith Exodus chapter twenty-one, verses twenty-three and twenty-four."

"You said a mouthful, Rev."

"Lather the sumbitch."

Afterward, Eddie lay unable to move, paralyzed with rage. He lay still as the Toccoa players stepped over him, as the last of the Chickapee players struck out, the whump of the ball striking the catcher's mitt, the muttered curses, the cracking sound of the lights being thrown off, the last clack of metal spikes on the packed dugout floor. He sat up in the darkness of the visitors' dugout— the game long since over, his hair an elaborate crystal of dried clay—and cried. When he found his bike was gone, he cried again, then sat down against the light pole with no intention of ever moving. The crowd was gone, the bank littered with crushed waxed-paper Coke cups and empty plastic tubes that once held peanuts, little triangular papers meant for Sno-Cones. The floodlights glowed tentatively. The moths were gone.

When he saw the figure approaching, he almost ran, but didn't. He simply sat and stared down between his feet at the blacktop.

"Hello, up there," called the man. "Hello."

It was Joe Barnwell, the skipper of the Chickapee team and a friend of his father's from the mill.

"What do you say, Edward. Looks like you might could use a bath."

Eddie said nothing.

"Sulled up, have you? Well, I don't blame you. Somebody said you were giving that preacher fella a hard time, though. Said maybe you had it coming."

Eddie shook his head, never looking up. "He didn't have no call to do me like that. I was playing was all. Contrary son of bitch. I ain't but fifteen. That ought to count for something. Being immature and all."

"Reckon he didn't exactly see it that way."

"I reckon he didn't. But I tell you this, I swear right here: the day will come when I whip his ass. I swear to that. I'll whip his ass or I'll know the reason why."

"Now, Edward."

"I swear on it."

The man leaned forward and considered this.

"Well, you can't go home like that. Come on down to the showers and clean up. Likely I might could even rustle up a shirt and pair of pants. Keep your mamma from seeing you that way."

"I ain't no charity case."

"Well, if you don't mind your daddy seeing you."

Eddie said nothing.

"Now, Edward."

He shook his head and whimpered. He could no longer tell the difference between the salt tastes of blood and tears.

"Well," said Joe Barnwell. "Come on if you know what's good for you. The mill was good enough to build a shower room, and I reckon you ain't too high on the horse to use em."

Barnwell labored back down the slope, cutting straight from first base toward third then slipped through the chain-link fence and was gone. Eddie waited, refusing to look up again. Finally, noticing the lights down past the third-base line, he stood and walked.

The doors were open, and inside it was bright and loud. Banks of fog drifted like weather fronts, and he could hear the sizzle of hot showers. He pulled off his shoes and socks and walked in, trying to act confident, found a towel in a bin and walked back into the shower room, where the last of the players were drying off. No one stopped him or paid him any mind. He rinsed until the tiled floor was a stain of dirty runoff, then toweled dry and slipped his pants and shirt back on, throwing his socks and underwear away. He stared at himself in the fogged mirror until the locker room was empty. The players were all out in the parking lot revving engines and shouting. Around the room lay dusty gloves and balls, seven or eight bats spilling from the mouth of an army duffle bag. One by one he picked up and set down the caps and discarded jerseys, the cans of snuff and pouches of Red Man, while outside the men grew suddenly quiet, motors silent, the night so empty

Eddie could hear cars humming along Main Street a quarter mile away. He peeked out the door. The players were circled, each on one knee. They were praying, and in the center, both hands open toward the heavens, stood the reverend. How long Eddie sat watching the man he couldn't say—long enough to memorize the road map of his hands, the gray slug of a mustache he hadn't noticed before. The rage seeped back into him until he was sweating, and he felt it pulse through his veins like traffic through a city. He stood, washed his face, leaned by the door, paced. The man was still praying. Eddie shut his eyes and counted to fifty: still praying. The players shifted, switching knees. Someone coughed. Eddie almost laughed. That was when, in the far corner of the locker room, sitting on a Bible fat with flyers and circulars, he noticed a bulging black leather wallet.

The house was as dark and still as a cave, no different really from any of the other houses. All along the streets that ran like spokes from the hub that was Chickapee Mill sat identical single-story homes, each with its black shutters and gas lights, each with its pitiful square of slanting porch. He was quiet on the steps—slipping past a ceramic black child eating a slice of watermelon, the figure's bulging lips cracked and striped peppermint—inside quieter still, shutting the door and latching it and three steps down the hall before he realized his father was sitting in the rocker in the far corner. He stopped then and unconsciously straightened his shirt, thumbed back his eyebrows. His father was all head and shoulders, silhouetted against the blue-gray window, his hands bathed in a slant of streetlight.

"Edward?"

"Yessir."

"Didn't hear you ride up."

"No, sir," he answered.

"Where's your bicycle?"

"I left it down with Tom Suggs," he said, "seeing as how the chain slipped loose and all."

"The chain slipped loose?"

"Yessir."

"Chain shouldn't slip loose like that on a new bicycle. You should have brought it. I could have fixed it for you."

"Yessir."

"Step up here by the window, Edward. I hate to turn on the light and wake your mother seeing as how she sat up some while worrying over you."

Eddie stepped forward, his fists tingling.

"You run into trouble?"

"No, sir."

"Then it just found you, I guess."

"Something like that."

"Well, it's late," said his father. "I think this conversation is best reconvened in the morning."

Out the window an owl called, keeping him from sleep, though he could not spot it in the trees. Instead, he counted the reverend's money: there was well over six hundred dollars in crisp twenties and tens and fives. His driver's license from the state of Florida showed a bald man named Frank Krebs, six foot six, two hundred and thirty-seven pounds. There was also a small parole card marked MIAMI-DADE COUNTY and punched in places like a ticket. He recounted the bills. Folding money, he thought, the only kind worth having. Don't give me none of that jingling shit.

Two days later Eddie walked home from school to find a high sheriff's car parked along the street.

Seven miles up the mountain from the Burdens' homeplace, old man Joseph Cory was keeping his daughter in an iron cage meant for gorillas, called it his calaboose. What it was, was an old trailer car he'd bought off the traveling circus twenty-some-odd years ago, marooned now in a sea of thigh-deep cattails and broom straw beneath a chinaberry tree and casting a jagged shadow across the yard.

He looked up from his welding, flipped back his visor. He couldn't see her, couldn't see anything, just a gaping darkness where the window was, couldn't even see the bars.

"Mary Anne," he called. "Mary Anne." He waited, the torch still hissing in his hand. Around him sat bottles of compressed air, some stacked but most scattered as if by storm. "Mary Anne, you best look at me, girl. You hear me?" She gave no sign that she did.

Cory started for his calaboose, lips tingling with anger. Ever damn since her mamma died, he thought. That was the thing. Every damn since then she'd been like this.

The yard seemed a museum for discarded junk: disc plows, a dunking booth, broken-down tractors, goalposts leaning out toward the pasture, cars rooted now on cinder blocks. He walked into shadows of the calaboose and grabbed the window bars—cool to the touch—squinted in at her figure. She sat huddled against the far wall, cross-legged and wearing pedal pushers. She wouldn't look at him.

"Girl, you know good and well I'm going about the Lord's business here. You hear me? You ort to answer stead of making me cross the got-damn yard ever ten minutes. You need some water?" He pushed his head up against the bars. She was looking at him, at the sweat pearled in his beard. "You hear me, pumpkin?" She nodded her head yes and Cory recrossed the yard and took the ladle from the rain bucket and passed it through the bars. She drank it quickly, water spilling over her chin and down her neck to wet the cotton of her shirt, and then shrank back to the floor.

"Ain't too hot in there?" he asked. She wasn't looking at him now. "I allow it ain't," he said. He turned to study the sky, a milky blue with films of cirrus clouds orphaned along the horizon. The sun was hot, the air thick. The shaded wood of the calaboose was maybe the coolest place around, short of dipping your feet in the river.

"I reckon when that devil woman's spell wears out you can come on out. You feel anything yet?" She wasn't listening, or at least not answering. "Well you holler if'n you feel something moving through you. I got to feed Big Ernie."

Cory made for the feed shed, knowing exactly what had happened. Hoghead Johnson had seen it all, had come up two days ago all sorry to be the one, hat in his left hand, his only hand, the other sleeve pinned neatly. It's the damnedest thing Mister Cory and I shore as God hate to be the one to tell you, and all such nonsense. Hoghead's Rottweiler hanging out of his truck window barking its got-damn head off.

"I ain't allowed time to stand and chitchat," Cory had told him, standing on his front porch, biscuit flour dusting his hands. "If you got something to say, I reckon you better out with it."

Hoghead had shuffled from foot to foot, hat flat against his stomach.

"I don't reckon you'd have a little taste setting about, would you?"

"You reckon a taste'll loosen that tongue of yours?"

"Yessir, I allow it might."

"Reckon it might shut that dog up?"

"Who? Burt Reynolds?" Hoghead turned toward his truck. "Hush up, Burt Reynolds. Hush up, now."

Cory had come back out with a pint of muscadine wine, and Hoghead took two fierce gulps, licked his lips, then settled into what it was he had to tell.

Now, Cory entered the coolness of the feed shed, the smell sharp, the ground-clay red with iron. He came out with a sack of sweet feed hoisted over one shoulder, headed for the fence line. Hoghead's wife had been up to see the old McCallister woman, the got-damn witch, and climbing out of the holler toward the road she had come upon two young girls. The girls had hid when they'd seen Mrs. Johnson, though Mrs. Johnson didn't mean em no harm, didn't even care what they business was so long as they let her pass, seeing as how that's just the kinda woman she is, real gentle soul, now you know that, now don't you, Mr. Cory? So she had walked on and not thought a lick of it till the next night. Hoghead had drunk down half the wine by this point, his tongue purple, cheeks flushed. Well, he went on, the next night he and the missus had headed over to the fish camp off Highway 76 and pulling in the missus had grabbed his arm and said, "God in heaven, Hog, you see what I see?" and by God he had, too.

Cory scrambled over the fence like a man one quarter his age, the forty-pound sack still on his shoulder. He was lively, he was, told everyone he'd quit counting birthdays after number seventy-five, but in truth he knew his age to the day: he was eighty-four years, four months and two days old and could remember every detail of every second of his life. Every moment with all three of the wives he'd outlived, the birth of every one of his good-for-nothing children, all thirteen of them, that had, at least twelve of them so far, abandoned him. Only Mary Anne was left, and then one-armed Hoghead Johnson shows up wearing his shiny Shriners jacket and telling his tale of abomination and woe. He would sooner have heard she was making the beast with two backs with some nigger boy, but that wasn't it.

What the Johnsons had seen there in the late evening dusk, coming up the dirt road toward the fish camp, was the two girls—Mrs. Johnson knew it right then, had grabbed Hoghead's arm, put the death grip on it—the two girls she'd seen hiking out of the McCallister holler. They were sitting in the backseat of a Chevy Nova, kissing each other on the neck and lips like boy and girl. One of them was Mary Anne.

"I allow the McCallister woman put a mojo on em," Hoghead had said, trying to tongue the last of the wine from the corners of the pint bottle. "I told my wife many a time not to go see that crazy woman, but I ain't got no say over what she does. She's a good woman other than being hardheaded. The missus, I mean." He hadn't mentioned the other thing his wife had said, that being: "Hog, I do believe them girls is attempting sexual congress."

Cory had sent Hoghead and Burt Reynolds home with another pint, and the man had thanked him and taken his leave. Now Cory crossed the pasture down toward the creek, sidestepping cow patties and rattling the bag of sweet feed. He saw Big Ernie, his bull, coming hard and direct over the crown of the hill. Cory put the feed pan between him and Ernie. Ernie was prone to wildness when hearing the rattle of a bag, charging at the sound. God help me the day I shake a empty bag in front of him, thought Cory. Except there ain't no such thing as God—had to keep reminding himself of that.

"Come on, big fella," he called. "Come on and get it now."

A mojo—the damn witch had went and set to preying upon the sole girl-child left to him. If it wasn't for pressing business, he'd head over and learn the McCallister woman a lesson she not soon forget. Pistol-whip the crazy bitch, see then how bright she was on putting a curse on an otherwise respectable girl.

He slit open the sweet feed and poured it into the feed pan, and Ernie lowered his head to eat. His horns were wide and peeling, flecked with calcium and mud and tree bark. A bubble of mucus swelled from one nostril, burst. Flies circled his eyes and rear end. His tail swished, absent of thought. Cory touched the thick hide of the bull's neck, and the bull turned one glassy eye on him, though only for a moment. Ernie kept eating. A whole bag of sweet feed was liable to founder a cow, even one the size of Big Ern, but Cory was feeling reckless. He knew time was running out, that the Lord was coming soon, and when he did, Cory wanted out.

She was standing, arms out of the bars, calling, when Cory came back up out of the pasture. She sounded like her old self again, and Cory nearly spoke thanks aloud before catching himself. It was an old habit—praying—that he'd sworn off years ago. Cory had been a prophet once, an itinerant minister who traveled on foot preaching revivals, trekking deep into eastern Tennessee and western North Carolina, once walking as far as Kentucky. But after his second wife had died, he'd asked the Lord God for a vision, and a vision he'd got. He saw the world eaten by fire; he saw three women laid in the earth; he saw a string of thirteen abandonments, lined like charms on a bracelet. And he saw himself forsaking the Lord and His world, spitting out the Bread of Life and escaping.

She called again.

"What you say, pumpkin?"

"They's a snake in here."

"What's that?" He came at a fair pace, almost running. Mary Anne was pressed against the bars, a sliver of face visible, both breasts round and pushing forward. She was growing up on him, was almost grown.

"I said they's a snake in here, Daddy."

"Got-damn. Where?"

"Over by the door." Her voice was high and caught in her throat. "Curled up right over there. A bunch a bees, too."

Cory unlatched the calaboose door, creaked it open.

"Aw shitfire, Mary Anne." He picked up a tiny thing that curled over his hand and wrist. "That ain't nothing but a little old garter snake." He let the snake slither away into the grass.

"Well, let me out, Daddy, please. I'm hot in here, and thirsty."

"You ain't coming out till that mojo's off you, girl. You felt anything stirring?"

She nodded yes.

"You wouldn't lie to me, would you?"

"No, Daddy, I have, honest. I was all cold and trembly a while ago. Now please let me out."

"Let's make us a rule bout kissing other girls first."

"Please, Daddy."

There was that submarine tremor in her voice. He stepped back and let the door swing open.

Yellow jackets circled the hand pump. Cory shooed them, flicked away a praying mantis, and began pumping. The pipe gurgled, spilling cold water into a zinc bucket. Eveningtime. His favorite time of day. A man could rest a little come eveningtime, could put the day behind him, let his mind go a little, maybe have hisself a little taste. The sky was just beginning to streak, catching fire to the west, burning out somewhere overhead. Someone had told him once that polluted air was the root cause of sunsets. But he needed no more proof of its iniquity. This is a dirty world, he thought, heading back toward the house with his bathing water, a dirty, filthy place.

He heated the pail on the woodstove and called for Mary Anne. She'd said nary a word during dinner, just mopped the ham gravy off her plate with cornbread, drunk a jar of water, scraped the plates into the sink. He walked back toward her room and called again. Nothing. Just like today, he thought, ignoring me. He went back to the stove and felt the water—still tepid—then, by chance, caught something moving out of the corner of his eye. He leaned into the window and saw her going over the fence down into the pasture, a croker sack slung over one shoulder.

"Got-damn, female," he muttered. "Put that sack down, Mary Anne. Quit rattling that sack."

Cory ran out to the yard and called for her. Mary Anne looked back once, mouthed words he could neither hear nor understand, hiked with one hand at her crotch, and then went on running down the slope, the sack swishing on her shoulder.

"Mary Anne! Mary Anne!"

He scrambled up the fence, lost his balance, fell headlong into the tall grass hearing something in his ankle pop. He stood, collapsed in pain, tried standing, couldn't.

Dark was coming on. The sun was all but gone. He kept calling until his voice failed, swallowed by the insect sounds, tree frogs, and whippoorwills. Beneath the hum he imagined he could still hear the fabric of the bag. Darkness spilled unevenly, leaving patches of bone-colored light. He wasn't even whispering her name anymore. He might have prayed had he believed in God. Instead he started crawling, headed for the house to fetch his boots, a shovel, and his 30.06. The last thing he'd seen was old Ernie charging over the hill into the dark bowl of the field. Then the cicadas had started. Just because they had no language, Cory thought, didn't mean they couldn't speak.

Time passed, and with it the drone of work settled over the orchard, allowing James to find his own lonely routine. He would rise late, dream-haunted, having fallen into a fitful sleep sometime just before dawn. Bobby would have long since left out, rising and heading into the orchard just as James finally succumbed to fatigue. He was, Bobby said, at the point in his life where he no longer needed sleep, where it was just a void or absence, a place that left you not rested but regretful. James came to realize that the orchard itself was a sort of absence. Over the years, as money became less and less a concern, Bobby had left many of the trees unpruned, abandoning whole stretches of the orchard so that where once neatly trimmed figures bristled over the grass now stood hankering beasts, woolly trees marooned in seas of rotten apples and gloating insects.

It was not money Bobby desired, James realized. It wasn't even help. It was human company, and if that came in the form of an old friend or in the form of a migrant worker, well, so be it. Desperately, he wanted James to go see his mother.

"I just don't want to see you wind up like me, James. You stay gone long enough people will start to treat you like you're from off," Bobby said, walking onto the porch. "Like you can't do for yourself."

James took a bite of his tomato sandwich. "It ain't about that at all."

When he was alone, James would shoot up and sit on the porch until Bobby came up for lunch. They ate ham and tomato sandwiches and watched the migrants eat. After lunch he would wander deep into the forest, following the Chauga River upstream or down, lost in memory. He thought often of his wedding day, Ellie in her Sears-Roebuck dress, her black hair loose and sliding down her back like dark water. She'd felt like a breath, so clean and light, almost the idea of a woman, the very word whispered in a single exhalation. He remembered all her aunts in their pink taffeta dresses, sugary confections, they'd seemed, seated in the front row smiling and dabbing eyes. The same women who'd abandoned Ellie after her father had been sent away to the state penitentiary, ashamed of her then and leaving her to the auspices of the state, but suddenly proud, hypocritical, and pink.

Then, sometimes, he was a boy again, standing in his mother's kitchen and watching her chop cabbage for kraut or canning beans. Sometimes he sat listening to one of his father's sermons, the pew beneath him hard and splintered so that he sat perfectly still, not daring to shift for fear of a splinter.

"You need to go see them," Bobby said one night on the porch. He was peeling a peach. The Grand Ole Opry was on the radio, some old mountain tune, fiddle and bow, banjo and mournful voice. He glided the knife beneath the skin, the peel sliding away then hanging in a sort of helix. He halved it, tossing away the pit, and then cut it to quarters, then to eighths, the meat bright and firm. "You hear me?"

James took a sip of Old Granddad. It was dark out, a paring of moon, the harsh rustling of katydids and cicadas. "You want some of this?"

"Yeah." Bobby took a pull off the fifth. "Drank out the neck and shoulders, I see," he said holding the bottle up to the porch light. "You want a bite of this?"

James shook his head. "You know me about as well as anyone, Bobby," he said.

"So why don't you go and see em, James? You good and well know they're looking for you."

"Why? So I can go find out there's another 'monster of the dark corner' on the loose? That I'm poisoned? Go on and bury my whole life? Pass that back."

"Don't talk like that. God Almighty. Let the dead rest."

"Pass that back if you would. Bury my whole life," James said, and then drank.

"Hush now. Listen to that boy pick."

"You're a good man, Bobby. You got that medal in there to prove it."

"Hush, James," said Bobby. He tossed the peel out into the yard. "You know that don't mean a thing in the world."

"That's why he hasn't come over here. Mamma neither. You know that, don't you?"

"Who?"

"My father."

"Don't speak ill about your daddy. He's a good man."

"He feels it, too, Bobby. He's knows just like I know. It'll drive him to the grave, Bobby."

"Listen to that high lonesome sound, why don't you."

"It'll turn his heart black. Eventually it will."

"Hush, James."

"You remember what's it like when they're shooting, Bobby? When they're gunning for you?"

Bobby was quiet for a moment then said, "Yeah, I remember."

"I heard some tell that when they was hit they could just taste it, the metal. But it wasn't like that for me."

"I heard that too," Bobby said.

"The way it felt, yeah." James nodded. "Well, all the time, Bobby. All the time."

And then there was James's dream. Every night he dreamt the same dream, lost in some hellish dreamscape, part war, part collage of memory. His mother was there. Kin that lay long dead and forgotten during daylight were there. Time twisted, doubled back on itself—every night the same dream.

In his dream, James was a child of indeterminate age, standing on the front step of a house like those he had seen in neighborhoods outside Atlanta and Richmond: each house identical but for the gold numbering on the door. Two friends walked by up the street and James called to them, asking where it was they were going.

"To Trichelle's," said one. "You don't know her."

"Yes, I do," called James. "Let me come."

"No, you don't." And they disappeared up the walk.

Then the dream shifted.

There was no sense to anything. He was in a large banquet hall, dressed in a tie and sitting in an orange-cushioned pew, with two large men on both sides of him.

"Now it's your turn," one said.

"For what?" asked James.

"To take the ride."

The man handed him what felt like a small flashlight but was actually a tiny Luger pistol.

"When the light's on you," the man said, "go crazy. Scream and holler. We're going to tranq you in the neck and carry you out. That's the cover."

A spotlight fell on James, and for a moment he was dumbstruck before managing to yell and brandish the Luger. He might have even managed to fire a shot into the arced ceiling before the darts hit him, but this was never clear. Then he was being rushed out, a man at each arm, trying vainly to paw at his neck, his vision collapsing at the frayed edges. He rode in the back of a car to a place more beautiful than any he had ever seen. Long hedgerows and fountains jetting plumes of blue water.

"There's one more thing," said the man.

James, now the child James, pressed his hands against the glass of the back-seat window. "One more thing," said the man. Out the window were the faces of those he had forgotten: friends from childhood, distant cousins, men dead since his infancy, now resurrected from the blue dust of memory. He waved. No one waved back.

A man, a single man, led him up a series of outdoor stairs to a small, rectangular hole in a brick wall.

"In there," said the man. The hole was no wider than a foot, no more than a few inches tall. The man indicated that James was to climb through.

"I can't fit through that," James said.

"Fine, then," said the man, and he proceeded to stretch the hole wider. "How about now?"

James climbed through. Inside sat a large, high-backed chair, not unlike that of a dentist. A woman was waiting, squat and older, perhaps sixty, with a tangle of steel-gray hair.

"Sit," she said.

The man fastened James's wrists and ankles with leather bindings.

"No one's going to shock you," said the man.

"Why did you throw up?" the woman asked James.

"I didn't throw up."

"When they tranqued you. You threw up when they tranqued you."

"This is the last thing," said the man cinching the straps.

"I had just ate," said James. "I must've threw up cause I had just ate."

"This is the last thing," repeated the man.

The woman picked up what appeared to be a two-by-four plank and struck James's right shoulder. His breath left him, expelled in a sudden cough. He panted. He found himself fully grown. She struck him again, working now from his left shoulder across his upper back to his right shoulder. He tensed, muscles catching, trying to rear them like armor. How long she went on striking he could not say, but abruptly she stopped to say something to the man in a language James could not understand. Not Korean, not Chinese, German, perhaps—the language of childhood fears. The man walked forward with a shovel and briefly, in the rusty spoon of its head, James could see his bent reflection. White bandages were wrapped around his forehead. The woman struck him directly in the face, then the ear, jaw, left temple. Then they were burning him. The woman held a butane lighter against one wrist, against the naked flesh of his stomach, and finally he woke enough to cry.

"This is the last thing," the man reminded him. "The last thing, then you're one of us."

A tongue of flame sharpened to blue.

"No, I quit," cried James. "Please, for Christ's sake, I quit."

"Fine, then" said the woman, putting away the lighter. "You quit. It's over."

James's head sank.

"It's over," the woman said.

"Congratulations," said the man. "You made it."

"He quit," said the woman.

"She's lying to you. She's like that. Congratulations."

Here time and place again shifted and James, older now though not grown, found himself walking on the deck of a ship, a blanket pulled over his head and shoulders, his back prematurely humped. He leaned against the railing and watched a series of rocks pan past. The people on shore gestured and called to them, though he heard nothing but the groan of the ship's engines. A man stood beside him.

"They say they're gonna sail this thing all the way down the Yalu to let us off," said the man. "Everybody's saying it even though it's impossible. I still got a mind to believe em, though."

James walked away, finding his mother sitting with a blanket wrapped around her, her back pressed against the cold steel of the forecastle. She looked up at him. Her hair had lost its color and appeared broken, stringy, and disheveled. He could see the pale curve of her scalp. Her face was a sour white, sagging and adhering poorly to her bones.

"What have they done to you, James?" she asked, and touched his forearm. "What have they gone and done?"

He said nothing.

"Have you seen your brothers?" she asked.

He nodded. "I saw Enis, Mamma. I saw Roy too, but it's too late for him, he ain't coming back. But Enis, Mamma."

She was crying now.

"There's so much evil in the world, James. Such an evil place. It started with Cain—"

"I saw what they did to him, Mamma." And he had, he was certain, though how he had come about this knowledge he had no idea. "They cut him up, Mamma. Like he's a girl now. They said he had some disease and there wasn't any penicillin but I don't believe em. They just went and cut him up."

His mother held at his forearm as if for leverage while clots of tears ran down her face. "It started with Cain," she began to babble. "Slapped his own flesh down with a jawbone in cold blood. Saw a bright light at the end."

"Mamma."

"A bright light. And the Lord put a mark on him."

"I saw them cut him, Mamma. I saw it, but it wasn't me."

She went on crying.

"But it wasn't me, Mamma. Hear me, Mamma?"

James woke in the orchard to the night sounds of crickets and tree frogs, sweating from the dream, from Freud's castration dream. Only not his own.

Three weeks to the day after arriving, James met his youngest brother. James was sitting on the back porch at Bobby's, eating barbecue from a Styrofoam plate. It was near six and the migrants had quit work for the day. Bobby had driven into town, leaving out with Sharon's forgotten dolphin on the seat beside him. James sat barefoot in a rocking chair, eating, trying not to think. He knew the time was coming to visit his parents, to reopen that wound, and he was scared. Things felt inevitable, moving toward some inexorable point. Bobby with his hand-me-down leftover knickknacks, Ellie with her homemade curtains and bottle of gin, Korea, heroin—the slow accrual of things, real and imagined, the way things latch on to us.

A junco went hopping through the grass. The breeze rustled. Slowly, the air was thinning, losing its humidity. Fall was coming. So many things, James felt, were coming.

He didn't bother walking around front when he heard someone pulling down the drive, figuring it was Bobby. Until the apples started coming off the trees in heavy numbers, traffic would be almost nonexistent, the place a no-man's land.

James watched the junco scatter into the air before realizing a man stood at the corner of the porch watching him. James wiped his mouth.

"Can I help you?" he asked.

"How's that barbecue?" asked the man.

"I could just about eat my weight in it. Bobby ain't around."

"I know he ain't." The man walked around to the bottom of the step, facing him, thumbs tucked behind his belt buckle. He was smiling with a toothpick in the corner of his mouth. "Maybe I ought to introduce myself," he said.

"Maybe."

Sometime later James found himself inside, tearing through his duffle bag, finding the syringe, his heart's needle, his savior. Brother. Blood kin. *What were they like when you were little, Mamma and Daddy?* Same eyes, hands, same cut of the chin. Same questions. *You didn't recognize me at first, did you?* Questions, the lapses where instead of words or memories there were spaces in the throat, empty and hollow; where instead of stories there were only wishes, said and unsaid. *I went, too. Just like you. Roy was already over there. But I never saw no action. What was that like, when it finally happened?* James stumbled out into the yard, trying to gather his breath, feeling it swirling around him. Brother. Blood kin. He pulled off his belt. The sky fell away, twirling in soft color. He found himself on the ground. He found mown grass beneath his hands, the imprint of blades, the smell of spring. He sat up and found air.

Here I've spent my whole life wondering about you and there you sit.

Then a voice said: "Why do you do that?"

James looked up to find a girl standing over him, the girl he remembered from his first night here, her hair dark as plums. He dropped his belt, instead cinching his arm with a piece of bailing twine just above his left elbow. His veins danced. The sweat was coming.

"Aren't you supposed to be working or something?"

The girl shrugged, tottering from foot to foot as if dancing. She was perhaps ten, maybe twelve, wearing a feed-sack dress, a string of beads, no shoes.

"Somebody's bound to be looking for you," said James.

Again, she shrugged, rubbed the instep of one foot along the opposite calf. He released the twine, exhaled, sat for a moment panting.

"Your English is awful good."

"Why do you do that? Why do you make yourself bleed? My daddy said it was because you were sick and it was to make you feel better, but I don't believe him."

He wiped away the blood with his sleeve.

She kept looking at him. "You have sweat in your eyes," she said. "How can you see anything?"

"Get on now," he said, without looking up again, sitting until he was certain the girl was gone. *Get going, brother. Blood kin.*

Deep in the forest he crossed a shallow stream bedded with rocks the color of sand. Nameless birds crowded the upper works of a tree. In a few weeks the leaves would begin to color, then fall, a season one tasted like pennies beneath the tongue; a stillness would befall the mountain, but for now the world was humid with life. He walked on up a steep slope, ignoring the switchbacks while the morphine began its creep, moving outward like ripples worrying a pool. His legs grew light. He had no arms. He chattered his teeth, feeling nothing, simply the awareness of contact, of vibration, nothing more. His was detached. He looked down at his feet and felt they belonged to someone else, an old lover, a friend, some forgotten relative, and for a moment he seized with some great compassion, some great worry for that traveler that journeyed without his feet.

James crossed the ridge then rested on a jutting shoulder of limestone. Below him, flickering like quicksilver through the dense canopy, ran the Chauga River. He sat to wait for the full push of the morphine that filled into the hollow places, that seemed to expand him, to comfort him. Thy rod and thy staff. He was faintly aware of being watched, even glanced down once to catch a rustling of the laurel bushes below, but did not care. If someone had followed him, well, let them follow. If they planned to waylay him, to steal the twenty-year-old paratrooper boots off his feet, let them do that as well. Let them come for him, family, blood kin, lover, and foe alike. He was searching for someone, and there was a surety here, a sense of not wanting, and there would be no undoing of that.

What will be will be, his mother had told him. This remark had been prefaced by his saying he had no intention of dying in Korea nor anywhere else, and his mother's response had chilled him. He had sought assurance. He had sought her definitive response, 'No, my son, you will not die. You are my son and you will not die. I won't allow it.' But none of that had passed her lips—what will be will be. And in the end, this too shall pass. Now, he was searching for God, haunting the trunks of fallen trees, could sense Him in the laurel thickets.

"I won't let you get away," he mumbled. "Not again, I won't." Not after coming so close. But God's will. Not his own.

Likely he had joined for all the usual reasons: boredom; a faint sense of duty; to test himself; because if you were young and poor it was what you did; to get out of the corn patch, maybe; to sink a marriage that was already listing, to sink it before she could find him out, see through him, to punch that final, irrevocable hole in its hull—be honest, that was it, now wasn't it? Funny thing about him, he had no sense of nostalgia, no desire for imagined better days. Whatever rose-colored glasses men and women are fitted with at birth—James had smashed his years ago. After joining up over in Greenville, he had been sent to Parris Island then Camp Lejeune, where he finished basic and then quartermaster school at Camp Pendleton. After that he had spent five months filing arrest reports for the Shore Patrol in San Francisco, walking the narrow streets, tracking up and down the humps of the city, fairly addled by the great expanse of bay.

In Okinawa he had waited, drank, waited and drank, had sought the company of no one, shunning those who called him hillbilly just as he shunned those who were called it. He had no friends. Then he was in Korea, and suddenly men were dying. At Taejon they had died in droves, bodies sundered by artillery shells, and he had felt some strange brotherhood with men ravaged by grapeshot in the Civil War. From there they had retreated south to Pusan and then the landing at Inchon, then the retreat from the Chosin Reservoir, where he was captured, raced north across the Yalu River just ahead of the U.N. advance, arriving finally at a POW camp deep in Manchuria. Shortly thereafter they were moved again, to a camp south of Pyongyang where men lay prostrate and whimpering during air raids. He had sent one letter home via the Red Cross, a letter to Eleanor in which he set out in detail the method by which he intended to kill himself. Likely it had never made it through the censors, Communist or U.N. That he never bothered to kill himself wasn't, he felt, from a lack of courage. It was simply too much trouble.

Dreams—he saw the camp now only in dreams. The First Marine Division had crept closer, and faint tremors had turned from distant flashes to unmitigated beautiful violence, the constant shelling that drove men mad, that left one cowering on the ground, eardrums shattered, tearing his fingernails loose against the frozen earth. When it was clear the Americans would arrive in a matter of days, the rumor ran through the camp that they would all be machine-gunned. Then one day they woke to find the camp empty. A platoon of marines arrived later that afternoon. After that it was a field hospital in the south, then Japan, where they removed most of his stomach for reasons they could not explain. Next came two months convalescing at a sanatorium near Fort Dix in New Jersey. The morphine was the only constant, his single abiding companion.

It was from Fort Dix he had written Eleanor to try to explain things, to explain why he couldn't live with her, be her husband, be a man, a human. It wasn't selfishness, he wrote. I am simply no longer a part of this world. Things, he told her, things will be what they will be. But he never sent the letter.

God's will, he thought, not his own.

When he came down the bank, the girl was standing along the river watching him, as still as an idol. In her hands she held what appeared to be tiny, rounded stones.

"I brought these for you," she said.

"I thought I told you to get on."

"Don't you even want to see?" She pushed them forward. "Mushrooms. They're like what you take, my father says. Except you won't have to keep making yourself bleed."

He took the mushrooms from her.

"I found them down in the pasture," she said. "They were growing down there."

"What's your name?"

"Mercedes."

"Mercedes. Well, Mercedes, I don't think they'll work the same way."

"But they still might make you feel better. My father says they might."

He nodded. "Well, come on, Mercedes," he said. Night was falling. They walked back to the bunkhouses.

Roy piloted his midnight blue Fastback along SC 28 down the mountain toward Seneca and Highway 123, past the café and the firehouse and the movie theater, its marquee blank but for the numbers 455 and 700, numbers rendered meaningless by their lack of context; past the Dairy Queen, with its three-foot plastic ice cream cone; past the AMC bowling alley. Late September and the day was hot and clear, heat shimmers warping the blacktop. Roy kept the window down, sipping on a thermos of ice water propped between his thighs. To his right and left stretched fields heavy with late-summer corn. A tractor moved along a furrow. Johnny Cash was on the radio.

Past a sign for Clemson University, Roy saw a boy walking along the road's edge, bag slung over one shoulder. He slowed and honked.

"I'll be damned if you don't look familiar," he called.

The boy squinted back, his eyes nearly drawn shut by the sun.

"That's one sorry-ass excuse for a spindle."

"Who the hell are you?" asked the boy.

"I got a mind to say you're Tom Gathers' youngest."

Roy eased onto the shoulder. The boy stepped closer. "Roy Burden?"

"The one and only. Where you headed?"

Eddie spat. "You wouldn't believe me if I said. Fella tried to law me. Some traveling preacher. Said I stole his wallet."

"Did you?"

"Hell, yeah, I did. Now I'm getting out of town. Don't matter where to. Might just wind up in California."

"California?"

"Damn right. They got women there, don't they?"

"California's west."

"No shit."

"You're going east."

Eddie looked down at his feet. "I reckon a man can walk any which way he chooses," he said.

Roy reached across the seat and opened the door.

"Well, you better get in then. California or not, I reckon I can't leave you standing in the dust."

Eddie threw his bag into the backseat and climbed in.

"I appreciate it. Ain't nobody even slowed down all morning."

"Don't mention it."

"I ain't headed nowhere particular."

"Well, I reckon I can get you there."

"California just sounded nice was all. The beach and all." Roy nodded. "Hey, I don't reckon you might have a cold something to drink, day like this," Eddie said.

"Try the cooler there in the back."

Eddie leaned over the seat and fished in an Igloo cooler filled to the rim with melting ice and cans of Strohs, his hand coming out pink and dripping and clutching a beer. Roy pulled out onto the highway.

"Want one?" asked Eddie.

Roy shook his head no as Eddie began to drink. The apple of the boy's throat bobbed violently.

"I heard you was some kind of pilot once upon a time," he said when the beer was empty.

"You might have heard right."

"Heard you killed more gooks than God Almighty hisself."

"Seven confirmed Migs. Russian jets. Which makes me an ace. You only need five to be an ace. Got five of em with Sidewinders. Two with guns. Just blew the shit out of em. They smoked down like fireworks, embers or whatever they're called." Roy looked from the road to Eddie back to the road. "Flew eighty-one sorties. Hanoi. Haiphong. Shot at a hell of a few times. At one point Haiphong was the most heavily defended place on earth. Maybe still is."

"No shit? What'd you fly?"

"An F-4 Phantom."

"And you flew it off one of them ships?"

Roy nodded.

"You ever get hit?"

"Never a scratch. Not so much as a broken fingernail. Watched SAMs go past me to hit other guys like it was magic or voodoo or just some sorta miracle."

"That's lucky," said Eddie.

Roy shook his head. "No. That ain't luck."

They drove on a while past fields of grazing dairy cows, past a chicken-processing plant, past the leaning relics of sharecroppers' cabins, past bulldozers cutting red gashes in forests of dwarf pines—the precursors to tract housing. Outside a gas station, men sat on upturned milk crates. A pack of beagles skirted the edge of the highway then disappeared into the woods.

"This is not exactly what you'd call a bucolic paradise," said Roy. "More like a dark place, a shadowland."

"What's that?" asked Eddie.

"Everything. This whole place. I used to hunt in them very woods."

"Who with?"

"My brothers. Whoever was going. Sometimes old Bobby Thorton would take us. Old Bobby practically raised me and my brothers. Like a daddy to us. Used to take us catfishing. Man taught me how to shoot, how to bow hunt."

"Not your real daddy?"

"My daddy would go into these long funks. He's what you call a pacifist." Eddie looked at him.

"Means he hates guns," said Roy. "Man won't touch a gun. Only gun in the house is one Mamma hid from him years ago. A .410 belonged to my brother. He don't even know it's there."

"No shit? And all three of you went off to the service. That's something, I reckon."

"Strange world. They razing it all now, anyway. Ain't nobody gonna be hunting them woods. Put up a strip mall, maybe another subdivision, a nice big parking lot."

Twenty minutes later they pulled up outside a large block building. Sunlight glared off its slant roof. The sign out front read UPSTATE FABRIC & APPAREL. Several pickups and an old Impala sat in the gravel parking lot.

"Wait here," said Roy.

"If this is my get-off, I wouldn't mind taking one or two of them cold beers with me."

"This ain't your get-off. Just wait in the car. I've got a job interview inside."

"A interview?"

"Can't suck that government teat forever, Gathers. Just wait out here. I won't be but a minute."

When Roy came out, the boy was asleep, beads of sweat running off his face down the collar of his shirt. He knocked on the front glass and Eddie jerked awake.

"Hey, what say, Roy. Man give you a job?"

"What do you think?" said Roy climbing in and starting the car. Cool air poured against them. He eased the car into reverse.

"I'd say you don't much talk like a man that just got a new job."

"I'd say you don't much talk like a man that knows when to keep his mouth shut." Roy pulled out onto the highway. "He said he'd let me know," he said after a moment. "How about a little drink to take the edge off this heat?"

"You the boss," said Eddie, reaching into the back for two cans of beer.

"No. There's a place up here. A nice establishment. Real civilized."

They pulled into a gravel parking lot and walked inside. The honky-tonk was nearly empty, except for a few other men bent over beers or tumblers of amber whiskey. A red BUDWEISER sign pulsed against the front glass casting a pinkish pall over the room.

"What you know good, boys?" asked the barkeep.

"Let me have a whiskey. Double for myself. How bout you, young Gathers?"

"Same, I reckon."

"Couple of doubles," said the barkeep. "Jack all right?"

"Old Jack'll do just fine."

Roy reached for his wallet.

"Naw," said Eddie. "This one's on the good reverend."

"You sure the reverend don't mind?"

"I have yet to hear him complain."

"Well, I ain't got a mind to argue then."

By four the bar was beginning to fill up with worn-out mill hands and masons and day laborers. Roy and Eddie had lurched shakily to a booth against the far wall. Waylon Jennings's voice faded. Men kept ambling through the door, flooding the dim bar with sunlight as sudden as a flashbulb before bellying up to the bar.

"Tell me about flying," said Eddie.

Roy shook his head. "Now why go and ruin a perfectly decent afternoon?"

"Just wondering was all."

Eddie shrugged and sat up taller in his seat, tapped his nails against the Formica tabletop.

"I need to take a piss," said Roy.

"Hold on now a minute. That man over there's got an eye on you, Roy. You know him?"

"Which one?"

"The one in the corner there. He keeps looking over here. Got the khakis and red shirt. Looks like something out of some damn Sears Roebuck catalog."

"Well, let him look."

The man did look, pointing, and then conferring with two friends.

"He's coming over this way."

"Well, let him come. Free country, Gathers."

The man walked over and stood, hands in pockets, at the edge of their table. Roy finished his drink.

"Excuse me, gentlemen," said the man. "But my friends and I were conferring on the subject and we believe that you might be Roy Burden."

"You and your friends have conferred correctly," said Roy, staring at the saucer-sized buckle on the man's belt.

"Well, I thought as much. And I'm afraid there might be something of a problem."

"No problem here," said Eddie.

"Keep your mouth shut, boy," said the man. "There is a problem, a real problem, cause as we understand it, your friend here's been keeping with a girl by the name of Faith Abernathy."

"Never heard the name," answered Roy.

"Well, I doubt that," said the man. "I do doubt that."

"Free country," said Roy. "Doubt what you want. Now if you don't mind stepping aside for a man to take a piss. Or maybe you'd like to help out? Doctor did tell me not to be lifting anything too heavy."

"Your friend's pitching a little drunk, is he," the man said to Eddie.

"This ain't about him," said Roy.

"You're damn right about that," agreed the man. "My friends and I actually know as a matter of good fact that you're keeping up with this girl and the problem, my friend—"

"I'm not your friend," interrupted Roy then burped.

"The problem is, that girl is all set to marry a good friend of ours. Peyton Fowles. You might know him."

"I might know him to be a first-rate asshole."

The man nodded, a bemused look coming across his face. "You acting big in front of your little friend but I'm willing to bet you're all talk."

"How much, partner? Lay it on the table. We do live in a free country here."

"Well," said the man, "I think therein lies the problem. Now you seem to think there's some correlation between pussy and, let's say, beer. See, one a man might not mind sharing. But the other, well, the other—"

"Look," said Roy rising in the booth. "We didn't come in here looking for any trouble. I do know Faith, and I know Peyton too." Eddie watched as the fingers of Roy's left hand wrapped around a silver napkin dispenser, squeezing it so tight they went white, Roy keeping his eyes on the man the entire time. "I appreciate the concern of you and your friends," said Roy.

"But I want you to know"—and he swung the metal dispenser against the left temple of the man who staggered back a half step, his knees buckling, reaching gently to touch the area where he thought his head should be—"that I don't take to assholes ruining my drinking."

A single napkin opened like a parachute to float down against the floor. The man recovered, lunged forward, and Roy struck at him again. This time the man was prepared, blocking the dispenser and landing a punch solidly in Roy's solar plexus. He fell backward against the wall, his head bouncing off the concrete, and then stood in the booth. The man's friends were scrambling over by now.

"Come on, Gathers," said Roy, and he kicked the man in the chin. "There's gonna be hell to pay, and I'm broke as shit."

The sound of the man's jaw clamping echoed off the block walls. The barkeep began to yell then grabbed the phone off the wall and began to punch numbers, then gave that up to reach under the bar for a pistol. Eddie and Roy leaped out of the booth and made for the door. Halfway across the room a bottle caught Roy behind the left ear, spraying against Eddie's cheek. Roy staggered onto all fours, kicking free of the man trying to pull him backwards.

"Come on," he yelled, running into the parking lot and starting the car. They sped away, a curtain of dust rising behind them. In the rearview mirror, Eddie could see men swarming in the parking lot like yellow jackets.

"Can you drive?" Eddie asked.

"I reckon if I can"—Roy hiccupped—"I reckon if I can fly eighty-one times over Haiphong and not get myself killed I can drive home drunk."

He leaned forward as if the car's wheel were a ship's, turning using his whole body, batting his eyes and now and then reaching up to finger the back of his skull. His fingers came away bloody.

"Son of a bitch," he said. "They anybody back there?"

"No," said Eddie.

"Son of a bitch. There's something wrong with this road, Gathers. It keeps twitching on me."

"Pull over."

"Do you know how to drive?"

"I can learn real quick."

They pulled over onto the grassy shoulder.

"Son of a bitch," repeated Roy. "I believe I cracked something against that wall." He paused for a moment, staring into the dusk. "This ain't the direction you were planning on heading, was it?"

"Well, not originally, but I sure as hell ain't headed back toward that snake pit."

"Good man. Drive then." They climbed back into the car. "And remember," Roy said, "those painted lines ain't suggestions."

Roy dozed with his head against the glass while Eddie drove as tentative as a child. Near Seneca Roy woke. They drove through alternating pools of light and dark, chains of lamplight puddled along the street.

"She drives true, don't she," said Roy.

"Was that true what that fella was saying, about you and that girl?"

"Watch the damn road there."

Eddie jerked the car back toward the centerline. "I got it."

Roy sighed. "Hell, Gathers. I feel responsible for you now."

"I can take care of my own self just fine."

"Well, are you looking for work or something? Or just to run away?"

"Work, I reckon, so long as it ain't near the mill. It don't matter."

"You give up on school?"

"Reckon I did. I figure they probably give up on me, too."

"Well, I might could help you. With the work part, I mean."

"You know a place hiring?"

"Might be."

"No offense, but why don't you work there then?"

Roy said nothing. Sometime later, staring out the mirrored glass, he said, "Yeah, it's all true about me and Faith."

Bobby was removing an alternator from a truck marooned on four cement blocks when they pulled into the yard. He walked forward, shielding his eyes from the headlights that illuminated the shed, a single stark tree behind it.

"Now who might that be?" he called.

"Hey, Bobby."

"I'm not much anymore for guessing voices."

"Roy Burden," called the approaching figure. "Ain't gonna have to club nobody with your wrench tonight. Got the Gathers boy with me."

"Well, hellfire if this ain't the new Burden family reunion hall."

"James still up here?" asked Roy, offering his hand. Bobby wiped his hand down the front of his coveralls. Old Gus came loping down the porch steps.

"Big James is here, Enis come by, the whole lot of ya. Hell, Roy, what happened to you?"

"A little misunderstanding.

"They God Almighty. Looks like a big misunderstanding."

"It escalated, you might say. This is the Gathers boy."

"Gus Gathers's boy?"

"How do, sir," said Eddie offering his hand. "Tom's boy. Gus is my uncle."

Bobby pumped his hand once and let it fall.

"Any truth to that ugly rumor the law's after you, son?"

"Just an ugly rumor, that's all," said Roy. "Can we sit for a minute?"

"You look like you might need to sit longer than that. Let's walk inside."

Bobby emerged from the back room with three cups of coffee balanced on a silver serving tray. "This is the good silver," he said. "Sharon never would let me use it."

They took the coffee. Roy removed a flask and topped off his cup.

"Might want to pass that over for just a nip, Roy."

Roy passed it to Bobby, who offered it to Eddie, who declined.

"The boy's looking for work, Bobby."

"The boy speak for hisself?"

"I do," said Eddie.

"Well, can you pick apples?"

"Yessir."

"Can you drive a tractor?"

"I can learn."

"You ain't above working with Mexican folk?"

"No, sir. Work's work."

"Yeah," said Bobby. "I keep hearing that."

Roy walked down the front steps into the yard past the streetlight. The sky was star-blown, fleets of fireflies moving and flashing in cadence. He walked around the back of the house and studied the sleeping bunkhouse while mosquitoes whirred about him, angry and blood-drunk. He could hear the desperate thump of luna moths striking the streetlight back over the shed. He looked down to where shoals of mist appeared caught in the orchard trees, unmoving, gray yet bright with the luster of starlight. All around him the night seemed to nurture a fragile, uncertain hum.

He walked down through the damp grass until he saw the shapeless hulk of someone sleeping. The air was bloated with the smell of rotten crab apples. He picked one up, tossed it.

"James." Roy tossed another. "Big James."

"You don't have to whisper," said the shape.

"Well, hell." Roy walked forward. "I do if you're giving off the impression of the living dead. Good to see you."

James sat up. "What time is it?"

"That how you greet all your brothers? I'll tell you what time it is—it's time for you to get your ass up and give your brother a hug."

"I'm asking cause you woke me."

"Hell, I don't know. Late."

"What you doing up here, Roy?"

"Been what? Nearly twenty years and that's all you got to say to me? Surprised you even recognize me."

"It ain't been that long."

"Well, damn near twenty years, I'd say. You know Enis don't even know what you look like."

"What are you doing up here?"

"Brought a boy up looking for work. Heard you were hiding out."

"I ain't hiding out. That what Bobby said?"

"Enis came up looking for you, too."

"I talked to him."

"You give him a big brotherly hug? Now get up, come on up to the house, and we'll have a drink."

"You already smell like Jack Daniel's toilet."

"You should too then, you son of a bitch. Come on, I'm being serious here."

"I don't drink no more."

"Bullshit."

"Leave me alone, Roy."

"Well, just come on up to the house and we'll talk."

"Mamma send you up here?"

"Shit, James."

"Eleanor?"

Roy shrugged. "I ain't seen her."

James nodded.

"Well?" said Roy.

"Well what?"

"God Almighty, James." Roy ran one hand through his hair. "You know Eleanor didn't want your money. Sent it all to Mamma, and Mamma never touched one red cent of it. It's all sitting in the bank downtown."

"What are you talking about?"

"Your war pension, mister hero, what you think I'm talking about?"

"You know about that?"

"No, James. I damned just channeled her spirit and the words came out my mouth."

"You say Ellie didn't want it? Well, I don't want it neither."

"Well, hell, guess don't nobody want it then. I mean it's just money."

James said nothing.

"You are one hell of a conversationalist, James. I'll give you that much. Now come on, you're giving me a headache."

"Let me sleep, Roy."

"Well, it's good to know some things haven't changed."

"I'm going back to sleep now. Come down here in the morning and we'll talk."

"I can't believe you. All these years and you just lay there."

"In the morning, Roy."

"You gonna be here in the morning, you AWOL bastard?"

"Come down and find out," said James.

Roy made a motion of dismissal, turned, and walked back to the house.

Will Burden's world moved behind an opaque curtain, a window fogged with child's breath—early signals, he knew, of the formation of cataracts. Still, he drove the logging truck himself, down along the twinned ruts that wound from the highway stretching before him on into the forest down to a small clearing, where the ground lay turned as if by teams of plow horses. Mosquitoes and gnats sought standing water, gutted mud holes, and teary eyes. Rain seemed to fall every night, and the land had flowered a lush green of indescribable richness. Morning found the ground pooled and deltaed with water, little levees formed from footprints and tire tracks. The air was laden with moisture but cooler here than in the towns at the foot of the mountain.

The foreman came over to stand on the running board of the truck. He grabbed the side mirror with one three-fingered hand, and Will leaned out to hear him over the idle of the engine. The man waved into the distance.

"Down that way," he mouthed.

Will nodded.

"Across the river there. They're waiting on you. Empty em and bring back what they've got."

"No problem."

"Where's that boy of yourn?" asked the foreman.

"Enis?"

"Yeah."

Will made a motion meant to show ignorance, and the man nodded, as if this were the way of the world, as if fathers were meant to lose track of sons as certainly as they lost track of old lovers. Enis seemed to skip work as often as not these days—the foreman knew as much. Will shifted the truck into gear and it jerked ahead out of the clearing, the payload of timber in the bed shifting for a moment then settling.

Enis didn't want him here. He thought Will too old, said he was having dreams at night, premonitions. Enis claimed he was seeing suffocating murders of crows rising from barren fields. Will had dreams, too. He dreamed of his own father. He dreamed of the only real thing he remembered about the man: the way he had died. The awful wrenching of death, sudden and sharp, the part Will had played, just a boy, an unwilling part, but a part nonetheless. Somewhere deep inside him, Will had probably known his father needed to die, but he could never separate his father, the man who had raised him, clothed and fed him, from what the newspapers later called "The Monster of the Dark Corner."

Will never saw this dark side, at least not until the last day, though looking back he was often mortified to have missed so many signs: the absences, hearing his father come in panting at night, hushing his mother, the young girls who would wander into the yard. But then his mother had missed them, too. Or at least ignored them.

Will had tried to raise his sons differently. He had renounced violence and attempted to impart the single real skill he remembered his father teaching him: how to fry a fish. There were other things, of course. Gardening, hunting, clearing bottomland, but those he'd forgotten intentionally, washing them from his mind during all those years of schooling, then, when they resurfaced, crediting another source. But his father, monster that he was, had been a magician frying a fish. He knew the meal perfectly, dusting the fish, then flipping it only once, knowing precisely the moment when it turned a crisp brown.

"You flip only once, son. Never more."

Only once. One chance. Anything more was decadent, wasteful. Big-knuckled hands a harsh brown in the clotted cornmeal.

Will gripped the wheel with two hands. *I have failed as a father,* he thought. *I am not a monster, but one need not be a monster to have failed.* He loved his sons. But he had always loved them from a distance. The same distance he held Maddy. It had been different with his first wife, Alta. When she had begun her slow three-month spiral into death, Will had sat for days on end in the chair beside her bed bathing her forehead with a wet washcloth, sifting her vials of medicine, holding a zinc bucket while she coughed up her lungs. He would lift her wasted body and slide the bedpan beneath her. Cleaning it, he never once flinched: it was part of her, and he imagined her dying away in rotting pieces. The doctor had worn a cheesecloth over his mouth, but never Will. If he died, he died. That was what love meant to him, its definition, its very context. .

When she finally had died, he shut her eyes and sat by the bed for what seemed hours. He hadn't wanted it to end like this. He knew, of course, that it would, still he had never really understood it. *There is a difference,* he had thought, *between knowing and understanding.* To be left with useless dresses, the sour smell of her in the sheets and a square of yellowed sunlight stretching lazily on the floor—that was understanding. That night while she lay on a cooling board, attended to by the women of the congregation, Will had stayed by her empty bed to study the impression left in the mattress and sheets.

Things had been different with Maddy, and in turn with the boys. He loved Maddy, of course, and their love had gone now to a place he imagined few loves ever find, a certain contentedness. But he had been older, and more guarded. You love recklessly only once. *That,* Will thought, *is the great tragedy of this life.*

The road ran down to the south bank of the Whitewater River, where trees had been cleared and a shallow ford discovered. Will eased the truck to a halt and paused for a moment to study his passage. Upstream and down, the river frothed whitewater, but here it ran still, so still he could now and then see slim brook trout moving lazily along the bottom. A man with hair to his waist walked down onto a thumb of sandbar across the river and waved a red handkerchief, sweat glistening down his face. Will let off the brake and the truck went forward, water washing over the tires. The man waved him on. The truck lurched, hesitated, and then moved up the far bank before stopping.

"Keep it coming," said the man, walking up to the cab window. He sucked smoke from his cigarette then tossed it into the current. "Stay on it," he said. "On the gas."

"I am."

"Hold on," said the man. He waded into the water. Will watched him study where the back tire disappeared into sand.

"Stuck, old-timer. Try backing up then coming forward again."

Will did. Nothing happened.

"Hellfire," said the man. "You got any ideas?"

"I just drive it, son."

"Right. Well, let me study on it a minute." He walked from sight then came back to stand on the running board. "You know I seen a man once back all the way up and ford it backwards-like. When he came to the near bank he gunned it and when the timber slid backwards he hit the brake and that lifted him out. Think you could try it backwards?"

"If I can get out of this sand, I will."

He could. Will backed the truck back across the river then turned, point after point, in the narrow clearing and began to ford backwards, the stalks of trees piled in the bed rearing ahead.

"Now gun it," called the man when Will reached the far bank.

He nailed the gas and the engine revved, bucked backward.

"Brakes," called the man.

But when he hit the brake something happened. The logs moving forward suddenly switched direction and began to slide off the rear of the bed but never made it fully off. Instead they slid halfway down, bucking the cab of the truck into the air, which finally threw off the logs. With no weight to hold it, the front of the truck dropped forward into the soft river sand. It was a terrible mistake. Will understood that now. *You love recklessly only once,* he thought, then flew from his seat into the windshield.

"Hellfire and damnation," said the man. He climbed up the front of the truck, heavy-lidded, wooden with incomprehension, and peered through the dusted spiderwebbed glass. Within the cab, the old man had crumpled forward, eyes shut, seemingly at peace with the world, his face as serene as that of a newborn baby.

For whatever luck or charm or grace of God her sons carried, Maddy Burden knew the wars had hurt them. She refused to acknowledge what the wars had done to her. She had been raised hard, but the day her husband climbed the attic stairs to lock the door behind him, she had encountered a hardness that she had never imagined existed, a hardness that had lain otherwise locked away in some distant place. His first retreat, in '42, had lasted only a few weeks, but he had spent almost two years in the attic in the mid-sixties, his mind so warped he thought it was Hitler and the Nazis and the Japs all over again. That had nearly been too much. Now she scrubbed clean the frying pan, left it on a rack to dry, and walked out into the morning sun, a basket of wash in her arms. Fog hung across the yard, all but obscuring the bulk of the mountains that encircled the house.

One by one she hung the wash along the line to dry, lost in memory.

She thought of Will. They had married in 1928, Maddy seventeen years old and desperate to get out of her parents' house. They were sharecroppers in the lower part of the state, all but itinerant, moving with the seasons, always looking for a better deal, some return that would allow them for once to get ahead or at least to break even. Like other sharecroppers they relied on a network of hearsay—word of mouth that was revered enough to send families packing in anything they could strap wheels to: wagons, trucks, flatbed trailers pulled by mules. Half the time they had lit out in the dead of night, owing some landlord money, staying one day ahead of starvation or jail. Her defining memory of childhood was of crouching beneath the feedbag tablecloth that lay over a large wire spool, and watching her mother bludgeon a cat with a broom. The cat had climbed in through the broken stove flue, and her mother had finally cornered it, batting it like a toy until the cat went limp, a slim trickle of blood bright against its white teeth. Maddy had not moved, had bit at her lower lip while the tears ran, while her mother sat on the board floor and cradled the dead cat and wept.

By the time Maddy's father had come in, the cat was in a brown paper sack which was just beginning to discolor.

"I wish you'd toss that in the Pee Dee on your way," said her mother.

Her father looked warily at the fast-soiling sack, a blood as black as ink beginning to accumulate.

"What is that?"

"Just garbage is all."

"I thought I heard a cat in here before."

"No," said her mother.

Maddy's father looked at his wife with hard, gray eyes. He worked his mouth in a slow, thoughtful manner. Her father was gentle. He babied her. It was Maddy's mother who'd kept them alive.

"Lord, Grace, you didn't go and kill some poor cat, did you?"

"No," said her mother, but she choked this out. Her legs were mapped with veins. Cobwebs blunted the high corners of the room in gray. "No, I most certainly did not."

"They Lord," said her father, who left a few minutes later with his lunch pail in one hand and the dripping sack in the other. I ain't never going to know hard like that, Maddy thought. I ain't never going to know hard so bad I snap and kill a defenseless creature. But Will's ascension had been something close, perhaps something even beyond it. Like stumbling barefoot into a stone-bottomed creek bed, she had waked to a staggering pain. When she was young, Maddy had almost drowned during baptism. They had beaten the water from her lungs. It had been like that all over again: that gagging emptiness.

That night, the night of Will's ascension, she had climbed the stairs and knocked, waited, knocked again. Through the door she could hear him speaking, reading the Bible aloud, the Book of Psalms blurring with the words of ABC Radio News. She thought of him wearing the death smell of dried flowers. She thought of him dead. She sat down against the door and cried, then slept on the couch, hoping he would come down. He didn't, and the next day she called the doctor, who rode up around suppertime.

"He's taken with something," she said. "Something in his heart."

"Like a murmur you mean?"

"Not like a murmur. More like with his spirit."

As year after year passed without word from James, she had not dared confess her fears to Will, ignoring her worries while she read through the door the weekly letters from Roy at sea and, later, letters from Enis seemingly all over the Pacific.

She was lonely among her people, without sons or blood kin.

The wash bellowed now like sails, like empty angels filling and swaying in the breeze. An old flower print dress, her Sunday dress, as soft as chamois. She fingered it thinking of the day she had bought it at the dry goods store on Main Street in Seneca. She and Will had ridden down in the cab of the truck with Enis on the seat between them, then walked the street like aristocracy, stopping for a vanilla Coke at a fountain, taking in a picture—Olivier in *Richard III,* she remembered it like yesterday and not some fifteen odd years ago—before buying the dress. She had worn it the Sunday after that, a wave in her hair that she tucked and pinned beneath her hat, the old Wesleyan women nudging and murmuring, shamed by her puffed-up indulgence. She and Sharon side by side on the back row, smiling at each other. She'd been beautiful before life cut into her like a scythe. Before arthritis had claimed her hands—the fruit of years of work on the line at a garment plant. But pride was a sin, and maybe the Good Lord had seen fit to give her something to trouble over, something to take her mind off the petty things, to distract her from the cold splendor of sin, for that was what she saw it as. Life ain't colored ribbons and play pretties and cooing babies, her mother had told her. Life ain't no pie cooling on the window sill. You want to know life, you go hoe a row a cotton, see how your back feels round about sundown. Get your bones brittle. Sleep on the ground to work the kinks out. Wake up with a circle of ringworm on your cheek, lice in your hair. It was pride, after all, that made the angels fall.

After James went missing, she had smashed the small mirror of her compact. Nineteen-fifty and she'd been a thirty-nine-year-old woman, but it felt like more than that, as if there were some special dispensation for mothers, time measured differently—days weeks, weeks months—when children were away, when children were missing, when mothers were left alone in the company of ghosts. She loved Will, but he seemed distant, detached, almost as if he were merely sojourning among the living, biding his time until called on high. She had visions sometimes of what Glory must be like, visions that came in snippets of songs and hymns, and once, lying in the sanctuary of blackest night, Will snoring and groaning beside her, she had put her hands down beneath the covers to let them rest between her legs, and touching herself, the words to a hymn had come unbidden and she felt shame, a deep tremulous shame so that when she woke her eyes ached from crying through the half-sleep of night. She feared something, though she knew not what, longed for something she could not name, and in the end declared it the vanity of vanities and chalked it up to the simple, symmetrical perfection of sin.

Her only pleasures she took now in prayer and the everyday accomplishments that number life, the miracle of a cake rising, the unadorned beauty of a made bed. Then too there was memory. But who was to say memory was not so much duty as pleasure?

After the wash was hung, she sat on the porch breaking snap beans into a washtub. After Enis had left, Will had started coming down in the evenings, and they would walk the fence line or up the road out toward the main highway, saying little, letting night settle about them. She loved Will, had grown to love him, despite, or perhaps because of, their ten-year age gap. When she married him, she knew his first wife had been tubercular and had died years ago in a little blood-spurting fit, a spot of rose flowering on the bedsheet where it tucked beneath her chin. She knew he was a quiet man, quiet in the pulpit, quiet around the house—his God in the vacant hollows. The only time she ever remembered him raising his voice, come to think of it, was that first night in the attic, that night reading aloud from the Psalms. So she found her husband, as he found his God, in the spaces, the empty pauses where one might otherwise find words. For what is God, she thought, but silence?

When the last of the beans were broken, she walked inside and stood washing her hands. The pantry shelves were lined with canned kraut, chow-chow, and beans, and she tucked the washtub beneath them, shutting the door, then pausing, hearing something. A car was coming down the drive. Two years ago the sight of a strange car would have broken her, shattered her—at least it had years before—and she still couldn't help but feel that same tension, imagining two small American flags snapping in the September air, conciliatory words on the lips of a stranger wearing his dress uniform. The wash, the car—it all felt so much like before. Once, she prayed. Once for a mother is enough. She could just read the lettering on the door panel: UPSTATE TIMBER. She dried her hands and walked out onto the porch with just the slightest twinge of curiosity.

Millie licked her lips and said, "Oh, I got something for you, sugar."

Enis smiled, looking from the road to her back to the road.

"Mm-hmm, I do," she said. "My parents are going away again. For over a week this time. I'm serious as a heart attack." She motioned toward the sidewalk. "Park up here for a second. They're going to Charleston with Faith. Her betrothed's ship is coming in, literally, for ten days." Enis looked at his hands on the wheel. "Well, you might as well be happy about it for us, Enis. I hate it for Roy just as much as you do."

He stared over the wheel at the rain-lashed street. A woman ran from awning to awning, a newspaper held over her head, before disappearing into the Winn-Dixie. Two little girls left in the cab of a pickup walked back and forth across the seat, pressing their faces to the back glass.

"I know," he said. "And I am happy about it. Real happy. Roy can fend for himself."

"Exactly," she said, curling against his arm. "After all, he's a big boy."

They pulled out and drove on up Main Street and parked a block down from the movie theater. Rain drummed against the roof. The car sat idling, Enis hesitant for a moment, unwilling to turn the switch.

"We should go on in," she said, but didn't move. The rain blew. "When I was a girl me and Faith would sit and chew sugarcane. I just thought of that just now. The rain reminded me of summer, I guess."

"Whenever you're ready."

"At my granddaddy's. Hadn't thought of it in years. There was this cane-brake out past his house."

"Just any second now," he said.

"Just this old canebrake and we'd sit out there and here was Mamma calling for us and we'd just laugh and laugh then tell her we couldn't hear her over the ice cream churn. Mamma fit to be tied."

"Any second."

"Well, I'm patient, Enis."

He looked at her. "We're the king and queen of patient. We're royalty when it comes to waiting."

"I know," she said.

A car sluiced past throwing up a fan of spray.

"I'm sorry about your daddy, Enis. I know he'll be all right, though."

"Millie." The change in his voice made her look up. "Let's get married, Millie. What do you say?"

"We're going to, baby."

"No, I mean now. Tonight. I'm not kidding," he said.

"I can see that."

"I mean you said you didn't much care about seeing the movie anyway, didn't you?"

"Enis Burden! I know I said I didn't care to see the movie, but good Lord, still."

"Still what? You've always said you wanted out of that house as fast as possible, what with your daddy running around and your mamma swallowing up nerve pills. I want to get down to the regular business of living, Millie, of living with you. That's the only thing in the world I want."

"It's the only thing I want, Enis. Still, maybe we should plan a little. Maybe I want a church wedding."

"Why?"

"Why?" She sat up in the seat and pulled a compact from her purse. She studied her lips. "Enis Burden," she said. Her voice was level. "Are you honestly going to sit there and ask me why I want a church wedding?"

"I want to settle down with you, Millie. I love you. I love you, but I can't take this driving and dating and waiting for your parents to be out of town so we can spend more than an evening together. Lord God, Millie, I'm twenty three. Twenty-fucking-three."

"I know how old you are. You don't have to cuss like that."

"I mean how long have we known each other? Remember that first date, that first night?"

"Please. That wasn't me. That was an act. That was me playing my sister."

"I loved you that first night."

"Don't give me that. I love you too, Enis, you know that. From that very first night I've loved you. And I will marry you."

"So say I do."

"I do," she said. "But not tonight."

They sat through the first show of a double feature, then crossed the street to the Seneca café and took a booth in the rear.

"It bucked up on him basically," said Enis. "Dropped him a good ten, twelve feet. Man on the bank said he'd never seen anything like it. The dumb ass. Probably his idea to start with. Daddy's too old to think of trying something like that on his own."

Two laminated menus lay flat on the table: HAMBURGERS, HOTDOGS— ONE MEAT & THREE VEGS., ROLL/CORNBREAD, TEA—HAMBURGER STEAK W/ MUSHROOM GRAVY—HOUSE SPECIAL!!!

"They ever heard of a thing called service in here."

"It's late," said Millie.

"It's not late and the place is practically empty. We should've went to the Time drive-in."

"Everybody's always there. I hate it. It's just like the drive-in movie."

Behind them a door swung open and a woman strode toward them.

"Oh, hell," said Enis.

"What?"

"The waitress," he whispered.

Millie looked up.

"Is that—"

She walked up flipping open a small blue pad, licked the tip of a miniature pencil. She looked older, worn, though he knew her around the eyes. The same eyes as the woman in the photograph album. Then he knew her face, finding it in some deep locked place. He knew beyond knowing. He even remembered meeting her once years and years ago.

"Evening. I see y'all saw the menus"—then she stopped, seeing a ghost, fingering an old wound that wouldn't scar.

"Hey, Eleanor. I'm Enis. This is my girlfriend, Millie."

"Well, hey," said Eleanor.

"I didn't know you worked in here."

"Yeah," she said brushing back a strand of hair. "Few months now. Marlon took me on. I'd kind of been working all over the place. How's your folks doing?"

"Mamma's fine. Daddy got hurt, but I guess you've probably heard about all that."

She nodded. "I was real sorry to hear it," she said. "Real sorry. Was y'all looking to order?"

They ordered and, when their food arrived, did not speak. Eleanor smiled, or attempted to smile, the chap of her lips showing as she placed the plates before them, the bill face down on the edge of the table.

"That was odd," said Millie after Eleanor had walked away.

"Scared the living daylights outta me."

"What's she even working for? Didn't James send her all his pension or whatever?"

"She wouldn't take it. Signed it all away to Mamma."

"My God. Really?"

"Then Mamma wouldn't take it neither."

"My God. Well, you think she's seen him yet? She hasn't, has she?"

"No. No, I'd say she's seen him all right."

Footsteps. Three days later Enis woke to the sound—cold, measured and even—not really believing it at first, phantom steps perhaps, muffled on the cinder block steps then the porch boards. Then he heard the dogs rouse and a voice hushing them. Soft knocking. He was stretched out on the couch wearing only his drawers, a bedsheet thrown over his legs, throw pillow propped behind his head. The TV pitched steep shadows across the room. Knocking again. If he didn't move, it might go away.

"Hello." A whisper through the window screen. "I know somebody's in there. Come on, now. Open up, I can see the TV on."

The damn TV. It reflected against the window. Good Lord, thought Enis. He tried to find his watch, couldn't, pulled a pair of fatigue pants on over his BVDs and flipped on the porch light.

Bobby Thorton was on the porch, one hand up by his face.

"Shit, I'm sorry to wake you, Enis, but I didn't know where else to go. I didn't wake your mamma, did I?"

"I wasn't sleeping. What's wrong?"

"It's Roy. We need to go get him."

Enis could feel the cool night air against his damp shoulders. A shiver ran through him. The dogs had settled back to sleep.

"Well, where is he?" he asked.

"Down at the Last Chance. I wasn't down there with him. I reckon the Gathers boy, Eddie, told em to call me."

"Hurt or drunk?"

"Hell, both, I reckon. Come on, I got the truck out here."

"Well, good God. Just like Roy to wait till everybody's asleep then make trouble."

"I didn't pick the time. Hell, trouble ain't never particular about bedtimes no how."

"I know it. Gimme two minutes here. You want to come in?"

"Naw, I'll wait out here."

"I didn't see you pull up."

"Kept the lights off. Figured your mamma was sleeping."

"She is, but come on in. I'll put some coffee on."

"I better not."

"Just gimme a minute then."

Enis pulled on a shirt, scrubbed his face with Noxema and stared into the water-streaked mirror. A bit of soap clung like glue. Hairs wreathed the grate. He needed to brush his teeth but didn't bother with it. He looked closer at himself. He was going gray at the temples and saw a glimmer of his father staring back.

He crept down the hall to peek in at his mother. She lay wheezing, a thin gray bulge, a corner of bedsheet stirring now and then, in sync with the roving head of an oscillating fan. He fingered the grooved wood of the doorjamb trying to think. He didn't see any sense in leaving a note.

Bobby sat on the porch rocking.

"All set?"

"Yeah. What time is it?"

Bobby looked at his bare wrist. "Late. Real late." He slapped his palms flat on the arms of the rocking chair and stood. "Let's get to it," he said.

Along the roadside they saw gully grass and trash caught in the beams of the headlights, paper cups, an empty Dairy Queen bag floating over kudzu. Bobby kept both hands on the wheel, his skin rough and dotted with purplish liver spots, a fat blue vein forked and tunneling down along his wrist. His hands trembled, delicate on the wheel. The truck pitched forward down the mountain roads, sliding into the curves, straddling a flattened opossum.

"You planning on doing the highway department a favor and straightening the road for em, Bobby?"

"Drunk as hell. Ed what's-his-face owns the place called. Drunk as hell and roughed up a little. Ed's an ass anyhow."

"Ease up so we get there."

"Drunk son of a bitch." He looked at Enis. "No offense to you or your daddy. Your daddy's a good man. He still unconscious?"

Enis nodded.

"Damn. I do hate to hear that. Swear I do."

The wheel slipped through Bobby's hands, his thumb catching here and there on the rubber knots. The window was down.

"I been one to drink, now. And I'll be the first to admit as much," said Bobby. "Reckon the law appreciated God giving me two hands and not but one mouth. I seen better days though. I'll shit you not, my better days are behind me."

Enis stared out the open window. He could smell honeysuckle. Something metal rattled in the bed of the truck.

"Where's the Gathers kid now?" he asked.

"He was with Roy. I reckon he still is."

SC 28 flattened at the base of the mountain to run parallel to the railroad tracks. Crossties swollen fat with summer rain and left to split in the heat lay abandoned along the roadside. The hull of a freight car was stranded knee-deep in willows, a blood-colored rust corroding the sides, SOUTHERN RAIL smeared from oxidation. Past the trees they could see Main Street, here and there fingers of pipe gouging the nighttime sky. In the gravel parking lot sat Roy's Fastback, the vinyl top torn and hanging.

"You coming?" asked Bobby. He was out of the car and leaning against Enis's open window.

"Yeah, just lemme study on this a second here."

Bobby paced.

"You coming or not?"

"Right behind you."

A Rottweiler hung barking from the window of a pickup. No one sat outside on the crates and the log bench. Inside, the bar was dim with smoke hanging just above eye level. A television rolled black and white, the light bouncing on the faces of old men hunched around the bar. The place seemed tired, beyond rest. The fireplace was cold and empty but for two crumpled cans and a film of ash.

"Hey, buddy."

Enis looked up.

"Yeah, you," said the bartender, the man named Ed something. "Wanna be buddies? I said wanna be buddies?"

"Not particularly," said Enis.

"Shut the door, asshole."

"Ease up," Bobby said. "We down here looking for Roy Burden, all right? You the one that called us."

"Well, you're a day late and a dollar short, Bobby. I called you a good hour ago. Look at that in the back. See that? The light back there."

Over the dark felt of a pool table hung a long fluorescent light tube, above it the remnants of what had once been an elaborate stained-glass shade.

"Where is he now?" asked Bobby. "This here is his brother."

"Is it now?" Ed was drying the inside of a glass. "The good brother finally went and showed up, did he. Which one are you, the Marine or the vagrant?"

"He in the back?"

"He ought to be in the poke, is where he ought to be."

"He back there or not?"

"See for yourself. You realize I'm gonna have to replace the table felt to get all the damn glass out?"

The pool players ignored them. Bobby disappeared into the shadows and Enis leaned against the wall, trying to think.

"I took her back down toward Yellar Branch falls," said one of the men, chalking his cue. "You been back there, ain't you, Hog? Down across from the Tunnel?

"Oh, yeah. Purty in there. Pur-tee as a picture. But I took Bobby Jean down in there and saw the falls and all and I tell you this, I was moved. I was. We stood there looking up at them falls and I said to her, I said 'Bobby Jean, these falls done went and moved something in me and I tell you what, for one year I will only hit you with an open hand, no fists.'"

The men broke up laughing.

"Uh-uh. You didn't."

"Swear to God I did."

"Tell the truth."

The man raised his right as if to swear an oath.

"You full of it, Jed," said Hoghead.

"Only thing I regret was not saving it for Valentine's Day."

"Shit."

The balls went clacking. A man fished a wad of tobacco from his mouth, flicked it away, packed in a fresh chew. Enis tried again to think then spotted Bobby standing in the corner with a bottle of Bud.

"You want one?"

"I thought you come to look," said Enis.

Bobby took a slow pull. He exhaled.

"They God Almighty. Just got a little thirsty was all."

"You sure he called from here?"

"He didn't call. Ed called."

"Well, if he's here I don't see him."

"He's here," said Bobby. "You check the toilets?"

"No."

"Try the toilets. I'm gonna get another."

Roy's head was propped against a urinal, his blue gabardine pants crusted with orange vomit, a white film in the corners of his mouth. One eye had nearly closed, shaded as if he wore dark makeup. Along the stall door amid dates and phone numbers and fart jokes were old bumper stickers rippled with air bubbles. THEY CAN HAVE MY GUN WHEN THEY PRY IT FROM MY COLD DEAD HAND. AMERICAN BY BIRTH, REBEL BY THE GRACE OF GOD. I LOVE MY COUNTRY, BUT I FEAR MY GOVERNMENT. Enis lifted him onto one shoulder. GUN CONTROL IS USING BOTH HANDS.

"Lord God, you stink, Roy. Help me a little here. Come on."

A solitary light bulb dangled, swayed for a moment, righted itself. Enis pushed open the wafer-board door and headed for the door.

"Hey, buddy," called the bartender. "Your brother's got a tab."

"How much?"

"He's good for it, Ed," said Bobby. "Cain't you see the man's caught hell tonight?"

"Shut it, Bobby. I ain't running a charity here."

The bartender passed a scrap of paper over to Enis.

Bobby shook his head. "You got no couth, Ed. You was raised no-count is what you were. No count and you ain't got a lick of couth."

"I said for you to shut it, old-timer. I don't take no checks neither," he said turning to Enis.

Enis left a twenty on the bar.

"No couth," said Bobby.

They walked out into the night, the clouds low and blue. The Rottweiler was asleep now.

"Can you manage with him?" Bobby asked.

"Just get the door for me. No Gathers in there?"

"None to speak of."

"I ain't half surprised."

"Keep his head up," said Bobby.

"I'm trying."

Roy's head rolled about his shoulders, then fell forward, knocking against the dash.

"His head's soaked."

Enis nodded. "He'll live."

"I never allowed he wouldn't."

They drove on down Main Street. The streetlights were on, bright globes on shadowed poles, the storefronts all dark mirrors. A heavy chain sealed the door of the Western Auto. Bobby had the window down, the air thick with exhaust and honeysuckle.

"You know where he's living these days?" asked Bobby.

"More or less."

Roy mumbled something unintelligible.

"What'd he say?"

Enis leaned close. "He says he can't spit. Says he's got no spit."

"That's about right," said Bobby.

The night was still.

"A safe bet would be Peyton Fowles's friends, wouldn't you say, Bobby? Peyton Fowles's friends."

"Who's that?"

"Fiancé of the girl he's been sleeping with."

Bobby kept his eyes on the centerline.

"I wouldn't know nothing about that."

"Gonna wind up one night on the wrong end of a gun."

"I wouldn't know a thing about it."

"Turn up here," said Enis.

The balustrade of the house laid pencil-line shadows along the street. They lifted Roy, his back wet and cool against them, moved forward beneath the cone of a streetlight. The wind blew, swirling the air with leaves.

"Mind the vomit," said Bobby.

Inside a light came on, then the porch light.

"Ah-oh. Shit, Enis. Put him down. You know she was in there?"

"Bring him on."

"Turn around and let's just take him on to my place. Let him sleep it off."

She stepped from the door, watched them. Her cigarette lit for a moment, glowed, disappeared.

"Is he drunk or dead?" she asked.

"Drunk. More or less," said Bobby.

"Well, it better be less. He's breathing too, then."

Faith held the door for them.

"Couch or tub?"

"Christ. Couch, I reckon. It's his couch." Gray ash fell to the carpet. She let the screen door slap shut. "Y'all want some coffee?"

Enis shook his head. "No. We're going on. Thanks just the same."

"Where was he?"

"The Last Chance."

"Figures." She looked down at Roy and brushed back a lock of hair. "Oh, baby, why do you want to do this to me? Why do you want to treat me this way?"

"You all right with him, little miss?" asked Bobby.

"Fine, yeah." She kept brushing his hair, not looking at them. "Thank you," she said. She was still looking at Roy. "Both of you."

From the door they could see her sitting on the arm of the couch touching his head, her lips moving, fingers, hands.

Lights flooded the cab of the truck. The road bent and the beams disappeared, straightened and reappeared. They were halfway up the mountain, just past the ranger station.

"What the hell?" said Bobby.

"Just kids. They'll pass you."

"They God Almighty they will. Tailgating sons a bitches."

"Tap the brakes."

The lights flashed again. Bobby cursed under his breath.

"Think they want something?" Enis asked.

"They about to by God get something."

"Pull over here, Bobby."

"Do what?"

"Pull over. Let's see what they want."

"You sure?"

"It's fine."

"The hell it is."

"Go ahead."

The truck eased onto the shoulder of the road. Enis cracked the door.

"I don't like this. Here," said Bobby reaching under the seat. "Take this with you."

"What is this?"

"What's it look like? A tire iron. Take it."

"This is how people get killed, Bobby."

"Shit, this is how people stay alive. Take it. Take it or I'm getting out myself with it. Go on. I ain't whooped nobody since nineteen hundred and forty-five. Take it. I'm serious here."

"Me, too."

Enis held it for a moment, testing its heft.

"Go on with it or I'm getting out myself with it."

Enis stepped out, shut the door, and dropped the tire iron in the truck bed, one arm up shielding his eyes. Two figures stepped from the car.

"Who is that?" he called.

"Cut the lights, Shine," said a voice. "You blinding him."

"Who is that?" said Enis.

He walked on past the bumper, the lights flaring and wheeling against a wall of dark. The figures came on, one stumbling in the brush, one gagging and then vomiting. Enis let one hand drift back into the bed of the truck.

"Who is that?"

"Is that one of the Burden boys?"

"Maybe. Who asking?"

"Enis, thought that was you. Gene Clanton. How the hell you doing?"

"Had me a little spooked, Gene."

"You know Shine Addis, don't you? Coach Addis's boy. Hardest-hitting son of a bitch ever to live."

"I do." They shook hands. "Linebacker. I remember."

Shine was chewing what appeared to be the cap off a bottle of Maker's Mark. "Fourteen games. A hundred and ninety-four tackles. Twenty-one for loss," he said.

"What's going on tonight, fellas?" asked Enis.

"Hell, we heard there was a fight at the Last Chance. Somebody said Roy Burden got jumped, so we just cut out from the plant. They can fire my ass if they like, I don't care. I ain't one to back down from no fight."

"You know anything about it?"

Enis shook his head no.

"Well, where you been then?"

"Working," he said. He hooked one thumb toward the truck. "Old-timer up there was driving me back."

"Working this late?"

"Yeah. Reckon somebody's got to earn a living."

"Who's in the truck?" asked Gene.

"We planning on by God whupping some ass before this night is over or knowing the reason why," said Shine Addis. His eyes were bloodshot and held steady the promise of some future atrocity not yet realized. Both men reeked of whiskey.

"You know, Shine, he gets drunk he's got him a mean streak a mile wide. Who'd you say was up there?" repeated Gene.

"That's old man Thorton. Owns the apple orchard in Long Creek."

"Bobby Thorton? I know him," said Gene.

"Well, shit," said Shine. "That old fart hates my guts but I ain't gonna let it spoil the fun. Come on and go with us, Enis. You can put some of that Vietnam kung-fu shit on 'em."

"We figured if somebody had done went and ganged up on Roy," said Gene.

"We figured to kill their ass is what we figured."

But Enis had already turned toward the truck.

"Go home," he said. "It ain't your fight. Go home and go to sleep and leave it be."

"Now, Enis—"

"It ain't your fight."

"Who was that?" Bobby asked when he was back in the truck.

"Gene Clanton and Shine Addis."

"Shine Addis. Why do I know that boy's name?"

"The linebacker. Coach's son." The car tore past them, laying rubber on the asphalt then disappearing around the bend. "Me and another fella were down at Myrtle Beach once, Ocean Boulevard they call it, and we saw Shine across the street. He'd been down on the beach for two hours drinking Pabst and swinging a five iron like a bat. All sweaty. Looked like he'd been at the gym."

"Yeah."

"Right then we see him walk over and hit some black guy with one of the clubs, the five iron, maybe, I couldn't tell which, and the black guy, he goes down on one knee and grabs at his head. Looks up and we see he's got his left ear in his hand."

"He's a mean son of a bitch to know," said Bobby.

"Knocked the guy's ear clean off. I told em it wasn't their fight."

"Did you now?"

"You dadgum right I did."

"And you think it's yours?"

Enis turned in the seat to look at Bobby. "If it ain't mine," he said, "whose is it?"

All day James wandered through the forest and along the back roads, emerging along a plumb line of blistered macadam. A sign pointed in one direction for Highway 76, in the other for the Georgia state line. He followed the road into Georgia and there stood thinking of his father and watching the Chattooga River expire against the concrete of the Tugaloo Dam, the lake a frail green, glowing like phosphorus. Heading back, he hitched a ride with a man in a long Cadillac who drank Canadian Club and trailed his left hand out the window grabbing air, hungry for it, worshipful, his right hand green with the dashboard lights, the road tumbling away like a scarf and the car thumping over potholes and the crests of hills, while James slept a sleep meant more for angels than men.

When he woke, he knew what was to be done.

He walked the sterile, antiseptic halls of the hospital, wandering like a child before a nurse took him by the elbow and led him to the door of room 212.

"You want me to knock or you think you can handle that much?"

She was joking, he thought, but then he looked so confused there, so sallow and thin, that she actually reached for the door.

"I've got it," he said. "Thank you. I'm fine."

She nodded and left, and he watched her glide up the tiled hall in her white tennis shoes, swinging her ponytail and twice looking back over her shoulder at him. James had seen Enis in the lobby, asleep in a plastic armchair, a Dr Pepper sweating onto a stack of old magazines, each with the mailing label cut away. No sense waking him, but James had stood there for some time imagining Enis, the inner workings of his mind and life, like a clock that goes on ticking long after the hands have worn away. Enis had admitted to almost worshipping James as a boy. War hero. Survivor. His eyelids fluttered, and James knew him to be in deep sleep, unbroken and unhurried, a sort of remembering, if he dreamed anything like James dreamed. A wheelchair squeaked up the hall, a janitor with mop and bucket. No, James wouldn't wake him, not from his dream.

He opened the door. Inside his father was asleep, sitting in traction at a thirty-degree angle, his arms strapped to his sides. The cotton stuffed in his nostrils needed changing.

"He's sleeping all right," James said. "Appears to be."

His mother stirred, clicked on the lamp beside her chair.

"James."

"Hey, Mamma."

She pressed the small Gideon's Bible she'd been reading against her chest. "James," she said again.

"Roy said to tell you they were having a prayer meeting for him tonight. Up at the church, I reckon."

"You saw your brother?"

He nodded. "Both of em."

She stood and grabbed him then held him out away from her as if to shift him toward better light. "Let me just look at you here, James," she said. "It's been so long." But he shrugged away from her, moved across the room so that the bed was between them.

"Oh, if I could only tell him you were here. To see you again, James. We had heard, from your brothers—"

"Mamma."

"Oh, James."

"I just come out to see how he was. Roy said his back was broke." She nodded.

"Is he paralyzed?"

"They don't know. He's only woke up once, when they were pulling him out of the truck. It's funny. Enis kept worrying about him going up there."

"Some damn fool thing, him out working at his age."

"Please sit and talk Christian, James. Understand how I feel seeing you again."

She wiped at her eyes. The Bible fell to the floor.

"When they came up that drive to fetch me, James, I thought for all the world they were coming to tell me you were gone. That I had grown lazy with my praying. That the good Lord had done gone and sent a messenger to deliver one of them wartime telegrams. That I was lazy and thought the war was over and my boys were safe, even if I didn't know where one of them was, but I'd grown lazy with the Lord and now he was coming to tell me he had taken you away and what a burn it was, James. What a burn. And I cursed myself, and I cursed the world at the idea that here they were taking you from me, James, and I hadn't even seen you. I hadn't even seen you, James."

He moved across the room.

"Oh, James," she said.

"Tell him I came by," he said, and slipped out the door.

Roy woke late the next morning, his thoughts torn between the bright glow of the pine board roof and the mounting pain that was throbbing behind one matted eye. The ceiling must have once been the old drop kind, sheets of asbestos probably, but was long gone now so that he looked up at the whorled and knotted boards that rose to a peak. He'd never noticed it before. Stray sunlight was everywhere. He touched his chest with his fingertips, hesitantly, afraid of what he might find, then touched his head. Dried blood. Swelling around one eye. His knuckles were split and scabbed black. Damn he was thirsty. He tried to sit up, but everything felt precariously balanced, as if moving too quickly might topple a house of cards. His stomach flipped. His throat was parched. He shut his eyes—pink glare through the lids, the delicate trace of veins—tried to sleep.

Thirst woke him the second time. He rose from the couch and walked back to the bedroom, buried his nose in the pillow searching for her smell, then walked into the kitchen, drank a glass of water and then another, waited, found some orange juice in the fridge and drank from the carton. There was a note from Faith on the counter. *Miss You!* He crumpled it but left it there by the empty carton. It was after ten. He couldn't remember what time she'd said she was leaving, but likely she was in Charleston by now, maybe already with him.

"Let me tell you a story here." Always he wanted to tell her this story, always wanted her to just stop for a second, think, baby, really think. Memory. Dream. Whatever it was, just think, baby. Listen. "There was this man and woman, couple of real hardheaded sons of bitches—"

"This isn't some fairy tale, is it? I've always had a real aversion to fairy tales."

"No. No. True story here. Happened a long time ago."

"Go on then."

They had been sitting in the Foothills Diner staring at their reflections in the glass. Faith pushed a pack of Virginia Slims around the table as if it were a child's toy.

"This man and woman," Roy had continued, "they had something, something special, you might could say."

"Oh, Christ. Was the man by chance a war hero? Feted all his days for never getting shot?"

"Yes, actually he was a war hero. I can't attest for the feted part."

"I can. Go on."

She'd lit a cigarette.

"The girl—"

"Woman."

"Right, woman. The woman loved the man. Deeply she loved him. And he loved her. It was almost, you might say, a fairy tale. But it wasn't. The man begged the girl to go with him, to love him, to give in to her love, but she wouldn't. She didn't. Forty years later she had another husband and four kids and twelve grandkids and a warm house with a fire burning in the grate and it was Christmas and the radio was playing carols and the TV was on and she was miserable. The saddest, sorriest thing you've ever seen. And the man was just as bad off. Sad. Very sad. Two sorry lives."

"No, no, no." Shaking her head and blowing a ring of bluish smoke at the glass and then smiling, studying the smear of lipstick on the tip of her cigarette. "I've already told you: sad or not, I don't do fairy tales, especially the endings."

He took two aspirins and showered then dressed and left. He had nowhere to go but couldn't just sit still. He needed movement, he needed to not think about her in Charleston. He drove Highway 28 up the mountain, working his way through the upswing of the gears, the open window a sort of flue for the onrushing air, the road white hot and falling away along its soft shoulders: Highway 28—the same path he'd traveled a thousand times before. He turned off on Whetstone Road headed for Earl's Ford, stopped for gas and bought a six-pack of Michelob and a tube of Lance's salted peanuts. Several old men sat out front talking about hunting dogs and Clemson football, their chairs and camp stools tilted against a drink box that read DRINK PEPSI COLA.

Roy leaned against the boot of his car and drank the head off the first beer, threw the tube of peanuts onto the driver's seat. Now and then a truck went past weighted with hay or bushel baskets of tomatoes or ears of corn. A yellow jacket lit in the cool dark spot where some beer foam had spilled. He finished it and tossed the empty across the road into the woods then opened another, thinking of flying. Operation Rolling Thunder—that had been his. Swallowing green meanies to get up for another run, Seconal tablets to come back down. The navy corpsman passing out white dailies and yellow weeklies. One pill had all the answers; the other would save your soul, *just you wait and see, sir.* Up and down, up and down, it went.

Waved forward and lashed into the catapult then leaving the deck in pairs.

"Watch for me today, lieutenant."

Looking out at his wingman: "Likewise."

Low brainlike clouds they would escape through. Finding their carrier again like a piece of flotsam adrift, descending out of the clouds, and there it would sit like a miracle, like salvation, and some little thing inside him would burst and that little thing was pure joy. The tiny tow hook grabbing the cable.

"Watch for me now."

"I'm with you."

He remembered the day they learned General Thanh was dead, the summer of '67, the warm beer they had drunk, the celebration. They had been after him for months. It was only later they learned it hadn't been bombs but cancer.

A motorcycle pulled into the yard driven by a boy in cutoff jeans, no shirt, and a crew cut. The boy was wiry, with long, sinewy muscles. A poorly drawn skull wrapped its vacant eyes around his left shoulder. Behind him was a girl who looked all of fourteen, climbing from the motorcycle in high heels and cutoffs that rode into the crack of her fleshy ass.

Roy sipped his beer. He could feel the vibration of the bike run through the asphalt, up the tires of his car to the trunk where he leaned. Then the engine cut, and there was a sudden calm, so quiet he could hear the cicadas whirring, hear one of the old men softly intoning, *I'm going home to see my Savior. I'm going home, no more to roam. . . .* The girl teetered into the dim store while the boy walked over.

"You Roy Burden?"

Roy finished the beer, wrapping his fingers around the neck, before answering.

"Could be," he said.

"Well, I'll be damned," said the boy. "I done heard about your exploits."

"Which might those be?"

"Shit, all of em, I reckon. Or all the good ones at least. I'm Billy Staples's boy, Martin. Private First Class, United States Army. Damn fine to meet you."

"Billy Staples's boy."

"Yessir."

Roy shook his hand.

"You don't know old Henry Staples, do you?"

"We don't claim him, but he's kin. We're cousins on my mamma's side."

"Me and Henry used to run together. Years ago."

"He's got a boy now. Six or seven."

"Ain't that something."

"Sure does. A little devil." He looked at Roy. "Listen, you mind if I talk with you here a minute?"

"You drink a cold beer?"

"Hell, did Sherman burn Georgia? I reckon I could suck the bottom out of a case."

"I don't have a case."

"Shoot, that's all right."

Roy passed over a beer and the boy sucked off the foam.

"Said you're army?"

"Yessir, I am. Headed for Vietnam directly here. Got all my schools in and everything down at Benning. Finished airborne third in my class. I'm all set."

"That a fact."

"Yessir it is."

"Well, I'm sorry to hear that."

"Shit, why you say that? I can't wait to get over there."

Roy wrenched the cap off another beer.

"I suspect you won't much find it to your liking."

"Hell," said the boy smiling. "Anywhere I get to sharpshoot some slope son of a bitch right in the eyeball is to my liking."

"Yeah."

"Yeah is right. I can't wait."

"See if you're still saying as much six months from now."

"Well, hell, you went over there and loved it, didn't you?"

"I went over."

"You love it?"

"It was the happiest time in my life. But that don't mean I'm glad I went."

"Shit. I heard you was a motherfucker to them gook bastards is what I heard. Why'd you get out anyhow? Everybody said you'd be a general someday."

Roy shook his head, looked out at the stretch of blacktop. Along its edges were hard, sun-dried things, dead things, the skins of frogs, husks of small animals, tiny brittle bonework. A big Nova came barreling over the rise, downshifting and disappearing in the next bend.

"Here comes your girl," said Roy. He motioned with his bottle. She staggered out into the violent sun, blinking, slow to regain her vision, then stood with one hand flat above her eyes staring over at the motorcycle.

"She's looking for you."

"Hell, she'll find me. Hang on a minute," he called at her. "She ain't even really my girl. Just something to ride till the time comes then I'll get me some of that Vietnamese poontang, if you know what I'm saying."

"I know exactly what you're saying," said Roy.

They watched the girl walk over and stand by the boy's bike.

"Don't touch nothing," he called. "She's the damn touchingest thing you ever did see."

The girl looked bored, fingering her hair, standing on first one foot then the other. She bent over and scratched at one instep, adjusted the strap of a heel.

"Yeah, buddy," said the boy. "She's just the flavor of the month, is all."

Roy nodded. "What did you say your name was again?"

"Martin. Martin Staples."

"Well, Martin Staples, how bout I give you a little advice."

"I'd take it as a considerable favor. I mean that. Seriously."

The boy looked eager. Roy turned toward the road where a turkey buzzard was picking its way down along the roadside.

"Take that girl home. Hear me?"

"Yessir, I do."

"Drop her off, tuck her in bed, kiss her good-night, whatever. Then go home and kiss your mamma good-bye, shake your daddy's hand and get on that bike and don't stop till you hit Canada. Pack warm. You see what I'm saying."

"Canada?"

"Or Mexico. Six of one, half dozen of another." He cracked the last beer. "You don't want none of what's going on over there. Take it from somewhere who's seen it and knows."

"Shit. I ain't no damn coward. I'm a blue-balled patriot or I'm a son of a bitch."

"You'll be a dead son of a bitch you go over there. Or you'll at least wish you were once you get back. My mamma told me two things growing up: eat when you get hungry and scratch when you itch. I'll add a third to that: run when somebody's looking to screw you."

Roy drained the beer, wiped his mouth along the back of his arm and flipped away the empty. He walked around to the door of his car.

"I ain't no damn chicken," said the boy following him.

"Ain't nobody saying you are. Your girl's waiting on you."

Roy opened the door.

"Why you son of a bitch," said the boy. "I thought you was somebody. I thought you was a damn hero."

"Somebody lied to you. I ain't nobody."

"That's the truth of it."

"You better get on."

"You don't tell me what to do. By God, I'll fight you right here, you son of a bitch. You think I'm afraid of you cause you flew some damn jet plane? I love my country, you son of a bitch. My uncle died in fucking France, shot like a hog by some Hun bastard he never even seen. Get outta that car and fight me like a man."

Roy could see the boy was near crying and then was crying, his fat bottom lip trembling, cords of muscle tensing along his arms. Despite his build, his face still held pockets of baby fat.

"Get outta that car, damn you," he cried.

It was useless. Roy rose slowly from the car and the boy staggered two steps back.

"You motherfucker," he cried.

When the punch came, Roy dipped, hooked the boy's arm and spun it behind his back, pressing the boy face first against the car's side. Snot bubbled from the boy's nose and his shoulders splotched red.

"You dirty son of a bitch," the boy cried.

Roy pushed him away and sat back in his car. The girl had come half over but stopped, uncertain of what to do. The boy was bawling, his face gleaming. A little clear bubble puffed then burst by one nostril.

"Somebody told me you was something. Somebody said you was a damn man."

Roy shook his head. "Somebody lied," he said.

Part Two

Memory

Bobby Thorton was headed into the Western Auto when the high sheriff spotted him. He wheeled his car around, parked, and walked inside, almost blind in the sudden dimness. No lights were on, only the morning sun that poured through the front glass, leaving half the store in shadow. A teenager sitting behind the counter stood at the sheriff's approach. The sheriff knew him from somewhere but couldn't say where. It was getting more and more that way. Once being sheriff had been everything, burning through him like a fever. Now he was drifting from the people he was elected, paid, and sworn to represent. The job was becoming an abstraction. More and more he wanted only to sit at home on his front porch and smoke and drink tea with his two girls, his wife, wave from his rocking chair at the lazy cars that swam up the street. There's a reason they give you a rocking chair at retirement, he thought. But he was a long way from retirement.

The boy started to tuck in his shirt, then stopped, the right side tucked, left side dangling.

"Morning, sir. Something I could help you with?"

"Just looking. Appreciate it, though."

"Yessir. Let me know if I can help anything find you, I mean, help you find anything."

The sheriff nodded and headed down one of the shadowed aisles. Like entering a cave, he thought. A cave lined with fishing tackle, spinners, jigs, plastic worms, Zebco rods, packs of Eagle Claws, then, farther down, radiator hoses, wiper blades, cartons of motor oil, power steering fluid, random castaway items. He made the corner and there stood Bobby filling a paper sack with threepenny nails, a tube of caulk under one arm. The sheriff brushed the dust from the top of a box of wood screws.

"What say, Bobby."

Bobby squinted in the dark.

"Sheriff Ellcott."

Ellcott. Bryan Ellcott. That is my name, thought the sheriff. So long with-out hearing it, existing behind this badge. His name rang like a bell—his mother's voice, his second-grade teacher, a girl he'd known in Sunday school.

"Shopping, are you? How's the apples gonna look this year?"

Bobby said nothing. Sloped against the wall behind them was a fire-red two-seat go-cart with an eight-horsepower Briggs & Stratton motor. The sheriff ran one finger along its slick tubing and whistled.

"Sure woulda took one of them as boy. All we had was an old soapbox racer. Made it out of a vegetable box, put wagon wheels on it."

Bobby counted out nails.

"Thing wouldn't steer," the sheriff went on. "Remember my brother took it head on into a big catalpa tree once. Lord. Mamma liked to flip. Always held me responsible for whatever happened to him. You still listen to the Carolina games, Bobby?"

"I'm trying to count, Sheriff."

"Sorry."

Bobby moved down the aisle, started counting out roofing nails.

"Heard you got some puppies off your hound Gus?"

"Didn't get no puppies," said Bobby, head still down. "Wasn't but four in the litter after the runt died. Woman I studded Gus out to said four puppies ain't worth the labor."

"That's a shame. Gus is a good dog."

"Mm-hmm."

"You ever get any puppies off him let me know. I'd like to buy one for my girls."

"Yeah."

Bobby dropped in two final nails, twisted the bag top and made a nota-tion on a scrap of paper.

"All right, Sheriff. Say what you aim to say and let me get going."

"Building something?"

"Something like that."

"Reckon you need more room now. All the house guests."

Bobby shifted his false teeth. "I keep waiting for you to pay a visit."

"I know. I been tied up with this whole Joseph Cory thing. The state's got involved now. Sent some people up."

"His daughter?"

"Yeah."

"I been around livestock all my life, and outside a Mexican bullfight not once have I heard of anybody getting gored to death. Let alone some girl in an open pasture. I tell you the truth, Sheriff, I find the whole thing pretty damn hard to believe."

"I know. It's the damnedest thing."

"She could've just run off on him."

"That's kindly what I figure."

"As prideful as they say he is, he wouldn't tell. He really building a spaceship?"

"What everbody says."

"They God Almighty. World's a strange place."

"That it is. That it is."

They stood for a moment, the sheriff fingering the go-cart again, touching the gas pedal.

"At some point we're gonna all have to get together and have us a sit down, Bobby. I'm content to wait for the moment till all this Cory mess blows over, but the time's coming. The Gathers boy's daddy's been on me, too. Twice I've had to stop him from coming up the mountain to your place."

"Tom Gathers ain't worth spit. You know that as well as I do. If he's at all interested, it's because he thinks he can somehow get a buck off somebody."

"That may be so, Bobby, but he's still his daddy. He's still got rights."

"He's a good boy, Sheriff. Real good boy. Hardheaded, no denying it. But that don't make him no criminal."

"Stealing a wallet does."

"He didn't steal no wallet. I'm just trying to do right by him."

"We'll sit down and talk about it. Oh, and I was sorry to hear about Sharon."

"Yeah. Reckon everybody's heard by now."

"People are bound to talk. I'll not keep you any longer."

The boy behind the counter started to stand, but the sheriff waved him off. He drove along Main Street to the foot of the mountain, passed a produce stand erected out of the back of a Ford pickup, some old-timer sitting in an aluminum lawn chair whittling.

Twenty minutes later he'd made the turn down Old Man Cory's drive, the dirt road overgrown, surprisingly free of tire tracks. The sheriff figured nobody had been up yet to check on things. Low priority then, he thought. Good.

Cory was waiting on the porch when the sheriff got out.

"Good morning, Mr. Cory."

"Is it?"

"I got a mind to say yes. Sun's out. Sky's blue." He walked over. "You don't mind if I smoke, do you?"

Cory shook his head no. His right ankle was wrapped in gray gauze, and he leaned on the balustrade. The sheriff lit a cigarette, inhaled, tipped the ash in the right cuff of his pants. A bluetick roused from beneath the porch, hackles flared along its back.

"Go on, Memphis," Cory said. "Go on. Git now."

The dog trotted behind the house.

"Nice dog."

"It'd tree a elephant if it ran crossways of one. Sit there till it died or the elephant fell, one."

"I had a dog like that once. Used to keep me up nights barking," said the sheriff. He cleared his throat. "I reckon you know why I'm up here," he said.

Cory stood on the porch. "I can figure as much. Had bout done give up on you coming."

"Is she around, Mary Anne?"

"No, she ain't."

"Well, where is she?"

"She's dead."

The sheriff propped his right leg on the porch. He was wearing thin-soled dress shoes, the polish flecked now with mud. He tipped his cigarette.

"That was what I figured," he said.

"Well, you figured right."

"What happened?"

"Bull got her. Gored her oncet in the chest, another round the back."

The sheriff nodded.

"Word sure does move quick down the mountain, don't it, Sheriff?"

"You bury her?"

"What do you think?"

"May I see the grave?"

"No, you may not."

"Now don't be like that, Mr. Cory."

"Like what?"

"You know what I'm talking about. You're being belligerent. Hardheaded."

"I ain't being like nothing. You come up here with a writ or a warrant or whatever it is and you can poke about all you like. Till then, you can stay the hell away."

"All I want is to look around the yard."

"What you want with seeing her grave anyhow? She was my baby, my youngest. Pumpkin, I called her. I don't reckon you'd understand the attachment between a father and a girl-child."

"I got two daughters," said the sheriff.

"That a fact?" Cory peered out over the yard. The door to the sheriff's car was open, the small dome light barely visible.

"You want me to put that bull down?" asked the sheriff.

"Big Ern? Hell, I done the deed myself."

"I reckon the county can dispose of it if you like."

"Dispose of it? Hell, sheriff. I'm gone eat that bull. I reckon I loved that bull like a child."

They stood for a moment looking around the yard.

"You got another of them smokes, have you, Sheriff?"

"Here." The sheriff held up a light.

"You still want to see her grave?"

They walked to a knoll where a sugar maple overlooked the trace of a creek that parted two hills, Cory leaning on his walking stick, the bluetick, Memphis, trailing on their heels. The ground here was dark and freshly turned. A bluebottle fly lit in the dewy grass.

"I carried her up here and said good-bye. She was still warm time I buried her. This is the purtiest spot around."

The sheriff sat on his heels and touched the loose dirt.

"Lotta dead Christians in this ground, Sheriff."

"You didn't call nobody?"

"Who would I call? You know anybody that could bring her back? I reckon I coulda called the McCallister woman, seeing as how she was responsible, but I don't see much sense in it."

"What'd the McCallister woman have to do with it?"

"Hexed her."

The sheriff hunched on his ankles, sifted loam through his fingers. After a moment he asked, "How deep is it?"

"I reckon I've lived long enough to know how to bury a child, Sheriff. I reckon I've lived that long."

"Sorry. I know you have. I shouldn't have asked that."

The sheriff stood.

"She's about five feet down," said Cory.

"You want me to help you find anything for a headstone? A rock or something? We can mark it."

"I allow I'll not forget the spot."

"Well—"

"You ain't planning to dig her up are you?"

"No. No, I'm not. But—"

"But what?"

"SLED, the State Law Enforcement Division, I mean to say, well, they may wind up poking around. They may want to exhume her, perform an autopsy. I'm just telling you so you'll know, Mr. Cory." The sheriff stood. "I'm sorry about it. If it was up to me I'd just leave things be."

"You took a mighty while getting up here."

"I just want you to know what may happen, Mr. Cory."

Cory had looked away, chewing now on his bottom lip, a single silvery tear tracking his hard face.

The sheriff said, "We best head back before the sun gets any hotter."

"I wanted to ask you one more thing if I could, Mr. Cory." They were back in the yard, Cory laboring up the three porch steps, trying to keep his weight off his bad ankle. He turned at the top.

"All right. Ask."

"I'm sure you heard about W. J. Burden. The accident he was in."

"Truck wreck up on the Whitewater? I heard a little. It ain't got a thing to do with me."

"I know it don't. What I was wondering about actually was his father. My daddy was sheriff then."

"I remember your daddy well. He was a good man."

"Well, I thank you. But he was sheriff, and I remember him talking about something that had happened with old man Burden."

"Something did happen. I know cause I was there. But your daddy wasn't sheriff then. Hell, your daddy weren't but likely in diapers. I weren't but a young buck, myself."

Cory disappeared into the house and the sheriff followed him as far as the open door. He could hear Cory rattling about. A horseshoe was nailed above the jamb.

"Sheriff?"

"Yessir."

"Pull that door shut. You're letting mosquiters in."

Cory walked into the room with a thermos of coffee and a bottle of brandy, motioned toward one of the chairs.

"You ain't got nowheres to be, have you?"

The sheriff shook his head no, settled into the chair. The room was lit unevenly, sunlight coloring the floor a bright buttery gold. There were two sitting chairs, an old console radio, an H. L. Hackney calendar on the wall showing MARCH 1956, a few cardboard boxes, a framed sepia wedding portrait, little else.

"I made the coffin for her. All heart of pine. Dovetail joints. Planed it down. Just beautiful." Cory's eyes were glassy and distant. The sheriff looked away. After a moment Cory produced two cups and filled each from the thermos. "How do you take it, Sheriff? One finger or two?"

"Better make it one seeing as how I'm on duty."

Cory poured the drinks. "Maxwell Burden. That was his name. This was just before the Great War. I couldn't tell you the year but I reckon you can look that up." He sipped his drink. His lips were thin wet slits and seemed out of place in his dry, cracked face. He had a stubble of gray hair on his neck and chin. He settled back into his chair. "The devil is a busy man, Sheriff. I learned that much early on."

No one was home. The sheriff fixed a glass of water and then walked through the kitchen out the back door into the yard, sat in the swing, his legs folded beneath him, tips of his leathers in the dust. Jeanne must be out shopping, running around tearing up the roads, burning gas and rubber just because she could. The girls were at school. Driving down the mountain, he had thought about stopping by to see them, knowing all along he wouldn't. Just a quick visit down by the school, wouldn't have to go in, keep from scaring anybody, maybe just stand by the fence and watch recess, his two daughters on the monkey bars, Sarah maybe hanging upside down by her legs, spill of blonde hair like a waterfall, or following their teacher back inside, single file. Knew he wouldn't, kept thinking of it anyway. Wanted to by God hold them, squeeze them, after what Cory had told him.

He sipped the water.

His head pounded, and his throat felt like someone had poured concrete there. The brandy. He'd wound up taking four, maybe five fingers of it. He took another sip, looked around the yard. A plastic three-wheeler sat overturned by the fence, tassels along a single handlebar folded limp, pink seat faded now. Daisies printed as big as eyes. He downed the water, walked over and flipped the three-wheeler upright. For a moment a bumblebee orbited his hand. It lit on the plastic seat, lifted silently and was gone. He watched it go into the stillness, an empty glass in hand, an elusive prayer on his lips. He couldn't form it. His damn head. On the porch was an empty pie tin left for the cats. He tipped it with the toe of his boot, released it, left it wobbling. He walked inside and called in, telling the dispatcher on duty he'd check back in a bit.

"What'd you want me to tell em if they call?" she asked.

"If who calls?"

"Just whoever. Anybody looking for you."

He fingered the Graceland ashtray that sat on the nightstand.

"Tell em I'm indisposed. I've taken a hiatus."

He slept into the blue of late afternoon, waking to the whine of air brakes, his girls on the front steps, sunlight oozing from the corners. Long jagged shadows. The screen door swung shut. Their voices tinny and frail. He disappeared back into sleep.

They were on the couch watching *Dark Shadows* and eating celery sticks when he walked into the living room.

"You were sleeping, Daddy."

"I know, baby. What you watching here?"

He met Jeanne on the road, just a block or so up from the house, and she waved with a sudden flip of one hand, cocked her head just enough to express surprise. He shrugged his shoulders but was already past her, pulling to the stop sign and watching her in his rearview mirror as she turned into the drive. The flowers out front, their name scrolled on the mailbox in yellow curlicues. Otherwise the house was just like all the rest on the street, cut from a single mold.

He took a right toward Walhalla and the mountain.

He had spent almost an hour with the girls, quietly inhabiting their soft, floral world. They both smelled of Lifebuoy soap, citrus in their hair, little half moons of dirt beneath their nails. He watched *Dark Shadows* with them, trying vainly not to think of what Cory had told him when Quentin went for the neck, then *General Hospital*.

"Aren't y'all a little young for this?" he'd asked them.

The withering look they'd given him.

"Don't be silly, Daddy. We watch it all the time."

He was silly, he knew it. Already, even as children, they knew more than him, understood more. They were little women.

He turned off the main road to Bobby Thorton's, trying to convince himself that it hadn't been a wasted day. A sheriff's job was knowing things. Sometimes just sitting and listening.

Gus, worn-out and arthritic in his hind legs, never bothered to rise from his shallow hole, thumping his tail instead. The sheriff could hear the voices of men and women, scattered and distant, but saw no one, the orchard set below the horizon line. He looked around the yard. Bobby's truck was gone. The mail sat in a bundle at the foot of the door, and the sheriff climbed the steps to leaf through it. A flyer from a Classic Car Show in Pigeon Forge, Tennessee. An advertising circular from Powell Brothers' Tractor over in Seneca. A newspaper two days old. He cupped his hands and peered in through the glass. The house interior appeared in disarray, cut with late-afternoon light. A blanket lay draped over a couch. An empty fifth sat in the windowsill. The mantle was swept clean, and empty curio cabinets sat stacked in one corner. He knocked, looked, knocked again, decided to walk around back.

From the rear of the house he watched the migrant workers moving through the rows of trees—back and forth they went from tree to box, tree to box, dull red apples accumulating in crates. No one seemed to notice him. No one seemed to look up at him. So this is what life's like, he thought, this constant motion. Welcome to the future. Productivity, he thought, that was the word. Efficiency, cold and mean.

He was almost back to the car when he heard the screen door open. James Burden stood bare-chested and barefoot on the porch. Blue jeans, an olive drab towel thrown over his shoulders like a fighter between rounds, one cheek lathered with shaving cream, the other swept clean. The screen slapped shut.

"Didn't know anybody was home," called the sheriff.

"Bobby's gone to town. The Gathers boy, too."

The sheriff nodded and walked over.

"I seen Bobby. And I ain't looking for the Gathers boy. Actually," he said, "I was hoping I might talk with you, James."

James nodded, not indifferently, the sheriff thought, but not with any real interest either. He was simply there.

"Didn't mean to interrupt your shaving. I don't know if we've ever met. I'm Bryan Ellcott. I was a few years ahead of Roy in school. I can wait while you clean up, if you might have a minute to talk with me. I reckon you know I'm here about your daddy."

"What about him?"

"Well, that's what I want to talk about."

The sheriff waited on the back porch, sitting in a rocking chair and watching the migrants again. But it was a depressing sight, such efficiency, and instead he decided to study on the sky, on a squirrel that went barking through the yard, a murder of crows that set down like locusts in the mown grass. A few minutes later James came out dressed in jeans and a T-shirt, hair combed, once-white Keds sneakers on his feet.

"All right, Sheriff."

James sat down.

"Call me Bryan," said the sheriff.

James nodded.

The crows lifted like a dark cloud.

"How much do you know about your granddaddy? On your daddy's side?" asked the sheriff.

"How much should I?" said James.

"That's a good question."

The sheriff talked for a good half hour, cataloging the grandfather's sins, James silent but listening, staring out at the yard, at some distant imagined something above the tree line, at the tea-colored light that was spilling along the horizon.

"I don't much see what this has to do with me," James said when he was finished. "Seeing as how that was all years ago."

"You're right," conceded the sheriff, slapping his knees. "Nothing. It don't have a thing to do with anything. I just thought you might want to know."

"That I might want to know I come from a line of degenerates?"

"I don't know," said the sheriff. "I just thought you might want to know. I'm sorry I said anything."

James stared out over the yard. The sheriff watched his lips suck inward, conjuring a moment, perhaps, back through blood's memory.

"Sorry," said the sheriff, starting to rise, wondering why it was he had come. "It's just, well. I didn't want to go see your mamma with it and I just thought . . . Well."

"It's all right. I knew as much, more or less I did. For years now. Since before I left, anyway."

"People talk."

"They do. They do at that."

The sheriff stood, the rocker gently swaying behind him.

"I just thought you should know the whole story."

"I appreciate it."

"You mind if I ask you one thing?"

James looked at him, the sheriff felt like for the first time all afternoon.

"I was wondering driving up here, just sort of thinking. Why after so many years did you finally decide to come back?"

James sat for a moment, before shrugging.

"I can't explain it."

"You were out west?"

"For a while, yeah."

"Long way to come not to be able to explain something. Not that it's any of my business anyway. I was just wondering was all." He stepped off the porch, adjusted his hat, dug one toe into the dirt, smoothed over the tiny gouge. "Well, tell Bobby I'll come back by sometime when he's here."

James nodded. "I will. And I did have my reasons, Sheriff. I did."

"I allow we've all got our reasons."

"I allow we do."

When the wind chimes began to sound, Will Burden knew he was to be visited, though he knew not whether the visitor would be of this world or the next. In the end, they came in turn, first a man of the Lord, then a messenger from the devil himself.

Maddy was sitting in the front room watching the fire, listening to it hiss oxygen, when the headlights swept the far wall. Her first thought was that it was one of her sons. All day, it seemed, she'd had a cold feeling upon her, as if she walked in shadow or had found a vat of cool water streaming up through a lake bed. What she felt was that the devil was set on taking his due, that her good fortune—three living sons, a living husband—was too kind, too fair, and she had prayed through the day's work for deliverance. Her second thought, oddly enough, was that it was her father. His face burst in the darkness of her skull and for a moment seared itself on her retinas. Most likely her father was dead, maybe twenty, thirty years dead. The sound of footsteps and then dogs rousing brought her back to reality. Her father fled like the ghost she believed him to be. On the front steps stood the tall, mustached figure of a pilgrim she recognized from the flyers hung around town.

"Evening, Reverend . . . Leggett, isn't it?" she said, standing in the crack of the door. "No prayer meeting tonight?"

"None to speak of, Mrs. Burden. But please do call me Jim."

"Out visiting?"

"I am. And I wonder if I might come in for a moment. I've felt a calling from this house."

"From my house?"

"Yes, ma'am. Something's weighing heavy on my heart."

He sat on the edge of the sitting chair and looked at her. She stood, uneasy, the cold having found her again. The reverend watched the fire, and Maddy watched its reflection flicker in his eyes.

"I heard how they done you, Reverend. Somebody taking your wallet like that. I hope you don't judge us all on the actions of a few."

"Oh, I wouldn't dream of it, but I came over here—" He brushed something from his sleeve. "I came over because I wanted to see about your husband, Mrs. Burden. I wanted to pray over him if I could."

"He's sleeping, Reverend. He's most the time drowsy with the pain medication they give him."

"I'd like to lay hands on him, Mrs. Burden. I think it's the Lord's will."

He licked at the bottom of his mustache.

"Well," she said after a moment, "I ain't one to argue with the Lord."

The man was asking for Will's father, but Will knew not how to answer him. The man leaned closer, his face red, nostrils flared like a bull. A bull, thought Will. This here man's a bull. "Son," said the man taking Will's small face into the glove of his hand. "Look at me, son." Past him Will could see men milling about, kicking at the dust, squatting on their heels, two leaning against the gatepost passing a match between them.

"I said look at me." But Will would not. "Fine. You won't talk, you can walk. Outside with him," said the man, standing. Hands snatched at him, carrying him out of the house into the gloomy sunshine. The air smelled of dust, faintly of honeysuckle and wisteria. Down below the house he could hear the creek running.

"Lead on, child of God," the man said.

Then he was walking down through the pasture among the white-faced cattle that sat like weary dogs, legs folded beneath them there in the bright summer grass. Will walked with the man's hand on his shoulder. He could feel the calluses grinding against his bones, the other men strung out behind them, stepping gingerly as horses as they walked down the hill's steep shoulder. Here and there bluebottle flies buzzed around dark patties splattered onto the grass. A dragonfly lifted to alight on a willow.

Near the barn the men fanned out, balancing their shotguns in the crooks of their arms.

"Stay here with me," said the man. He waved the men around him and they spread around the barn. The cows lowed. "Now," said the man. "Take me to him."

He saw his wife standing in the door and meant to wave her forward but could not move. She came forward and stood beside him, and he could tell that she was stroking his head, though he felt nothing.

"Here is an angel," he thought she said. "An angel, Will."

But it was no angel. It was a man.

"He wants to pray over you, Will. He wants to pray with you."

He looked at his wife, and she emerged as if through a parting fog, and she was frail, showing her bonework, her skin loose and liver-spotted but her voice, her voice belonged not to her body. It was strong, resolute.

"To pray," she said again.

He made to nod, thought he did, moved his tongue about his great mouth as if it were a rudderless ship, too large and too heavy to guide.

"He wants you to sit," she told the man. "Sit there by the bedside."

The man sat and looked at him with his bright teeth. Over the bed was a picture of a blue-eyed Jesus.

"Will," said his wife, and he felt himself perched on a fulcrum, teetering between light and dark, but then the lowing rose again and he could hear nothing else.

The man pushed him forward and he tripped over his own feet. Blades of dewy grass fell across his toes and ankles, were crushed beneath his step. The man pushed him on into the dark cavern of the barn. The air was cool and smelled of hay and cow manure. Bags of feed and 10-10-10 fertilizer lay stacked along a distant wall. Tack was nailed all about, spiderwebbed with silvery gossamer. The cows began lowing.

"Shut up and listen," said the man, clamping a hand over his mouth. "And you listen good. Is that him?"

The boy nodded.

"That's your father? Whisper."

"Yessir."

"You're certain?"

He was.

"Sit then."

Will squatted on his heels and watched the man slip from his pocket a long double-barreled cap-and-ball pistol.

"Come on," he told him.

The rasping sound of his father mixed with the lowing, one feeding the other.

"Cows. He's talking about cows," said the reverend, walking into the front room. Maddy was back huddled in front of the fire, still cold, feeling as if she would never be warm again.

"He was talking about a bunch of white-faced cows. I would have thought him to have been in the lifelong service of the Lord."

Maddy nodded.

"He was. Is."

"Odd," said the reverend.

"It's most likely the medicine. The doctor said it might do that to him, to remember things. His father had a bunch of cows, I think. It's just the medicine talking."

"Most likely," said the man. He stood there as if addled, uncertain of which step to take next, and Maddy felt a certain twinge of guilt. *Whatever you do unto the least of these,* she thought.

"Reverend, would you care for a bite to eat?"

"I really couldn't."

"I could just heat you up something. Maybe some soup and a pone of cornbread. I've got some soup on the stovetop there. It being a cool night and all."

"I really couldn't."

"It's no trouble. I can turn on the TV news for you."

He sat at the table spooning soup then wiping it from his mustache. She sat across from him watching, listening to the tick of the stove flue.

"I should tell you, Mrs. Burden, one of my reasons for coming up here— and this is delicious, by the way. One of my reasons, though." He bit a chunk of cornbread. "I'm worried about your sons."

She nodded. "The Lord has been working on my heart about them boys. About my pride in them," she said.

He agreed. "He's been working on my heart as well. I feel a real burden for them."

"They're good boys, Reverend. The best I've ever seen or heard of. I've known none finer."

"But?"

She shook her head. "But nothing. You just get to an age when there ain't no pride left. You don't want nothing but for your children to know Jesus. Nothing else. But times is tough on all of us."

"Indeed. The war."

"The war. There's always that."

"They'll be no end to the wars, Mrs. Burden. So says the Gospel of Matthew: there will be wars and rumors of war unto the Last Days."

"I know Matthew well. I've spent many a day praying over it, Reverend."

"But it's over for them, for you."

She stared down at her tired hands; she suddenly felt tired, immeasurably tired.

"War, I believe, is more with the mind and heart than with the body. I don't believe it's ever really over, Reverend. I don't believe it ever is."

He looked at her as if there was more to say then dipped his cornbread.

"I wonder where I might find your sons, Mrs. Burden. I'd like to talk with them. Roy, perhaps."

She looked back at the fire: the coldness, the fleeing of air. We'll all suffocate in the night, she thought. In the end we all die.

"Under a rock," she said after a moment. "Under a rock or out running around. Wherever God's light ain't shining. I'd wager you'd find him there."

A moment later he made to leave.

"All I want is for them to do right. Pray for them, Reverend," she said. "For my boys."

"Oh," he said. "I'll do more than pray for them."

Then they came again across the divide for him, their claws digging, teeth bared, and he found himself in the barn, the girl's lips blue, her body naked and stretched out as if for burial. He heard the dogs, the sound of the guns. Two more men came climbing into the hayloft where Will and the man stood staring down at the girl.

"They Lord God in heaven," one of them said.

The man with the pistol was sitting on a bale of hay. "She ain't mine," he said. He motioned at the bits of girl's underclothing tacked to the walls. "Ain't none of them hers either as far as I know, and I ain't bringing her mother up here to make certain, that's for damn sure."

One of the men made to touch the girl but didn't.

"Jewish girl," said the man sitting on the bale, pointing with his pistol and almost laughing. "God's chosen people, how bout that?"

One of the men prodded the girl's ankle with his boot. Between her legs was a nest of gummy pubic hair. She wore a necklace of bruises.

"She ain't mine," said the man, standing. He looked down at ten-year-old Will. "She ain't mine. But I tell you this, one day her daddy's gonna come and collect what's his. The Devil, too. You can bank that."

In the kitchen Maddy washed the reverend's plate and glass, then stood in the center of the room trying to remember the words to "Old Rugged Cross." They were lost to her. She couldn't think straight. For a moment she smelled the old smell: dried flowers, death, those attic years lost to the pain of believing. Don't worry, she told herself, standing, shaking off the thought as much as the smell. Pray. Pray, and let God worry.

The apples were off the trees and in the cribs, and the migrants spent their last few days checking them for maturity—firmness, sugar content, seed, and skin color—before separating them by species: Mutsu, Granny Smith, Winesap, McIntosh, Red and Golden Delicious. Diseased or damaged apples were discarded. The rest were put either in large canvas bags for wholesalers or in bins for passing tourists.

"They're like ghosts," said Bobby, standing one day on the porch watching the men and women. "They roll in like the rain and then they're gone. Take it to heart, young Gathers. There's a lesson in that if you study on it long enough."

The rain had indeed rolled in, and along with it a fog so dense headlights were as diffuse as heat lightning. The last of the mosquitoes and fireflies were long gone, and the air harbored the bright scent of fall.

In mid-October, Bobby, James, and Eddie sat around the front room of the house and listened to the rain.

"Sounds like somebody talking," said Eddie.

"Sounds like a woman," said Bobby.

"You're both delusional."

"Shit," said Bobby. "Like you ain't."

"Well, hell," said Eddie. "I guess that's it, ain't it? I guess now you don't need no seasonal help, do you? I reckon I'm gone be thrown back to the wolves."

"Or to your daddy," said James.

"Yeah, exactly. To my daddy."

"Ain't nobody throwing you to anything, young Gathers. I can always use a hand around here."

"Till the high sheriff shows up," said Eddie.

"Well, I cain't tell the future, son. But as soon as James kicks out on us—and look at him, that day ain't far off—they'll be plenty of digging to be done. Gotta bury his skinny ass. I figure we'll bury him standing. Use the posthole diggers. Shouldn't take long."

"You're a comedian," said James. "You've got a talent. You should head up to Nashville."

"Damn right I should," said Bobby. "Probably where Sharon's at right now, but I don't suspect I'll see her this side of the divorce court."

Eddie looked like a small animal caught in a trap.

"Ain't there nothing on the TV?" he wanted to know. "Ain't that Hawaiian detective son of a bitch on?"

He stood and walked into the kitchen, returning with a bowl of black-eyed peas.

"That the peas that was on the counter?" asked Bobby.

"I reckon," said Eddie, taking a bite.

"Well, they either is or they ain't."

"They was on the counter."

"They God Almighty, Gathers, I opened them peas two days ago. You eat them you liable to be ruirn't."

Eddie swallowed a heaping spoonful. "Hell, I already figured on that."

For the past month James had spent his days walking the banks of the Chauga with Mercedes, she as silent and ever-present as a shadow. For hours on end they would walk up-current, where the land grew steeper, less forgiving, barefaced into sudden flurries of falling leaves and changing weather. Along high limestone walls they found Cherokee and Seneca etchings hidden by brambles alongside the remnants of fifty-year-old stills shotgunned to ruin by federal revenuers. They scavenged through the pastures for mushrooms, in the process unearthing arrowheads and shards of pottery. And James became more and more reliant on the mushrooms, steadily trying to wean himself off morphine, enduring the sweats and bouts of vomiting, while Mercedes told him fantastic stories. The girl's family came from Texas. El Paso, she said. They had come across the border in '42 as *brazos* when Roosevelt was desperate for farmhands. She was born near a cannery in Louisiana. All told, she had lived in seventeen states.

She watched him cinch his left arm in baling twine.

She watched him fish through a duffel bag with a seemingly endless supply of syringes that was slowly going dry.

"Where'd you get all those?"

"Friends," he smiled. "Good friends. But not around here. Gonna have to find me some new ones pretty soon."

Wading the thigh-deep pools of the Chauga, he saw again the clear waters of Korea, a land not so different from the Blue Ridge escarpment, only colder, so much colder.

"They shaved the legs down on these big beds that five or six people would sleep on," he told her. "Really just more like tables about a foot off the ground. But they shaved the legs unevenly, so if one person moved just the slightest during the night everybody woke. You could never sleep. And the ground was frozen. You could never sleep on the ground."

"So why do you sleep on the ground now?"

"Because it's still. And it isn't frozen."

One morning they hiked along the Chauga to Low Water Bridge, emerging through the rhododendron and Indian thistle to find a man and woman sitting in beach chairs, fishing. Around them sat brightly colored camping equipment, a red Coleman tent, mosquito netting, sleeping bags. A Jeep sat in the clearing, and two children, a boy and girl, walked ankle-deep in the water, their Zebco rods propped against a poplar tree. Two Igloo ice chests sat in the shade, and a girl who appeared to be thirteen or fourteen lay on a lawn chair sunbathing in a patch of light. She fussed with her breasts, hiking the straps of her top, a look of bovine indifference on her broad, pale face.

James watched the woman nudge her husband, then motion toward them.

"Morning," said the man smiling. He wore a fly-fishing vest and boonie hat, Columbia shorts, trout boots, all of it brand new. "Y'all out walking, are you?"

James nodded. The couple rose and walked over.

"Where'd you come through from?"

"Just from upriver," said James, motioning up current. "Good ways upriver."

"Well, ain't that a pretty thing," said the woman looking at Mercedes. "Hey, brown-eyed girl. That your daddy there?"

Mercedes slid behind James's leg.

"Shy thing," said the man.

James nodded.

"We're just passing through."

"Well, sit and fish a minute if you like."

"Y'all had any luck?"

"None to speak of.

"It's about all fished out up through here. Maybe catch a sucker fish, one of those bottom feeders."

"Yeah, just out with the kids for the weekend, I reckon."

"Weekend?"

"Yeah. Nothing serious."

"What day is it?" said James.

"Twenty-first, I believe," said the man.

"No. I mean what day."

The man looked at him, eyes narrowing.

"What day? It's Friday. How long you been in those woods?"

The man stepped forward.

"I don't know," said James. "I got mixed up."

The woman turned toward the kids, who were now splashing each other, and made to herd them toward the Jeep.

"Where the hell you been, buddy?" asked the man. "You all right?"

"I'm fine."

"What's that?"

"Said I'm fine."

"You been smoking something, haven't you? Let me see your eyes."

James said nothing.

"Sure as shooting you have. Well, maybe you just ought to take the girl and move on before I get the notion to call the law."

He did, Mercedes looking back once as they passed under the bridge, at the woman and her two kids beside her by the Jeep, the boy poking the girl, the teenager still sunbathing, face down now. The man gauged their progress with his pinched eyes, a look that said don't come back—a look she had learned years ago.

In the late afternoons James sat on the porch with Bobby while the morphine and hallucinogens drained from him like bathwater. They drank white lightning as smooth as single malt scotch or fifth after fifth of Jack Daniel's while Eddie ran the tractor, hauling up cribs of apples they sold in bulk to wholesalers or by the bag to the occasional passing car.

"Quite a take," said Bobby. "High cotton, my friend. High cotton."

"I thought you said you wasn't rich?"

"Shit, I ain't. Yet."

In the evenings, James spread his bedroll and sleeping bag in the meadow beside the bunkhouses. He knew he was losing weight—perhaps less than one hundred and thirty pounds now stretched along his six foot two frame, giving him the look of some prehistoric bird: elastic, yet somehow powerful—but he felt his physical weight was being replaced by something preferable, something more abstract: the peace that passeth understanding.

What of his diet that wasn't taken intravenously consisted primarily of moonshine, whiskey, and the occasional dried jalapeño given to him by Mercedes's father.

The man swore that if James would travel back to El Paso and then Mexico with him for just one year, James's stomach would never trouble him again.

"I could make you better," he told him. "You eat things, peppers, seeds."

Then the rains came, and slowly, and then quickly, the trees were bare of apples and the work was done. The migrants left near the end of October, reversing their arrival of so many weeks before, the trucks cutting incisions as precise and fatal in the road as any left in a man's body. Mercedes waved good-bye and was gone.

The world fell still.

Part Two

James had not been to see his father since visiting him in the hospital. He knew now that his father was home, though not well. But he would not go to see him. It was more than his broken back, more than the frozen numbness that slept below his waist: memory had been loosed, some germ of madness planted years ago by his own father, by James's grandfather. The bond that tethered his father to humanity had snapped like worn rope. James felt the same fraying ties. And perhaps that was why he stayed away.

James was asleep in the front room the day the high sheriff's car pulled into the yard. He watched through the window as Bobby and the sheriff discussed something. Then the sheriff drove away. Bobby walked inside, meeting James by the front door.

"That traveling preacher man's something, ain't he. Son of a bitch. He really thinks that boy took his wallet."

"He did, Bobby. He says as much."

"Hell, I know he did but he ain't but a boy. Ellcott says he got a full-time fella to do all his lawyering for him. Said he woulda been up here weeks ago but he's been tied up with the whole Cory thing, the fella that's girl got gored to death or run off or whatever it was."

Bobby stood in the center of the room, his hands balled on his hips, thinking. Edging from beneath the couch where James was now sleeping lay his open duffel.

"Got a regular medical supply house set up, don't you, James."

James said nothing.

"I want you to keep that shit away from the boy. You hear me? He's got enough problems as it is."

James woke the next morning to the smell of Lysol, the itch beneath his skin, the sun in his face. He dressed in one of Bobby's faded chambray shirts, dungarees, and old work boots then walked out into the front yard to find Bobby and Eddie unloading sheets of drywall from the bed of the pickup.

The rain was gone and the heat had returned, as fierce as mid-August.

"You cleaning or something?"

"Well, look who's up," said Bobby. "Fancy seeing a loafer like you this early."

Old Gus thumped his tail at James's approach.

"Couldn't hardly sleep for the smell."

"Sleep? Shit, it's almost ten, James. Let us get this last one here."

James stood watching as Bobby and Eddie lifted the sheet of drywall off the bed, leaning it against the porch rail.

"That'll bout do it," said Bobby. "How bout some water, Gathers?"

"I reckon I could drink," Eddie said, and turned on the hose pipe, letting it run for a moment until the water came cold.

"Trying to clean up back there. The odor's strong, I know."

"It's fine. I was joking with you."

Old Gus settled into his depression by the hedges.

"It's done got hot on us, I reckon," said Bobby. "So, what's on the agenda today, big James? Aim to walk the river till dark?"

"Actually I wanted to ask you about something serious, Bobby."

They walked into the shade of the house.

"Don't drink too much of that, Gathers," called Bobby. "You'll wind up foundering yourself."

"I'm all right," called the boy.

"Shit, I'm sorry. What were you saying, James?"

"Wanted to ask you something, about a woman round here somewhere."

"They God Almighty. You ain't done went and took up with some woman have you?"

"Not like that. An old woman my Mamma used to know."

Bobby sat down on the porch steps.

"A woman that could talk the fire out of things," said James. "You ever heard of her?"

Bobby glanced up. He took a handkerchief from his back pocket, unfolded it meticulously, and wiped his forehead and eyes. "I got a mind to say I do. Reckon that would be the old McAllister woman. Only one I ever heard to talk out the fire. What about her?"

"I thought I might go find her," said James. "See if she might could help me."

"Help you? Shit, James. Lay off that water, Gathers. I'm telling you."

"I'm all right," called a voice. The hose pipe kept gurgling.

"Well. You know where she lives?"

Bobby stood. "I do. She's got a trailer down the mountain a ways, down toward Yellow Branch, I recollect. Off in the middle of nowhere. But what you want with her, James? Shit, you're doing all right?"

"But that's the thing, I'm not, Bobby. I'm weaning my way off it, but I'm not doing all right. And I'm running out. I heard she was a good woman."

"Hell if she is." Bobby leaned closer, conspiratorially. "I wouldn't say this in front of the boy, but I've heard things about her, James. Shit that would turn you green, inside and out. I wouldn't say it in front of the boy but bad things, James. Real bad."

"Wouldn't say what in front of the boy?" asked Eddie, coming round from the side of the house.

"You cut that hose off?" asked Bobby.

"I ain't done with it."

Bobby turned back to James. "You a grown man. You do what you want, go where you please. But I'll tell you this: they ran her out of the Pentecostal church. The *Pentecostals* we're talking about here, James. You better give it some thought."

"I ain't done nothing but give it thought, Bobby."

"They God Almighty you are hardheaded. Go down Highway 28 past the ranger station, then turn in toward Yellow Branch Falls, then keep going like you're heading toward the backside of the rifle range. She's in one of those hollers in there. The crazy bitch."

"I appreciate it."

"I'd give you the truck if I could, but I aim to get another load of dry-wall and lumber, and two storm windows before the day's out. But you be careful round that old woman, James. I'm serious now. How you plan to get down there?"

"I can hitch a ride. I appreciate it." James started up the drive.

"When you look to be back by?" called Bobby.

"Before good dark."

"Well, you see that you are. Wind up having a heatstroke walking. Wouldn't know it was fall by that sun."

"I'll see you."

James looked back once to see Bobby lost in thought, head down, hands on his hips. Then Eddie came up behind him, and they turned toward the remaining drywall.

A road crew picked him up, carrying him as far as the intersection of Whetstone Road and Highway 28, and James thanked them, then began walking knowing it wasn't far and that the road was mostly down-hill from here.

"You be careful in all this heat," said a man.

James waved, and the man sat down between two yellow Igloo coolers and nodded and the truck was gone. Past the ranger station he took a right down toward the falls area parking lot, with its picnic tables and glassed map. A green Forest Service pickup and a dirty Toyota hatchback sat in the parking lot. James started up the trail, following the creek and bending along the switchbacks, until far in the distance he could see the steeple of the Lutheran church pricking through the trees.

At the falls sat a boy and girl picnicking on a rock with a bottle of wine. The girl had a black and white Jack Russell terrier in her arms. The boy wore an orange Clemson shirt. James waved and walked on through the buttery leaves. There was no sign of the Forest Service.

He climbed past the falls and descended into a sloped meadow where jimson and vetch and broom straw crowded an old barbed-wire fence. Pieces of abandoned farm equipment, an old disc plow, another that must have been mule-drawn—all sat marooned in islands of weeds. The bugs were awful, gnats and dragonflies and horseflies circled his eyes and ear canals. He stopped down in the center of the bottomland. He could hear a creek running somewhere beyond sight. Twenty years, he thought. Bet nobody's been down here in twenty years. And the solitude was something—he could feel it. Being alone like that.

Through the bottom he passed a weathered barn with its oxidized roof and antique tack nailed to the walls, then found the creek and followed it upland out of the vale into the darker forest.

The air hummed and jumped. Ulcers of dark cloud had folded out from the once-blue sky, low and suppressed and quaking with electricity.

In the distance a state helicopter flew low, looking for marijuana. He kept walking.

The trailer and house sat side by side, shaded in a small dirt clearing perhaps a half mile past the barn, chickens in the yard, wheels rusted and useless but still visible on the trailer. For the life of him, James couldn't figure out how they had managed to get it in here. A rooster went tiptoeing across the yard, dipping its head as if it had lost something, and a dog came loping out at his approach. He rubbed one of its ears then climbed the steps and knocked on the trailer door. He waited. Knocked again.

When he turned to descend the steps, a woman was watching him. She stood barefoot on the steps of the house, a rug in her hands that she slowly hung over a line that ran from the porch rail to a catalpa tree.

"Hidy there, ma'am," called James.

"Ain't nobody live in there," said the woman. "They put it down here after I told em I didn't want it." She paused to study him. She was old, her hair up in an iron-gray screw she must have once thought a bun. "Clyde send you down here?"

"No, ma'am."

"Who sent you then? Them fools at the state hospital?"

"No, ma'am. Didn't nobody send me."

"What you want then?"

"I was looking for a Miss McAllister."

"What you want with her?"

"I've been sick. I need to talk to her. Are you Miss McAllister? Somebody told me she had the power to heal, to talk out fire. You know if that's true?"

"Could be."

"I don't mean her no harm. I wish you'd say if you were her."

The woman dusted the rug, slapping at it, arranging it on the line just so. The dog came up the steps to drop by her feet, yawn. She bent and pulled away a tick.

"Please. I'm trying to find her," said James.

"Well, I reckon you have," she said after a moment.

Her face was ravaged by deep cuts, blackheads across her nose and cheeks like a storm cloud of gnats. He followed her into the house, waiting in the front room while she disappeared in the back, reemerging with a large clasp-lock Bible in her hands.

"Say you want the fire talked out," she said.

"Yes, ma'am. Sort of."

He couldn't quit staring at her left eye, glazed and frozen in its socket. Then he realized it was glass.

"I'll have to eat something first. You wait while I fix dinner. Sit on down on the couch. I thought that good-for-nothing son of mine might have sent you up here."

"No, ma'am."

"Wants to send me to the old folks home and sell all this land for timber. By God's grace, I'll be in the ground when that happens. Sit on down and wait for me."

She shuffled into the back room, then came back out and walked out of the house without a word. James watched her go into the thick woods, wondering if he was meant to follow her but making no move. He leaned back against the couch that stunk almost beyond belief—a milky stench of rot and body odor. Thunder sounded. Something came scratching at the door, and he turned to see the dog panting at the screen. "Come on in out of the heat, boy," he said, and the dog came in to settle in the corner. Soon it was asleep. Soon after that, James was too.

The darkness seemed frighteningly personal, closing over him like a hood, like so many nights after the war, curled within an old Coleman sleeping bag by the side of some empty road, the tremors wracking his body. He woke to an incredible thirst coupled with the deep pangs of hunger. The last time he had drunk had been riding that morning with the road crew. He hadn't eaten since the night before. He walked into the yard.

Lightning bugs flashed. He called for the woman and, gaining no response, walked back inside. Maybe she had abandoned him. Maybe he was alone. Night seemed to insinuate all manner of things.

Maybe a half hour later the storm broke. She came in shortly after that.

"You up?"

He nodded.

"Hungry?"

"Yes, ma'am. Very."

"Well, come on then."

They ate a hoecake and green beans and a fresh sliced tomato dusted with salt. James downed four jars of water then leaned back against the chair and exhaled.

"Full?"

"Yes, ma'am. That was wonderful. I thank you."

"Help me clear the table here."

They cleared the scant dishes, and he told her why he had sought her out. She listened in silence.

"Morphine," she said. "That's a kind of painkiller, ain't it?"

He nodded his head that it was.

"Which war was yourn?"

"Korea."

"Korea. Clyde's is this one now. Vietnam. My husband was in the big one, the Second." She walked over to the sink. "You ever see a doctor working on a dying man?"

"Yes, ma'am."

"What's that?"

"Yes. I have."

"Talk at my left ear. Hearing's all but gone."

"Said I did. I have."

"Ever see the doctor or nurse or what have you get angry with a dying man? Curse him for dying on him? I know you have. You know why that is? Because humans is the only living creatures that lives in denial of their natural state. An animal gets sick or wounded it goes off by itself to die. We humans congregate, act like dying ain't in our nature."

James said nothing. The woman scraped the plates into the basin of the sink.

"Who'd you say your people was?"

"The Burdens. My mamma was a Nichols."

"The Nichols from Chow Valley?"

"From all over, really. Some might have been."

"I believe I knowed your mamma," said the woman after a moment. "We was on the line together at the mill for a while. She was a purty thing."

"Yes, ma'am. She still is."

"Uh-huh."

The shrill chant of peepers, tree frogs, whippoorwills. Bullbats came swooping out of the high trees to feast. Rain dripped from the trees onto the metal of the roof. James and the woman sat in the front room, the Bible on the couch between them and the woman bent close to James's heart, whispering fiercely. He could hear her, but the words were indistinguishable. She smelled like wild onions and dirt, metallic and clean and older than memory. Someone without antecedent or ancestor. There would be no scion, no children to follow. After a moment she rose and pulled at her sleeves.

"I don't know if that'll take or not," she said. "It's more for healing the body than the spirit. The spirit's between you and the good Lord. But I put it right into the heart best I know how. Are you washed in the blood?"

He looked at her.

"Is your soul washed in the blood?"

"No, ma'am, I don't believe it is. Not anymore."

"Why's that?"

"I don't know. I just don't think I am anymore. One time maybe. Before I left, they took me to the river."

"Dip you, did they? Well, it takes more than that to wash white your soul, boy."

"Yes, ma'am. I know it."

She nodded and stood.

"The youngest Cory girl come through here the other week, running away from home. I asked where or not she'd been baptized. She wouldn't say. I pray for that girl, ever day and ever night I do."

"Yes, ma'am."

"Well, it ain't my business no how."

James made to rise.

"You can't walk out and it dark. I don't know where the weather'll hold or not. I'll make you a pallet on the floor. You can get on in the morning."

"I'll not trouble you."

"Wait," she said. "It's no trouble."

She came from the back room with a pile of mildewed blankets and arranged them on the floor. They were musty but clean. James took off his boots and slipped into the covers while the woman stood over him, latching the door.

"You ought not to be able to sleep at night. I couldn't sleep in peace if'n I wasn't washed in the blood of the Lamb."

"That's right," said James. "I can't."

But he could.

He woke in the morning as lonely as something washed ashore. The old woman was nowhere to be found, but there was a jelly jar of cold water on the table. He drank that and left. He followed the creek down to the pasture and the barn then turned north toward the falls. The road wasn't that far away, and he could hear the expiring sizzle of cars passing on the blacktop. He walked on, a great itch rising, climbing him cell by cell, while around him the world appeared bathed in a soft, white light. Birch, poplar, pine—all seemed to gather and hold a certain phosphorescence pulsing just beneath their ridged and bitten skins.

On toward midday he was following a bluff when he heard a great crashing sound that echoed and rang through the trees, seemingly equidistant from every point about him. He hurried on in the direction of the road, and before he could reach the overlook, he heard sirens, then voices, more cars approaching, a chaos of motion. From the bluff he saw what must have been a blue car smashed and without shape now, a hulk of gray metal and spiderwebbed glass deposited against the guardrail. A transfer truck lay jackknifed across the center of the road. On the road's shoulder a man sat up on his elbows on a stretcher, his head swaddled in bandages, both hands wrapped like a prizefighter's. A crowd was gathered around the car's remains, and no one seemed in a hurry. The high sheriff was there, an ambulance, two wreckers. The county rescue squad came weaving up through the stalled traffic, and two men climbed out with what appeared to be giant needle-nose pliers. James turned to go, then, just as he did, he saw something. Two winged figures rising up from the car with something between them, a phantasm of swirling, white light. No one else seemed to see it. He stood watching as two angels rose into the boughs of the trees. Between them they held a fluttering spasm of light James knew without question to be a human soul washed in the blood of the Lamb.

For a week Roy staggered about like a man bent on destruction of some sort, be it self or otherwise. Afternoons he would stop by Bobby Thorton's to pick up Eddie Gathers so that he could drink in good company, or at least company of some sort.

"I got a mind not to go," said Eddie one afternoon.

"I got a mind not to take you," said Roy.

"Seriously. With the sheriff and all. Feel like I'm pushing my luck."

"You are."

"Hell, Roy. Why you want to go and say a thing like that? Damn."

Two days later Roy drove up to find Bobby on the porch sipping an amber solution from a Mason fruit jar, plastic Twinkie wrappers about his feet, old Gus dozing on his side, tail barely thumping. On the radio Carolina was kicking off to Wake Forest.

"Thought you might be the sheriff."

"Well, you must have not thought it too hard. Pass over that jar, how about it."

Bobby handed him the jar. Roy felt sinister these days, unshaven and hollow-eyed, two empty sockets cut into the pan of his troubled brain.

"You know what I notice?" asked Bobby.

"What's that?"

"You came home with almost something of a foreign accent, I kinda thought. British, maybe. All proper like. But it's about gone now."

Roy paid him no mind, studying instead the jar. Strings of something floating in an amber solution. It appeared to be the final resting place of some decomposed jelly fish.

"Rotgut?"

"Worse," said Bobby. "Try it."

"Gasoline?"

"Just try it."

Roy drank, winced, drank again.

"Looks like you started early."

"Day off," Roy said. "Where's that boy at, Bobby?"

"You find any work yet?"

"Hell. Hardly pays to work. Government takes it all anyway. Where'd you say Gathers was?"

"Bush-hogging down by the river, I suspect. Which is what I pay him to do. Least that's the theory. Seems I mostly just pay him to get drunk with you."

"You're rich, Bobby. You got plenty of hands."

"Rich my ass. Still wearing that shiner, are you?"

Roy waved him off.

"You got that no-count brother of mine to work, haven't you?"

"Shit. James? Keep expecting him to join that hippie commune up near Asheville they keep talking about. If he's not off in the wood eating mushrooms, he's sitting around meditating or some shit."

"Meditating?"

"That's what it looks like."

"Ain't no Burden ever meditated I knowed of."

"Well, that's James for you," said Bobby drinking. "He's some kind of world-beater, I reckon."

The following Saturday Roy drove up to see his mother. He ate dinner by the light of a single bulb shaded in purple crinoline, restless and near twitching. Faith was coming home Sunday afternoon, and he could feel something swelling in him, a bubble that was equal parts rage and relief. For the past seven days he had drunk his way through the image of her lying in the arms of her fiancé, of them eating on the porches of swanky Charleston restaurants, he in his navy whites, she in her Sunday best, her hair pulled up off her neck and garlanded with baby's breath. He stared out the dark window at his own vague silhouette. Outside the air was fast cooling, summer's heat all but gone. The leaves were beginning to color and fall. In a matter of weeks a carpet of dried leaves and pine needles would lie half a foot deep through the woods. The snakes were moving.

His mother walked in and scraped what was left of the gravy and country-fried steak onto his plate.

"Your father isn't making much sense," said his mother.

"No kidding. The man hasn't made any sense in all the years I've known him. I'd hate for him to take up something new at his age."

"I'm serious, Roy." She refilled his glass of tea. "He keeps talking about some white-faced cattle. About needing to hide them."

"Does he have any white-faced cattle?"

"You know he don't."

"Bingo. The man's a nut."

"It ain't Christian to talk that way, Roy. You wasn't raised to that. To take it all so lightly. You're starting to sound like your brother now."

"Which one?"

"Either. James, I reckon."

"Lord help me then. Reckon you seen the prodigal son then."

"He came to the hospital."

"He said he might. How thoughtful of him."

"Don't be that way, Roy."

He pushed a piece of cornbread in and out of the gravy toward the mashed potatoes. "This is good," he said. "I appreciate it."

"I'm afraid he's dying, Roy."

"Who? James?"

"No. Your father."

"He ain't dying."

"I'm afraid he is. There's things you don't know about, Roy. Things that happened to him when he was boy, with his father."

"Like what?"

She shook her head. "I don't know. I just know it's so, that something happened to him a long time ago. He's never talked about it, but it's weighed on him for years."

Roy sighed. "So what makes you think something happened then? All I know is that he'll live. He's too stubborn to go off and die. And that's the truth, Mamma."

She took his plate and set it in the sink.

"You and Enis, way y'all run around drinking and carrying on. It's pure foolishness."

"Well, I do it for the devilment of it."

"I'm trying to be serious here."

"Well, stop. Please. You always did want one of us to settle down with some good little Church of God girl, didn't you? Little hairnet. Won't wear nothing but a long dress seven days a week."

"You take it all so lightly."

"Aw, come on, Mamma."

"I worry about him, Roy. Your father."

His mother touched his hand, tentatively, and for a moment he was shocked at the lightness of her touch. She seemed so frail, her liver-spotted skin like parchment, her bones hollow. He thought her a small bird and suddenly he saw her for what she was: she was old.

"He ain't dying," he said, but softer this time, unable to lance whatever bubble was growing within him. Beneath it, he knew, was love, patience, a deep reserve of kindness, but he found no path, no relief, so he sat suspended between emotions. His mother sat looking at him, her eyes sad and full.

"Hope," he said after a few minutes, "is a four-letter word."

The road unfurled like some great river having flooded its banks to encompass new lands, constantly turning, switching back on itself as if dissatisfied with its lot. He passed Deadman's Curve, just below the Isaqueena Falls Restaurant, and before him lay the dark valley pricked here and there with light. At the foot of the mountain he stopped at the Last Chance and stood for a moment in the parking lot staring up at the lozenge-shaped sign that read PABST BLUE RIBBON. Overhead, cirrus clouds strung like bits of wool. He walked around front, where several men sat, three or four on upturned crates, two on a bench seat cut from the trunk of an oak, all throwing their empties in a wire basket.

"L-T Burden," said one on his approach. "How's the world?"

"Still not fit for a working man."

"I figured as much."

He walked inside and up to the bar.

"What you drinking?" asked the bartender.

"Jack and Coke. Ed not around tonight?"

"Lucky you."

"He say anything about that lampshade?"

"Just that it ain't gonna fix itself, is all."

"I'm gonna get right with him on it."

"I figure he's holding his breath on that one."

Roy left a dollar on the bar and carried the drink over to stand in front of the fire that sat banked and cracking in the hearth.

"Where's that partner of yourn?"

Roy looked up from the mortar grooves of the fireplace and shook his head at the man addressing him.

"You talking to me?"

"Sure I am."

"Don't know who you're talking about, buddy."

"Sure you do," said the man looking down at him. "Rascally looking thing. Snatch a red hair like the devil himself."

"Who are you?"

"Probably the cause of that shiner you got there."

"I don't believe we've met," said Roy.

"Reverend Jim Leggett. And I don't believe I've seen you at any prayins."

"I don't believe I've been."

"Right," said the man laughing. "I heard that about you, that you were real quick with the wit."

"Well, I don't need any foot washing, if that's what you're getting at."

"Right. Right. That's funny."

"Excuse me, Reverend," said Roy, brushing past him, "but I do believe I hear my old friend Beelzebub calling."

The reverend cornered him again at the bar.

"I'll have what he's having," he told the bartender. "What is that?"

"Jack and Coke," said Roy.

The bartender passed it over to the reverend, who drank it down in a single head-tossed swallow, rattled the ice, exhaled.

"Drinking man, are you, Reverend?"

"I don't mind a nip now and then. I consider it my only vice."

"Me, too."

"That and keeping company with juvenile delinquents."

"Well," said Roy, finishing his drink, "two's still real good."

He started across the bar toward the door.

"I'm dealing these days in white-face cattle," the reverend called across the room.

Roy turned.

"What did you say?"

"Said I'm dealing these days in white-faced cattle. Met a man that said he had some to move. Needed to hide em, he said. A desperate old fella. My heart went out to him. Cain't remember the name though. You may or may not know the old fart."

Roy walked out, realizing with a sudden clarity that fall had begun.

And then she was home again. In the weeks following Faith's return from Charleston, Roy felt as if he had been granted a last-minute stay of execution. It was that overwhelming. It was that tenuous. But first, there was her return. The Sunday night she came home, he had waited for her on her parents' porch. To hell with the fact that all three of them would be arriving together. To hell with the fact that for the eighth straight day he was drunk off his ass. He had sat there all afternoon and into the evening, singing and yelling and then playing a harmonica while neighbors drove or walked past casting wary looks. Twice a deputy's car had eased past, and he had given the man his best shit-eating grin, and then waved for all he was worth. The deputy had only shaken his head, and driven away.

By the time he saw the Abernathys' Cadillac pulling up the street, it was past dusk but not yet full night. Headlights went prowling up the street, illuminating hedges, a stop sign, a single lonesome cat seeking refuge in shadow. Headlights prowled at his heart, fell across his face, and for the briefest of moments he felt his eyes flash green.

Mr. Abernathy lugged a suitcase and halfway up the steps stopped to stare at the misshapen figure that hunched in the swing. "Who is that?" he called.

"Boo," said Roy. "A bank robber come to rob your bank."

"Is this some sort of joke?"

"Been gone a long fucking time, ain't you?"

"Why you—"

"Go on in, Daddy," said Faith.

"I'll call the law on you, young man."

She ushered her parents inside.

"Go on. It's OK."

The house flickered to life then steadily went dark again. He thought for a while she wasn't coming out, that she was content to leave him there, but this didn't trouble him. He had sat so long in the swing that he—like his father, he realized—felt nothing from the waist down. Even if she did come out, he was not certain he would be able to speak. His mouth had long since cottoned. And were he to speak, what would he say?

When she finally did come out, having changed, having scrubbed the rouge from her cheeks, he tried to avoid her searchlight eyes.

"Look at you," she said.

"I'm trying not to."

"How long have you been sitting there?"

"Since you left."

They sat for a moment, the porch swing creaking, before he asked her to tell him everything. She sighed. "Do you really want to know? Why not let it go, Roy? Seriously."

"I can't."

"It's gonna happen no matter what."

He shook his head no.

"It's going to, Roy. You can't stop it."

The swing kept creaking.

She said, "I'm gonna wind up the death of you."

"I hope so. I do. That's what I want most."

So she told him. She told him how they had strolled along the cobbled walks beneath the flare of gaslights, smells drifting from the windows of kitchens and restaurants. She told him how they had gone hand in hand, he in gloves and his pressed whites, medals flickering on his chest. How he had smelled: the musk of aftershave, the shampoo he used to wash his hair. How he had laid her atop a bed and slowly removed every article of clothing from her body, pulling free her panties with his white, even teeth, teeth as white as chalk. How his tongue had explored her body, how it had come into her uncertain, then flounced, greedy for the taste of her. How she had quivered and then cried like a child. She spared him nothing. She told him of kissing in a porch swing, staring out at the buoy lights that marked the deeper depths of the harbor. About how she woke to the sound of a bubbling percolator and already he was inside her and she was tender and raw and how her mother kept finding little excuses for her and her father to leave the two of them alone. And they coupled. "We coupled—is that the word? It was sex, just fucking. Wild, uncontrollable fucking like two horses, two animals, is that enough? Does the animals thing do it for you? Is that what you want to hear?" She spared him nothing, and he wept silently into his hands, a prickle of alcoholic sweat freezing him. But then she was finished. The story was complete. She had said it all, and somehow it felt done to him.

"That's all?" he asked.

"Is that not enough?"

"I suppose it is."

And it was. Then he could let it go; he could compartmentalize it. There was *here,* he thought, and there was *there.* And she is here. I am here. So he fell into a sort of imagined bliss. For days he would not leave her side, and she acquiesced to his every request, ignoring the necessity of making wedding plans, ignoring even Dr. and Mrs. Fowles. They walked hand in hand up public streets; they double-dated with Enis and Millie to the diner and drive-in. They drove his car through the mountain roads, passing a bottle of wine between them, Roy driving with his left hand, his right shoved down between her thighs.

"Do you love me?" he wanted to know.

"You know I do."

"What about him?"

She stared out the window. He looked at her then turned up the radio.

One warm night they returned to find Roy's father's pickup parked in the street.

"Enis?"

"I'm guessing," said Roy. "That or Daddy's cured and out courting."

Inside, Enis sat on the loveseat in the company of the Abernathys. He wore khaki pants and a white button-down, his hair a single shellacked wave. He half rose when Roy and Faith entered. *Laugh-In* played silently on the TV.

"How do, Faith. Roy."

"Evening, Mr. Abernathy. Thought I might return a daughter to you here."

Abernathy stared at Roy then turned back to the fire, where he seemed to consider for a moment lifting a poker and charging. He thought better of it and turned and forced a smile.

"I'm obliged, Mr. Burden."

"I was out walking, Daddy," said Faith. "And Roy happened by and offered me a ride. Wasn't that gentlemanly of him?"

Her father nodded. Her mother stood and left the room.

"I'm just waiting on Millie," said Enis, his voice almost breaking.

"Well, goodnight, everyone," said Faith. "Thank you again for the ride, Mr. Burden. Goodnight, Daddy."

She skipped up the stairs.

"Maybe I'll wait out on the porch swing," said Enis rising, "nice a night as it is."

When the door was shut, Abernathy began to pace a tight circle as if he were caged or staked by a rope shorter than he might desire.

"Nice night out," said Roy.

"Yes. Yes, it is."

"That's some kind of heat wave we been having."

Abernathy nodded.

Roy sat, looking across the room at him.

"You're a grown man, Mr. Burden. And I know you've seen a lot of things, been a lot of places," Abernathy said after a moment. "You're grown, I know, even if I can remember when you were just a boy running around with a snotty nose. So I'm not going to get into this with you."

"She's a grown woman, too."

"You're exactly right she is. A grown woman living under my roof."

"I think I see where this is headed," said Roy standing.

Abernathy pinched the bridge of his nose between thumb and forefinger.

"Just, just please. Try to see things from my perspective."

"Why don't you just out and say what it is you want?"

"I'm trying to be tactful but I can see that's lost on you, but fine. I want you to be, just . . . try to practice some, some sense of decency here. Some discretion."

"Well, which one? Decency or discretion?"

"She doesn't love you, son. You're a distraction, you're just for fun." He kept pinching the bridge of his nose. He sighed. "Someone told me something once, Mr. Burden. A preacher. I think you might appreciate it. He was talking about salvation, this preacher, and he said to me, 'You either believe in it or you don't.'" He turned for the stairs. "She doesn't love you. And even if she does, it doesn't change anything."

Roy walked out onto the porch and lit a Marlboro. Enis sat in the swing. "How'd that go?" he asked.

"About like you'd expect."

"That bad?"

"No, brother. Hell, no. That good."

They were still laughing when Millie came out.

The three of them piled into Roy's Fastback and headed for the Isaquena Restaurant, making it only as far as the base of the mountain, where traffic was backed up.

"What the hell is this?" said Roy.

They rolled the windows down. Around the mountain's first deep curve, a line of cars disappeared upward. No cars were coming down.

"Wreck, probably," said Enis.

Along the guardrail grew mimosa and cape jasmine—a heavy floral scent mixed with what smelled like burned-up brakes. By the roadside were the shards of sea-green bottles, waxed paper cups, a single balled diaper.

"Will this top let down?" asked Millie.

Roy touched the roof, shook his head. "Not anymore."

"Well, turn on the radio or something." She sulked down into the vinyl of the back seat. "God, it's hot in here."

Neither Roy nor Enis answered. They were watching a growing stream of men and women walking down along the center line. Couples, a woman with a baby, another with a brood of three children, an old black man emerging out of a fan of headlight.

"Excuse me. Hey," Roy called to the man. "Excuse me."

The man was gray-bearded, wearing overalls and a hat that read PURINA FEEDS in red and blue scroll.

"Excuse me."

He walked over and put his fingertips on the chrome mirror.

"What's going on up there, old-timer?" asked Roy.

"Automobile accident," said the man nodding. "Real bad. Got a woman pinned in there."

"She all right?"

"Naw, she ain't all right. She dead."

"Dead? I'll be damned."

The man shook his head solemnly.

"Why don't they by God push her ass off the road then," said Roy.

The man just kept shaking his head.

"Is it about cleared?"

"Got a tractor-trailer done jackknifed across the road, but that fella he's all right."

"My God. You wonder what we even got a highway patrol for. How long you been up there?"

The man studied the air for a moment then seemed to divine an answer.

"Three, four hour. Truck's still up there. I'm walking back down now looking for a phone to call the wife. Done went and throwed me off. I'm usual to go to bed with the chickens."

"My God."

"It's a sight," said the man. "Y'all be easy now. Miss."

He tipped his hat and walked on.

"Y'all want to turn around?" asked Roy.

"How?" said Millie.

"Shit. Good question." They were boxed in by the cars directly behind and in front of them. "Guess we're waiting then."

An hour later they sat in a back booth eating hamburgers steaks and drinking Cokes.

"Somebody change the damn subject," said Roy. "Like we're sitting in a funeral home here."

"All right," said Enis. "How's this: we're getting married, Roy."

"Enis!"

"Well, we are."

"Not tonight," said Millie. "Not right now."

"But real soon."

"Well, my congratulations to the bride and groom," said Roy. "I guess this season will be a banner year for the Abernathys."

They were quiet after that, cleaning their plates then staring at the front glass. Behind them was a mural of some idyllic place, Valhalla, perhaps, the German garden of the gods, replete with a churning milk-stream, fairies, trees bearing golden apples, large-breasted Bavarian women holding steins of amber beer.

"I saw a place like that," said Roy pointing with his fork. "Saw it from eleven thousand feet then bombed the hell of it. All the little fairies were crying, their wings on fire, napalm in their little slanty eyes. Blew up a statue of Buddha. Killed their god."

Millie skewered a last remnant of beef, the tines of her fork scraping the porcelain plate. The jukebox lit, rattled to life.

"Does she love him?" asked Roy. "Millie?"

"What?"

"Does she love him?"

"She don't know, Roy," said Enis.

Millie shook her head. "You should ask her that," she said.

"I have."

"And what does she say?"

"I don't know. I can never bear to hear the answer."

He let them out by Enis's car and watched them cross the street hand in hand, faces like bright windows. "I'm killing everybody around me," said Roy. "I'm dragging em all with me to hell, which is just fine because I'd rather not be lonely." He spent the rest of the night drinking at the Last Chance, then drove to the house he rented on Elm Avenue but never made it out of the car, sleeping beneath his coat, now and then waking to run the heater. In the morning the weather had shifted again, and a rime of frost lay across the windshield.

Two days later he came home from another morning with Faith feeling light and happy. Early in the day they had climbed an abandoned fire tower and made love one hundred feet in the air, with only the birds that nested in the rafters for company. He had driven her to her parents' then come home to fix lunch. In the mailbox were two letters, both of which he had been expecting. The first said he was late on his rent, two months in fact. He either needed to pay or be out by the first of November. The second envelope was marked UPSTATE FABRIC & APPAREL and read:

Dear Mr. Burden,

As much as it pains me to say so, I find myself unable to offer you the position as sales representative due to a shrinking operating budget. Please don't take this personally. Everyone at Upstate, myself included, were very impressed upon meeting you. We simply can't make any new hires at the moment as we're fearful of possible lay offs in the future. Good luck and God bless.

Sincerely,
P. Roscoe June
Plant Manager

He crumpled both letters and threw them into the corner, began to fry a grilled cheese sandwich, took a beer from the refrigerator and cracked it.

He was no less happy, no less sad. The next day he drove up 28 to 107 to 130, then on up to the turnoff for the Whitewater River, where Upstate Timber made its camp, and found Enis.

"It's a simple plan," he said. "You were serious about what you said the other night? About getting married."

Enis wiped the sweat from his face. "You damn well know I'm serious."

"A time comes, Enis, when you got to decide what it is you want, and exactly how you plan to get it."

"I said I was serious."

"So here's what we do about it."

"I'm listening."

It was decided, collectively, though not with the boy's consent, that the best and quickest solution to the problem would be for Eddie Gathers to return the reverend's wallet, apologize, and then square off whatever debt had accrued by working at the man's tent revivals.

"I ain't no damn show monkey," said the boy. This he said in the presence of Bobby. In the presence of his father, the high sheriff, and the good reverend, it had been all nosirs, and yessirs, his eyes tacked to the floorboards. Now he and Bobby were cleaning out the shed where the tractor sat.

"Nobody's saying you are," said Bobby, wheeling out a new Troy-Bilt tiller. Sheetrock still leaned against the front porch, surrounded by several cardboard boxes marked SMIRNOFF.

"Well, they better not. They damn sure better not."

"They ain't, so cool it with all that. How much money you owe him anyhow?"

"A hell of a lot. Something like two hundred dollars worth. Two weeks' wortha work, they say."

"They God Almighty. You and Roy drink all that?"

"I reckon I—"

Bobby walked into the house and threw the door shut behind him so that he could not hear what else Eddie had to say. He moved about the room quickly, unable to alight in any one place, the harsh emptiness of the house striking him like a blow. His mind shrank, reeled, and suddenly he was sick with an animal hunger for touch, love. "Sharon," he said. "Oh, Sharon." He pulled a small piece of paper from the back of a drawer and read the first line: CITATION FOR BRAVERY AND UNCOMMON VALOR. What he'd felt that day was a terrible love, more even for the ones he couldn't save. The pitched squeal of the air raid, and this little five-foot-five joke of a man waving a wrench while Stuka bombers sailed and dipped like truants from the Book of Revelation. The colonel came through, and a corporal named Buddy Trent, sitting on the back of a deuce-and-a-half, had pointed over at Bobby.

"Guy over there pulled seven men out, Colonel."

"Who, Thorton?"

"I kid you not, sir. Plane was burning and he pulled them everyone out. Saved em ever one."

He and Sharon had spent years in honky-tonks, making trips to Atlanta or Asheville, once as far as Memphis, drinking and listening to steel guitars, trying to bury his war in new life. Working all day in a garage then coming home to his daddy's, and then his own, orchards. He'd been drunk the night Sue Ellen was born. Sharon had forgiven him. She'd forgiven him everything except this last, whatever that last thing was. Two of her coats still hung on hooks on the back of the door.

After a moment Eddie walked inside. Bobby was sitting in the center of the room cradling a wedding photograph.

"There she is," he said.

"Bobby?"

"Look at her back then."

He was crying.

"The sheriff's in the yard, Bobby."

Bobby nodded.

"I'm going on then," said Eddie. "I just wanted to say thank you."

"You're welcome," said Bobby, still crying. "Thank-you accepted. You better not make the sheriff wait, young Gathers."

From the backseat of the sheriff's car, Eddie could see Bobby at the window, the wedding photograph hugged to his chest with one arm. With the other he wiped away tears, tears that fell, Eddie thought, for no real reason, tears he could not explain.

The sheriff drove him down the mountain, passing a bald spot on the embankment where now stood a cross of plastic flowers blowing apart. Petals were scattered in the mountain laurel and across the road in the ivy-like kudzu. They lay wet and flattened and discolored on the asphalt. In blue letters Eddie read the word MOTHER. The sheriff said nothing, bit at his bottom lip. Eddie turned in his seat, his fingers pressed against the cool glass, and watched it slide by like a movie, unreal and then gone.

At the foot of the mountain they missed the turn for the mill hill.

"Uh, sir?"

The sheriff shook his head. "I know. I know. Call it a short cut. I want to show you something first."

They drove past the courthouse, then down the hill toward the Oconee Detention Center. "The lockup," said the sheriff, smiling. "Pretty, ain't it?"

The compound consisted of three narrow block buildings connected by a green awning and sidewalk, giving the center the shape of a large E. Along the fenceline the grass was uncut and dying in long, knee-high stalks. Coils of razor wire were fashioned like tinsel. They parked and walked inside, passing through a barred door and then a second.

"You ain't packing heat are you, young man?" asked a deputy, motioning toward a sign that read ALL FIREARMS MUST BE CHECKED.

"I'll vouch that he's not," said the sheriff. "Come on, Gathers."

Eddie followed him down a dim corridor. Overhead ran a network of pipes, and faintly he could hear water gurgling. The building smelled of ammonia.

"Where is everybody?" asked Eddie.

"It didn't take me but one trip down here when I was about your age to know which side of the bars I wanted to stand on. My own daddy was sheriff then."

He opened a second barred door and waved in the boy then locked it behind them. There was no AC here and the room reeked of men.

"Come on," he said.

All along the corridor hands as limp and heavy as slain birds hung from rowed cells.

"Got a visitor," called the sheriff. "Up and at em, my lovelies."

Someone hooted. A catcall. "Pretty as a picture," called someone else. The voices echoed. Eddie looked around him. "Hellfire," he muttered. "I ain't aiming to be nobody's bighouse bitch."

The sheriff kept walking, trying not to laugh. The hands multiplied. He looked at faces, bare bulbs of heads with shaved scalps and dirty teeth.

"This is medium security," said the sheriff. "B and E. Strong-arm robbery. Assault. Any longhairs that wander into the county making trouble, this here is where they wind up. Come on, I got something up here real special for you."

He unlocked a second barred door at the end of the hall but this time did not step through. Eddie stood looking at the cell: an opaque window shone high above the single board that comprised bed, table, and chair. On the wall hung the Savior: a painted Jesus on the cross perhaps six feet tall. The image was stunning.

"Go on."

The boy stepped inside.

"Notice the bed. When I was overseas I got five days' leave once and went over to Dublin and saw Kilmainhain Jail, where they locked up all the Irish patriots and got the idea from there. This is sorta my pride and joy. I don't know who painted the good Lord there. Go on now."

Eddie stepped inside, and the gate clanged shut behind him.

"Welcome to hell, Gathers. Better start praying."

The sheriff pocketed the key and walked away.

How long he spent in the cell Eddie could not say. Long enough to lose his voice screaming, long enough to cry his cheeks raw. Finally he was simply exhausted and sat, and then lay, on the wooden bench. On Calvary, Christ looked toward the heavens, hands and feet tacked like an animal's. Eddie tried to count the thorns along his crown but gave up, too tired. He was asleep when the heard a key turn in the lock.

"Come on," the sheriff said. "Let's go, kid." Something in his demeanor had changed. He seemed solemn, regretful. "Enjoy your visit?" he asked, but he asked it without conviction, his voice so low Eddie barely understood him. In the lobby stood Eddie's father, a suitcase at his feet.

"Your mother packed your good clothes. Wash," said his father. "Don't think this is an excuse not to stay clean or brush your teeth." He cupped his son's chin. "You hear me?"

"Yessir."

"Do what the reverend says. It's two weeks, son."

"Yessir."

"Two weeks and then I want you back in school."

Eddie looked away.

"Edward?"

"All right."

"I love you."

Eddie nodded.

"You hear me?" said his father, as if either his voice or his son's ears had suddenly ceased to function.

"Yessir. I love you, too."

His father nodded. "Two weeks," he said.

Outside, the reverend stood with his hands clasped before him, dressed again like a pilgrim.

"Go on," said his father. Eddie lifted his suitcase into the bed of the pickup and went to climb in. "Not there," said a voice. He looked up to see the young man who had accompanied the reverend at the baseball game sitting in the passenger seat. "In the back," said the man. "Hogs and niggers always ride in the back. You ain't no nigger so I reckon you must be a hog, right?" And he spit a long jet of brown tobacco.

Eddie rode back up the mountain with the suitcase in his lap for warmth, his back pressed tight against the back of the cab. The sky was heavy with color; then broke, spilling streams of red and peach and orange and purple, while overhead the stars began to emerge. Darkness fell, and it was night by the time they stopped. Eddie piled out.

Part Two

156

"Where are we?"

"Home, my boy," said the reverend. "Home sweet home. At least for the time being."

Before them sat a large white tent, a pallet of folding chairs beside it. Grass-less ruts like cow paths crossed here and there, boards laid across the deeper troughs. Eddie looked back across the street.

"Is that the—"

"The what?"

"That restaurant—"

"Indeed. The Isaqueena Restaurant, I believe it's called."

"Well, I'll be damned. I thought we were going cross-country."

"Afraid not, my child. Now, are you hungry?"

Eddie shook his head.

"Well? Are ya or aren't ya?"

"I reckon I could eat."

"Well, hell, child, let's go eat." The reverend pulled a small medicine bottle from his hip pocket and uncorked it, swallowed twice. "Come on. I never known a man to conduct a proper prayin on an empty stomach."

"The reverend's a genius. You got to understand that about him," said the man, whose name turned out to be Stump. "I've seen papers on him with his IQ. It's something like 160. You know what that means?"

Eddie shook his head no. They sat by the front glass of the Isaqueena Restaurant, staring across the street at the circus tent they had spent the last two days working beneath. The sun was out, and the tent looked clean and fat in the afternoon light.

"Well, it means he's a full-on genius is what it means, a super-genius. Except he's not really a reverend, but I spect you've figured that out by now. He's what you might call a chameleon. Man wears a coat of many colors."

"Well, if he's so smart, how come it took him so long to track me down?"

"Shitfire. You think he was looking for you all that time? The reverend's a patient man. He's helping me to set up my own scam with a lady friend of mine over in Anderson. Gonna clean out some old-timer. Rev says it's personal with him. Needs him a little payback, I reckon. Rev was just fool-ing around with you. I reckon you're like a pet monkey or something to him. Hell, this whole county is. He just likes hanging around is all, I reckon. The thing he does with his voice," said Stump, chewing. "That's full-on genius. He talks one way, right? Just like you and me. Then he's got another way a talking around the churchgoing folk, sometimes real down-home-like, sometimes real educated-like, just depending on the situation. He likes em to think he's a Puritan or some shit. I seen him go out to these free-love sorta commune places and just charm the ever-living shit out of college kids then turn right around and preach hellfire and damnation to some of them Primitive Baptist folk."

"Was he ever in prison?"

"Hell, the rev's been everywhere. Prison, the service, all over the world. I cain't confirm this," whispered Stump leaning forward, "but I got good reason to believe he was in with the Chinese Communists, Chang Kai-shek and all them, during the war, the big one, a spy or something, but you didn't hear it from me."

"What's your reason?"

Stump showed the palms of his hands.

"You didn't hear it from me."

Every night at six there was an open prayer meeting. At seven the reverend would stand behind the altar and on a large General Electric sound system sing hymns then mumble for a half hour while a jar of acid-laced Holy Water was circulated about the room. Women would pass out, men would swoon, then open their wallets, visions of Glory washing over them. By seven-thirty the singing began and the hat was passed again. By that point the reverend had slipped out the back, headed, Eddie felt certain, for the Uptown Gentlemen's Club in Seneca. It was Eddie and Stump's job to keep track of the money while selling jars of sourwood honey labeled THE HONEY OF CANAAN—DIRECT IMPORTED FROM THE PROMISELAND and priced at five dollars a jar.

"I believe I might be getting religion," said Eddie one night as they sat counting the money.

"Found your calling, have you?"

"I reckon I have. Sight of all this money'll sway a man."

"Well, religious or not, don't plan on skimming none of that off," said Stump. "He'll know. He'll figure you out one way or the other. You know the rev used to work for NASA, I heard. Rockets and the like. Helped put a man on the moon."

"Ah, that ain't even true. My granddaddy told me the government made that up."

"The hell they did. The rev was by God there. You just ask him about it."

For a week the revival went on until on the eighth night the reverend decided that damnation was now more or less a nonissue in Oconee County and that it was time to move on to Anderson or maybe Pickens.

"I've been charting revenue," he said. "It peaked on night five and has been in a steady slide ever since."

Stump winked at Eddie. "He's got the mind of a Vanderbilt," he whispered.

The following day they staked the tent in the dead center of the Anderson county fairgrounds, amid the rusted hulk of an abandoned Ferris wheel and a ring meant to hold gas-powered bumper cars. By late afternoon the rain had settled in. By dusk the wind was whipping and the tent shuddered like a giant lung. Eddie and the reverend sat on folding chairs drinking whiskey and playing spades.

"How come you to drag me along like this?" asked Eddie.

"How come you to rob me?"

Eddie shrugged.

"I might have had it coming," conceded the reverend.

"Stump says you're some kind of genius."

"Does he? No. You can't play that."

"Why not?"

"You've got to play a puppy's foot."

"Oh. But he says you are. Says your IQ is astronomical."

"He said astronomical? He used that word?"

"No," said Gathers. "I think he just said real high."

"Well, real high sounds more like him."

"How did you track me down, by the way?"

"Well, I'll tell you how I didn't find you. Your damn good-for-nothing high-and-mighty sheriff. He didn't help a bit."

"Ah, he's all right."

"Dereliction of duty, they call it."

"So how did you then?"

"Saw you out with some drunk clown. Followed him. Wound up going up to talk with his crazy daddy, who told me where it was you were staying, then proceeded to try and talk me into helping him hide some cows I am fairly certain are nonexistent."

"That would be Reverend Burden. He's a real reverend. No offense."

"None taken."

They played on into the early hours of morning, the wind tearing about them so that now and then they had to get up and pull on slickers to hunch out into the rain and tie down flaps that had blown loose.

"Where is Stump, anyway?"

"At some point I'm am sending you home for a day or so to visit your mother. I am not a tyrant."

"All right. Where's Stump at?"

"Some girl he knows in town. He stops to see her every year. I put em on to a lead now that they've got their own private hustle going."

"So y'all got a regular route then?"

"Yes," said the reverend, studying his cards. "Yes, we do. Rummy."

"I thought we were playing spades?"

"Fine. Spade, then. I win."

He collected the small pile of pennies, pocketed them, and disappeared into the whirling night. The next day Stump returned, a smile threatening to rend his face.

"Lucky night?" asked Eddie.

"No. Well, yes, but that ain't why I'm smiling. The spirit's done went and moved the rev."

"That a fact?"

Stump lightly punched Eddie's arm.

"We're going into the marrying business, Gathers."

Disassociation—that was the word they had used. He had felt disassociated from his fellow soldiers, from the situation at hand, from life, from himself, from death. A young chaplain explained these things to him at a field hospital somewhere in Japan, nodding and adjusting an IV that extended from James's right arm to a plasma bag.

As the marines had grown near, James had, he was told, disassociated himself from his body, because what was a body, after all, but a certainty of mortality, a guarantor of death? In Pyongyang a Chinese officer had machine-gunned two American officers, most likely CIA, who had been captured after parachuting black-faced behind enemy lines to dynamite bridges and highways. The men had been marched into the street with no ceremony—two North Korean soldiers and a single Chinese officer. Around them the city was crumbling, burning. A steady flow of Chinese and North Korean soldiers were fleeing north, crowding the streets, stopping only to wire booby traps and set fire to gasoline and ammunition depots too heavy to carry. The officer had faced the Americans, both of their faces swollen with dirty cuts. Clearly they had been beaten for some time. James had sat across the street with the other POWs, too tired to stand, while the officer took a submachine gun from one of the soldiers to cut down the men. They fell and lay dead and, for all James knew, were still there, staring blank-eyed up at the cold Korean sky in silent communion with the circling birds.

So that was the thought when it was clear the Americans were coming: They'll kill us now. After staying alive all this time they'll kill us now. But truthfully, it was not at that moment that James had felt divorced from himself but months, years before. His earliest memories seemed fabricated, as if it were not him but some pseudo-James, some young stand-in selected for his striking likeness. As a boy he had never felt comfortable. He had never had close friends. Late into the morning of his honeymoon night he had sat on the closed toilet seat and stared at a reflection he did not recognize. He had just made love to his wife for the second time ever, and when she opened to him he had tried to open to her as well, but couldn't. His overriding fear was that there would be nothing there to show. That she would know him for the imposter he was, that she would see through his opaque surfaces.

Eleanor's letter, he had not written that. That had been someone else, that ghost-James that lived in his skin like an obtrusive, unwanted guest. *For six months I've been shaving a little bit of rubber off the tires of the truck that sits in the yard. I now have a decent sized handful hidden about the barracks.* Disassociation: Freud. Kierkegaard: "Despair is the sickness unto death." All the books he had read afterwards in the Red Cross hospitals. *My plan is to heat the rubber into a four inch shank then drive it into my liver, breaking it off there, or pushing it on farther should I have the courage.* Courage marked through, replaced with strength. Surely that had fallen to the blade of the censors. Most likely the entire letter had.

A conference within his dreams, on the night he slept in no-man's-land, the abandoned POW camp caught between lines, North Korean artillery streaking in one direction, American and South Korean M7 howitzers answering, the sickening beauty of war fought at night. Eleanor had been there.

"You're not coming back to me, are you?" she asked.

"I can't."

"Can't or won't?"

Silence his answer.

"You don't love me, then? You don't love me if you don't recognize that the one thing that can come out of this, the single thing, is love."

He had mouthed the words: "There's two."

She looked at him.

"Two," he whispered. "Love. But also hate."

The other was hate, grief, despair—many-named but no less felt, no less realized.

So she had left him there in a field littered with the ruins of war, the present and past tense of lives both lived and unlived, ruined though perhaps no one understood it yet. "Life shattered like this whole fucking country," someone said once. "Two useless pieces."

Now James wanted to go back, back to before, however useless that might be. He'd come home to die but, having seen his wife, wanted suddenly to live.

He borrowed Bobby's truck and drove down out of Long Creek to Seneca and sat on a bench across the street from the café to wait on her. Traffic came and went, cruising without purpose up and down Main Street. For most of the night James had lain listening to the rain on the tin roof, listened to it blowing in, jarring the screen door. But the storm had subsided before dawn, and now the world seemed at an uneasy peace. The sun was up, and the mercury in the thermometer in front of the Blue Ridge Bank had pushed into the low seventies. It felt like spring again, and James was alive, breathing. That morning he had showered and shaved then lay for a half hour soaking in Bobby's deep, claw-footed tub, something he could not remember doing since leaving. Bobby had walked in to shave.

"That was Sharon's favorite thing," he said, lathering his cheeks. "Always her favorite, soaking like that." He rinsed his brush. "I been thinking of maybe getting the Gathers boy a beagle pup. Something he could take care of. Think he'd like that? James?"

James had shut his eyes and sunk. Later, he had driven over to his parents', parking by the road and walking the quarter-mile driveway. The gold letters on the mailbox still read REV. AND MRS. BURDEN. In the yard he called for his mother, but there was no response except for the beagles who came barreling toward him as if he had been gone days and not years. On the porch he called again for his mother. Most likely she was out in the garden in the bottomland behind the house, or visiting at the next house over.

He headed down behind the house toward the shed and the fields. The corn had been neither picked nor trimmed and now stood wilted and dead, pale yellow stalks shedding like snakes, broken here and there by rain or wind. Wisteria and jasmine and kudzu grew along the shed wall up the slope of the roof, where they met a vine of poison ivy that reared from a crack in the clapboard side. It would keep growing until nothing was left, just a bramble of vines and the idea of a place, a rumor that keeps surfacing, claiming itself a memory. The door hung, then gave, and he walked into the cool interior. Sunlight tangled in the filaments of a spiderweb. The air smelled metallic with fine dirt. His body lay a thin shadow across the clay floor. Something stirred, and James froze thinking snake, but it was only an old coon hound smacking its gums and rousing to resettle in shadow.

Old metal signs leaned against the wall. The trace of letters: SEE ROCK CITY. ROYAL CROWN COLA. BUY WAR BONDS. An old mule yoke encased in spiderwebs tacked to the wall. A wringer washing machine in the corner. An ancient glue gun clogged with an eel of white magma.

The cotton patch was empty. The grass brittle.

He walked a ways along the rusted fenceline, trying to eye the Herefords their neighbors had grazed here so many years before, then gave up and turned back toward the house, approaching from the rear, the gabled roof carpeted in a moss that overhung the eaves. Inside, his father lay propped in his upstairs study, his surplus hospital bed a tangled geography of metal tubes and handles and white sheets. A large white wrap encircled his chest, and all was still but for his lungs filling and then discharging rhythmically. James stood in the doorway and watched. His father never opened his eyes, simply went on with his labored breathing.

In the deep freeze James found blocks of deer meat wrapped in butcher paper that a neighbor must have brought over. Dressing animals, deer, rabbit, squirrel—he remembered how reckless Roy had been with his knife, slipping it through skin so that it hummed like a zipper. James had always believed in patience, precision. But not so much anymore. He let the freezer clap shut and opened the refrigerator, finding butter, eggs, two cartons of milk, a jar of Duke's mayonnaise.

Down the hall James entered what had once been his and Roy's room, later Roy and Enis's after he had moved down the hall to sleep in his father's study. The bed was made tight, the room swept and dusted clean. He moved about the room looking at the framed photographs. The two boys together just before Enis was born, James maybe fifteen, Roy five or six. Their mother standing in ankle-deep water, wearing shorts and a shirt cinched at her waist, a bandanna tied across her head. She looked maybe fifteen, and the picture had an old foxed looked to it, as if it had been burned along its edges. Then Christmas 1948, the three men in worn suits and heads slicked with pomade, their mother in a dress, seated in a ladder-back chair and holding the infant Enis. Their father looking young and sleek and powerful, their mother a simple willow, still young and beautiful with only the intimations of age and worry beginning to creep into the cracks around her eyes. There was an album on the nightstand, a whole book of the dead, someone's dearly departed, old men and women on front stoops, shadows for eyes and hands like barbs. Children. Babies that would never see first birthdays. It meant nothing to him.

He put down the picture and opened the closet. Back behind Enis's plastic-bagged uniforms he found what he had always thought of as his good clothes, a pair of pressed Levi's draped over a coat hanger and a faux-pearl-buttoned dress shirt. Leather penny loafers. Black socks. Except they weren't his clothes, but Enis's. He took one of Enis's white undershirts as well, changed, borrowed some aftershave, brushed his teeth, finger-combed his hair, then carried his old clothes into the kitchen, where he dropped them into the wastebasket beneath the sink. He found a knife and drove a fourth hole in his old belt so that the jeans would fit, then walked back to where his father purred in his sleep beneath the picture of Jesus. On the nightstand sat an unmarked bottle of pills. James opened them, sniffed them, odorless, poured them out in his hand to count them: seventeen. He dry-swallowed one, capped the bottle, then opened it again, swallowed a second, walked out.

Sitting on the street he felt clean and new and light, a mild glaze shuttering his thoughts as he waited there for his wife to get off work and walk home. Around three she came out and turned left up the street, never once allowing her eyes to settle on anything but what lay directly in front of her. He followed at a distance then hustled up beside her. She glanced, smirked, kept walking.

"You following me?" she asked.

"Sure am."

"Any particular reason?"

"Yep."

She stopped. "Well, don't you sound right chipper."

He fingered his new clothes. "Look at the sun, look around you. It's hard not to."

"You're all cleaned up," she said, and kept walking.

He fell in step beside her, passing a yard with an overturned tricycle, a rusted swing set with bees buzzing around the open tubing, a man washing his car with smooth circular motions.

"I wasn't really expecting to see you again, Jimmy."

"I know."

"Once kind of rattled me."

"Me too."

They spoke without looking at each other, walking quickly and methodically up the street.

"You're coming home."

It didn't sound to him like a question, so he didn't answer. He took her hand.

"Don't," she said. "Don't unless you mean it."

He didn't let go.

"I thought you might like a nice dinner," he said. "Maybe a night out."

"With my husband, you mean?"

He nodded.

"I'm serious, Jimmy. Don't. Not unless you mean it."

James lay on the bed listening to the shower cut off, the sound of the toilet seat being propped up, a tinkling of water, a flushing—the comfort of sound, knowing we're better never left in silence, never left alone. She came out with one towel wrapped around her body and another about her head.

"You're still beautiful," he said. "That hasn't changed a bit."

She said nothing.

"I'm trying to do better by you, Ellie. I want to do better."

She turned away, nodded her head.

He lay on the foot of the bed with his feet touching the floor and his hands propped behind his head while she changed. She held dress after dress against her body, asking this or that? over and over, and to each he smiled and nodded.

"I'm in no hurry to rush this," she said. "I'm afraid if I blink it'll all go away."

When they were dressed, they rode out to the Keowee Courthouse supper club and sat at the bar drinking rum and Cokes. James crushed a lime wedge into his glass, swirled it with the swizzle stick.

"Should we talk about this?" she asked.

"About what?"

She tried to smile. "About everything."

"Maybe one night when you can't sleep. Maybe then."

"That's fine then." She folded her hand atop his. "That's fine."

"You look so beautiful tonight, Ellie. I like your hair like that."

Whether consciously or not she touched her hair with the tips of her fingers, then mocked herself, feeling about her head as if it were a foreign object.

"Marlon said I look like a boy. I told him it's the fashion now. I think he's just glad I still wear a bra."

"Marlon's a dumb ass."

"He actually has a certificate on the wall that says so: certified dumb ass." She smiled, drank through a red-striped straw.

After they were seated and had ordered, a silence seemed to fall. A single candle flickered within a glass bulb, pulsing light along their fingers. James studied his hands.

"I saw Enis," she said, as much to break the silence as anything else. "They came in to eat. Him and that Abernathy girl. Think I scared him. He's taken with her."

"So I hear. She was in diapers last time I saw her."

"She wasn't even born, Jimmy. You're thinking of her sister."

He nodded. "Her sister was probably in a training bra."

"Not anymore."

"No, I reckon not."

"What about Roy? Have you seen him?"

James shook his head. "I've seen him, but I've got enough trouble without worrying over Roy."

"Somebody said he got ran out of that house of his over on Elm."

"Sounds like him."

"Marlon says he's going with that Abernathy girl, the older one, the one engaged. That some men had been asking around about him in a not-so-friendly way. That Roy's something else."

"He could set a man to worrying," said James.

The waiter brought over their dinner, and for a while they ate in silence.

"Where did you go after, Jimmy?"

"After what?"

"Don't be like that, all innocent. Just after. You know, after it all. After you were back."

He held a bite of steak before his face.

"Just wandered," he said. "Out west mostly. Saw Alaska, the Pacific Ocean. Spent some time in Montana painting fences. Worked in Wyoming. I'll save that, too. Another night you can't sleep."

"I'm gonna need insomnia to ever understand you, Jimmy."

He nodded. They ate.

"Take me home," she said when the plates were cleared.

The streetlights were just beginning to flicker on as he drove Bobby's truck up Oak Avenue. She had slid across the seat and leaned against him. Inside the house she pushed him back onto the bed and slowly undressed, then slid beneath the covers.

"I'm alone in here," she said.

He took off his clothes and lay beside her.

"You feel so thin."

"I know."

They lay listening to the night sounds.

"Is this real, Jimmy?"

Again, it did not sound like a question. Again, he did not answer. He felt her cool fingertips moving along his body, and he blushed there in the inky dark, thinking to himself, here I am, a grown man, blushing.

After making love he propped himself on one elbow and looked at her. Her short hair spiked across the pillow. Her mouth lay against his forearm. Then they slept in a dreamless web, that seam between day and night, waking twice. The first time she flailed wildly for his arm, grabbing his left hand and pinching the spot where his wedding band had once been.

"Where is it?" she asked, her voice husky with sleep.

"Shh. Go back to sleep, Ellie."

"Where is it?"

"Go back to sleep. It's OK."

Her eyes seemed to shut involuntarily. He listened as her breathing settled into a regular, shallow pulse, and then slept himself. He awoke again on toward morning, a hollowness having broken inside him, the sound of faraway footsteps echoing. Eleanor lay on her stomach, her hands held by her head as if she were a penitent. James pulled on his pants and shoes and walked into the street. The moon was up and full and a pallor of yellow light lay like gold dust.

From beneath the seat of the truck he pulled out a small tool kit meant to hold a ratchet set. Instead, wrapped in an oil-smeared rag, was a syringe he injected into his arm. He was sweating, panting. He sat in the truck until he felt his breathing steady, then climbed back into the bed.

"Where is it?" he thought she said.

"Shh. I love you."

"I love you," she seemed to say. "But you took something from me." She curled into him, her face against the tracked skin of his left arm.

"What?"

"You heard them?" she asked. "The steps. His steps."

He smoothed her hair.

"It's just the house settling," he said. "Go back to sleep."

Eleanor woke just before dawn to the dull footsteps of an unborn child, surfacing into a dream of water, into the submarine world of an empty womb where amorphous shapes moved slowly, thrashing and trailing streams of bubbles like the tails of comets. She swam the blue depths, probing the corners, the distant ends, chasing dark figures that seemed to quit one place just as she arrived. In the end, she swam, and then woke, alone, the bedsheets twisted, the sound of her husband, and not her unborn child, worrying the floorboards.

At the beginning of November Peyton Fowles returned, greeted like a prodigal son, the warrior who had not once seen combat, the faithful lover who had spent his pay on Hawaiian hookers and cheap Japanese porn, and the storms descended again over Roy Burden, as present and palpable as the rain that fell night and day in cold, drowning sheets.

All along the house was the smell of Old Spice, in every crack, in every place she felt it shouldn't be. She shut the door to the bathroom and held her breath, shut her eyes, then exhaled: Old Spice.

She sat staring into the mirror, her lips a coral red, eyes rimmed with silvery blue eyeliner. Someone knocked at the door.

"In use?" asked the voice.

"One moment, Dr. Fowles."

"Oh, I'm sorry, Faith, dear. I'll use the restroom down the hall."

She listened as he walked down the hall, heard the distant bathroom door shut. More damn bathrooms here than most houses have rooms. She opened the medicine cabinet. It was his Old Spice she smelled everywhere, a smell that she couldn't get used to. A bottle sat on the shelf, another in a cardboard sheath. She eased shut the cabinet.

Peyton stood waiting for her in the hall.

"Well?"

"I couldn't. The smell was making me sick."

"Dammit, Faith, what have you been doing there?"

She shrugged. "Sitting there."

"For half an hour? Christ. I can't quit pacing out here and you're in there sitting?"

"Your father scared me."

"Please. All you have to do is pee on a damn stick."

They stood for a moment.

"This is important," he said.

She smirked.

"I know," he said. "I'm sorry. I know I don't have to tell you that. But for God's sake, Faith."

"Just . . . just later, all right?"

Downstairs a door swung open and shut. Dr. Fowles called up that they were waiting for them in the car.

"Later," said Faith.

"Later. You promise?"

"Cross my heart and hope to die."

Gleaming refurbished Model-Ts rolled through the steaming horse droppings left moments before by prancing quarter horses. A flatbed truck heaved behind them, high school kids dangling their legs off the sides above a banner that read 4-H CLUBS OF AMERICA SUPPORT OUR TROOPS IN VIETNAM while throwing hard candy at screaming children. Then Santa high on his throne, the American Dream incarnate, the flesh-and-blood embodiment of getting and spending, anchoring the Thanksgiving parade.

Roy watched all this behind a gaggle of children wrapped in toboggans and scarves, their parents behind them leaning on their slight shoulders. But mostly he watched the Fowleses, past, present, and future. Faith and Peyton hand in gloved hand, the Dr. and Mrs. behind them, smiling beatifically. When he thought Faith might have noticed him, he melted into the shadows and started up the street against the flow of traffic. He passed empty faces, scaly from the wind, passed one-armed Hoghead Johnson snoring drunk in the bed of a pickup beside his dog. Two blocks up he spotted Enis and Millie.

"What say, brother."

"Enis. Millie."

"Enjoying the parade?" asked Enis.

"I saw Faith and her beau back that away," said Roy. "Just having the time of my life."

"Oh, yeah."

"We're supposed to be down there with them," explained Millie.

"That so?"

"But I cain't bear him," said Enis. "Not for a second, the nautical son of a bitch."

"Me neither," said Millie, and she gave a little shiver. "His mamma and daddy got money running out both ears and ain't afraid to tell you as much. The braggingest people I ever did see."

"They'll talk a blue streak," said Enis. "Knock the ears right off a billy goat. You know he calls the floor the deck? I mean somebody tell the fool he's on dry land, how bout it."

Roy nodded. For a moment they stood in awkward silence.

"Look coming here," said Millie. "Here y'all come someday."

Up the street came old hunched men in blue overseas caps that read VFW WWI. Behind them were vigorous, middle-aged men, WWII scrolled in gold twill.

"Hell, those are war veterans, Millie," said Enis.

"What do you think you two are?"

"Well, damn, Roy. I guess we are. I always thought of vets as old men."

"I always thought of them as honorable men. Now look here at us."

Both studied him. Roy sucked his teeth and watched the men head up the street, then cleared his throat. "I wonder if I might borrow this no-good fella for a minute, Millie." He winked. "Secret family doings."

"Well, I can't say no to that," she said. "Not on Thanksgiving Day, at least. I need to catch back up with Faith anyway. See you, babe."

They kissed.

"All right."

"Say hello to the family for me," called Roy.

"I'll do that," said Millie.

They watched her walk away.

"This ain't about Daddy, is it?" asked Enis.

"No."

"All right then."

"I'll tell you in the car. Remember my plan."

"Yeah."

"You still serious, ain't you?"

"You damn well know I am."

"Well, this is the legwork, my friend. The preparation. The way I figure we just got one shot at this."

They sat in Roy's car.

"Where is it we're going?"

"He's moved on us."

Enis wrinkled his mouth.

"He's moved on us," explained Roy. "On up the road to Anderson. We can't just up and pick up the girls and then just hope all will work out. We've got to plan this. Make sure it runs smooth."

"If you say so."

"Well, I do," said Roy, tapping his thumbs against the wheel. "And believe me, I've thought about this. I've thought this whole thing through."

Enis nodded.

Roy turned back to the road.

"I figure we just get one shot at this."

Will crouched on the ladder, his eyes even with the loft floor. Below him he could feel the man, his hand around Will's left ankle like a manacle, pulling and pushing at him. Across the loft floor was his father, grunting and panting down between two splayed legs. His father's pants were around his ankles and his belt buckle slapped at the board floor. Will could see little else. The man pulled him back down.

"That's enough," he said, and he pushed Will aside to climb the ladder. He grasped a rung in one hand, the pistol in the other. "Wait here," he said.

Then Will began to scream, opening his mouth and scaring the birds from the rafters. There was the sound of a scrambling up above.

"You little son of a bitch," spat the man then shot up the ladder. Behind them the door burst open and two men ran in.

"Grover?" one said. "Where's Grover?"

Will was halfway up the ladder, almost falling when he heard the two reports.

A moment later there were four of them in the hayloft, five counting the dead girl. She lay on her back, her arms by her side, palms to the sky, her legs spread, a glistening wet mess down between them. The man named Grover, the man with the pistol, walked around the room looking at the pairs of girls underpants tacked to the walls. A moment before he had touched the girl's blue lips then ran one finger through her long black hair.

"That ain't my Emma," he had said. He paced around the room then sat. "She ain't here."

Will sat on the ground.

"They Lord God in heaven," someone said.

All he saw of his father was a cocooned bedsheet weeping black blood. They threw the body into the back of a truck and dusted their hands.

"That girl up there was the Jewish farmer's girl," said Grover to another man. "What's his name. The fella out on Country Junction Road."

"She was missing?"

"About a week now."

"Christ in heaven."

"A Jewish girl," repeated the man. "God's chosen people suffering like that." Again, he almost laughed, then didn't. He looked at the boy, motioned at the cows that had settled back into the grass after the twin pistol blasts. "Them whiteface," he said, addressing the yard. "Kill em. Kill ever last one of the sons of bitches, then burn the barn."

A week after moving back in with Eleanor, James drove up the mountain to return Bobby his truck and collect the rest of what little he possessed. He climbed the front steps only to find the front door ajar.

He called for Bobby, peeked in, saw nothing, circled the yard. No one. Sheetrock was still piled against the porch, marked now by rain. Bobby's pipe lay on the rail. "Bobby?" he called. "Gus?" He pushed the door open and walked inside. Empty curio cabinets were pushed against the walls. Bobby lay on the bed in the back room, face up, arms spread as if crucified, naked but for a pair of bulging pink lace panties into which disappeared whorls of gray hair. He snored through a limp valve of a mouth, his teeth in a dry glass on the nightstand. A square of paper lay face down on his chest. James picked it up. Hopeless poetry, he thought. Pulling seven men from the corpse of a burning B-17, the act made silly in writing. He put the citation in the night-stand drawer. He could hear a woman's voice, singing, and splashing from within the bathroom. He touched Bobby's warm cheek and started to spread a blanket over him then didn't. A nightgown the size of a sail was draped over the TV. He knocked on the bathroom door, easing it open.

"In a minute," called the voice.

A bank of fog rolled as if released from a valve, and James fanned it away. The woman sang, *Will you miss me when I'm gone?* James cleared his throat.

"I said, in a minute, honey love."

"I'm not your honey love, ma'am."

From within the fog he heard a sudden splashing sound.

"I'm not coming in," he said.

"Who is that? Who is that out there, Bobby? Bobby? I got a pistol here in the tub with me, you mean-hearted bastard. What'd you do with Bobby?"

"I'm his friend, James. Bobby's napping, it appears."

"Oh," said the woman, settling back into the tub. "You're that Burden fella he was talking about."

"Yes, ma'am, most likely."

"Yeah, Bobby said we just get shed of one, and anothern shows."

"How's that, ma'am?"

"Could you give me a minute, darling? Let me dry here?"

"Of course."

"Bobby and I's married. But I guess you know as much."

"No, I didn't know it."

"Just one minute, darling."

James sat on the side of the bed, his weight shifting the mattress and lolling over Bobby's head. Bobby's tongue swelled between two bluish lips, appearing too large for his slack mouth. James turned the head away from him, and then noticed it, a leather flight bag marked LT. R. BURDEN USN sitting in the hall spewing clothes. He started to rise and inspect it then didn't, sat instead listening to the woman singing and moving about the bathroom. She came out wearing a honey-colored robe and toweling her hair: a large woman, skin a boiled pink, toenails painted silver.

"Where's the ring?" asked James.

"Oh, no time for a ring, child. We just up and drove over to that marrying preacher and let him do it all. Bobby kept waiting for you to come back with his truck. Finally that brother of yours drove us over."

"Roy?"

"Yeah. That one's a looker, honey. I guess you must have got the smarts."

"Could be."

"Turn away, darling."

James turned, watching her pale reflection in the window as the robe fell, her large pear shape and swinging bottom, legs like temple columns.

"OK," she said after a moment. She was wearing jeans and a red flannel shirt.

"What's wrong with Bobby?" asked James.

She made a motion of drinking. "Too much you-know-what, darling. Way too much. Plus I think he took some sorta trucker pills, so I give him something to take the edge off. Maybe a little more lovin' than he could handle, too. He's been sleeping like a baby for hours now. You got the truck keys, you say?"

James passed them over.

"How about a ride back down the mountain?" asked James.

"Is that brother of yourn going to be waiting at wherever you get off?"

"I thought he was staying up here."

"I thought he was, too, but I ain't seen him in a day or so."

"How long did you say you two had been married?"

"Oh, darling, who counts them things?" She looked at the blank spot on her wrist where a watch might otherwise have been. "Maybe twelve, thirteen hours."

James walked into the front room pulling the door shut behind him. The window had been replaced with a sheet of polyethylene sheeting sutured with duct tape. The house was a wreck. On hands and knees he reached back under the couch to pull out his bag and began feeling through it for the syringes of morphine. The woman walked in.

"Something I should know about, honey?" she asked.

She was wearing high-heeled boots now, lipstick as bright as ripe apples.

"Not a thing," said James, zipping shut his bag and slinging it over his shoulder.

"Well, how about that ride then?" She smiled.

"How about it."

"One thing, darling."

James looked at her.

"You forgot to wish me congratulations."

The day before, James had woken late and alone, a warm depression in the pillow where Eleanor had been. A note on the dresser said she was work-ing and for him to come down and have lunch when he could. He rose slowly, and for the second time in three days soaked in a tub of warm water, sitting until the last of the water had drained, his fingers wrinkled, a lather of bubbles and coarse hairs caught in the drain. He stood, dried and naked, studying himself in the bedroom floor-length mirror. He drew in his breath, held it, counted the deep impressions of his ribs. His skin appeared drawn as tight as that of a drum. It could go no tighter. He exhaled, sat on the side of the bed and trimmed his toenails. The bottoms of his feet were spongy and webbed with thick blue veins, a certain plasticity there to counter the cal-lused skin of his heels. He studied his face, his hands, the pockmark tracks that dotted the flesh of his left arm. Then he dressed, drove to the café.

They sat together in a booth, two milkshakes between them, and she tried to convince him to eat, to go on, please, eat, baby, you look so poor. Her eyes had a faraway hopeful look to them, a look delicate, fragile. They seemed to be pleading with him not to undo the little good he had done, as if her eyes knew too well the nature of man.

"Let's leave here," she said, holding his hands on the Formica tabletop. "Let's just go. We'll go west and just drive and drive until we're someplace sunny. California, maybe. You know, I've never even seen Atlanta? Never even been that far west. Can you believe that?"

He smiled.

"You ever had a moment when suddenly you realize something and right then, it don't matter what, you just have to do it. You know you have to or you'll die, or maybe you won't die you'll just . . . I don't know. I know that doesn't make any sense, but all of a sudden I feel it, Jimmy. Like we have to go, I have to go. We have to go now or never. We can't *not* go. With or with-out you, Jimmy—I thought that sometimes." She tucked a short band of hair behind one ear. "But now it'll be with you. You know, the biggest city I think

I've ever seen was Greenville. I've never even seen the ocean. Here you've been all over the world, and I've never even set foot on a beach. We could go live by the ocean."

He looked at her hands, at their hands.

"I could work and you could get better and then maybe someday we could have a son and a daughter and take them to the beach and we could never even talk about this place, Jimmy. We could never come here again. Never again. I'm not too old to have a baby, I don't think. Maybe I'm not." She looked at him, her eyes still holding that faraway light. "I love you, Jimmy."

"I love you, too."

"You'll go with me then? Please promise me."

"I promise."

"I've never even seen the ocean."

"You'll see it. We'll go."

Tension seemed to fall away, her shoulders dropping.

"We'll go. You've promised," she said. "We will. We have to."

The morphine he had taken the night before had settled into him, calming the storm he feared, but that, too, would run out. He needed to get up to Bobby's, but there were other things to do first. After he left the café he drove to the post office to collect the contents of the PO box his mother had sat up for him years before. He walked around to the counter where the postmaster, Julab Early, sat smoothing out the front page of the *Keowee Courier.*

"Morning. I help you with something?"

"Yessir. I've got a box here I need to clean out."

"I knew it. Reverend Burden's oldest, aren't you? Your mamma set that account up for you, right?"

"Yessir. Least that's what I heard. Can you check it for me?"

"You got that Burden jaw. Kindly squared off. Recognize it anywhere."

"Can you check if for me, sir?"

"No need to, son. It was piled up something high till she came and cleaned it out."

"I meant for her to take it. I thought she hadn't though."

"No, she did. Sure did. Ain't said nothing then, has she?"

"No. How long ago was that?"

"You staying up with Bobby Thornton, I heard."

"So where can I find my mail?"

"Old Bobby's something, ain't he? You ever hear about when his youngest was born? What's her name, Judy. Married by now, I reckon. Hell, probably got a mess of younguns."

"No, I haven't, but really I just come in—"

"Now hold on a minute, this is worth hearing. This was long about thirty year ago and Bobby's wife Sharon had went into labor and nobody could find him and she was just pitching a mortal fuss wanting to claw his head off. Finally somebody rode over to the Last Chance and found him passed out in the back, had really pitched hisself a drunk. Well, I drove him up the mountain and he about half woke up enough to go on and on about how he couldn't afford no child, let-alone a girl child, and about how the bank was set to take all his land and all and he just knew it, and one of the boys with me slapped him around a little and said, 'Now don't give us none a that poor mouth shit,' cause we all knew Bobby had a few hundred acres fat with apples and his daddy always had money in land too—"

"Mr. Early—"

"Now, listen to this now, this is the good part. So finally we get up to Bobby's place and throw his drunk ass in the shower he had rigged down near his shed, big old thing he sprayed cribs of apples with, and in the front room is Sharon and the midwife and Sharon's mamma's pacing, and her daddy's out on the porch smoking and pacing and looking like he might bite the head off a rattlesnake were it to look crossways at him, and don't nobody know we've snuck Bobby out back in the freezing cold and he comes out of there pink as the day he was born and I says to Jimmy, I says, 'Jimmy, that man is stone cold sober.' And we thought he was. Now, hold on, this is the part I was working up to. So we walk him back up to the house and he's dripping bare-ass naked on the porch boards, and I go around through the front and slip Bobby in by the back door, and a few minutes later he comes into the front room fully clothed and clean with his hair all slick. Only thing is, ever few minutes he keeps grabbing at the seat of his pants. Sharon's screaming and the baby's nigh on out but he can't quit digging. Finally he walks into the back room and I follow him in there and he drops his drawers and now listen to this, he's wearing Sharon's lacey underpants. Had pulled em on in the dark. You ever hear of such a thing?"

"Not often."

"Shit. Never. Oh Lord, that man could raise hell back in the day. Drunk the day he was born, hadn't been sober a day in his life since. Old man used to put white lightning in his bottle, and his mamma tit-fed him moonshine, but he's a good old boy for sure."

Part Two

"What about my mail, Mr. Early? Should I go up to see my mamma?"

"Aw, hell, no, son. Walk over to the bank. She sent it all over to a deposit box or something."

James walked up the street to the Blue Ridge Bank and fell in line among the others. It was lunchtime and the bank was full. Along the teller stalls ran snakes of garland, large oversized red bows. A teller sounded a bell, another. Several bells later James stood before a young woman with eyes that appeared flat and smooth behind her glasses.

"Yessir?"

"My name's James Burden," he said. "I believe there might be some checks here for me. It might be in my mamma's name."

"In what type account, sir?"

"I'm not sure exactly."

"Well, would it be, say, a safe deposit box? Or maybe a checking account?"

He shrugged. "My mother sent some checks over for holding. Her name is Madison Grace Burden."

She nodded. "Just a second, then."

After a moment she had returned with a man, the branch manager, to whom James again explained the situation.

"Of course," said the man. A few minutes later he had returned with a cardboard box of opened envelopes, a return address of Atlanta, GA.

"She deposited them."

"She did?"

"Had to. They would have expired. You got to cash them within ninety days. Plus the accrued interest. Put the stubs in a safety deposit box."

"Why didn't she cash them? Couldn't she?"

"Certainly."

"Well, why didn't she?"

"You'd have to ask her that, sir."

"Right. Well, how much is it?"

The man studied the paper. "Not too bad. Just over thirty-one-thousand dollars. Have a look."

James took the statement.

"You're a rich man, Mr. Burden. How much did you want to withdraw?"

"All of it. Ever bit of it. In cash, please."

"Normally we'd do a cashier's check."

"I need cash, please."

Sitting in the truck he had thumbed through the cashed check stubs one by one, maybe as many as two hundred in all, each marked DISABILITY AND

COMPENSATION, each for the amount of $114. He slipped the box of checks below the seat and what he figured to be about a thousand dollars cash into his jacket pocket and walked back over to the post office.

"You find em?" asked the postmaster.

"I did. Thank you."

"Wonderful."

The man went back to his newspaper.

"One other thing," said James.

The man looked up.

"I need to see about stopping my mail."

"Planning on dying or just not needing it for a while?"

"Moving."

"Hell, son, just get it forwarded."

"Let's do that then, please."

"Well, where you headed?"

"California."

"What town?"

"I'm not positive on that yet."

"Well, you got to have a town, son, even for general delivery."

James nodded. "I'll stop back by and let you know."

"You do that, James. Hey," the man called after him. "Your daddy get anything out of his garden this year, cause mine pert near dried up?"

James kept walking.

By the time Eleanor came in around four, James had cleaned the house, patched the front screen door, and cut the small yard in the back with an antique rotary push mower he found in the cellar among jars of long-forgotten canned vegetables. The sun was out and the yard lay rowed like an outfield. He liked that, the feeling of doing something purely good, something clean and measurable. Sometimes that was all a man could do, little true things, cut the grass, shave.

He put the money in the kitchen cabinet over the stove, not mentioning it to her. He'd have a surprise for her when they got out west. They'd buy a house, settle down.

They walked into the front yard.

"Well, look a here," she said.

"A seller's dream."

"Or nightmare."

"We could paint it first," he said. "Wouldn't take long."

She shook her head. "No," she said, the tip of one finger against her lips. "No, I've seen enough of this place to last me for good. We have to go as soon as we can. No painting."

"No painting then," he agreed.

That evening they sat in plastic lawn chairs on the back porch facing the late-day sun. Inside the TV was playing, and they could hear the music to *Laugh-In*, then *Hawaii Five-O*. They sat there quietly sipping beers.

"California," she said. "Warm. Sunny. Every day like this. Except warmer."

"The West for desire, the East for home."

"What's that, baby?"

"Nothing, just that you can't go home again."

"No." She thought on this. "No, you can't."

Tammy Wynette and George Jones sang on the radio, now and then drowning out the noise of the TV, and James imagined rolling in the spring grass, his hands clenched around her waist, little blades falling from their clothes. He imagined the summer sky, Perseus and Cassiopeia.

"You surely can't," she said.

Now he was riding down the mountain beside Bobby's Thorton's new significant other.

"I never caught your name," he said.

"Lorrie. Lorrie Torrie. It's a stage name."

"You're an actress?"

"Used to be," she said, one-handing the wheel. "Used to be in a traveling show some years ago. Out through the Midwest. Chicago. Milwaukee. But I live over in Anderson now. Or at least I did."

"How'd you meet Bobby?"

"Through a mutual friend. Fellow named Stump. Where is it you said to turn?"

"Right up here. I don't know a Stump."

"Well, nobody said he was *your* friend, sugar."

She turned down Oak.

"You got some kind of itch on that arm of yours, darling."

He nodded.

"Next one up," he said.

She pulled to the curb.

"Anything you want me to tell that brother of yourn if I see him?"

James thought for a moment. "No, I don't guess so. Tell Bobby I'll come by to see him before I go, get right with him for whatever I owe for gas and boarding and whatnot."

"You going somewhere then, honey?"

He nodded yes.

"Ain't we all. Well, good luck to you and yourn."

She winked and drove away.

Inside, James poured the contents of his bag onto the bed. He had begun to sweat, his hands to shake. He clenched and released his fists over and over. Cold sweat fingered along his scalp. His hands. Be still. Christ. The wind chimed knocked against the house. He dug through the scant clothes once, then again. Nothing. He sat on the bed and tried to think. The last of the morphine was missing.

James left a note for Eleanor saying he was with Bobby and would be back by dinner, then walked up to the Main Street Diner.

"Can you get me a cab?" he asked the man behind the counter. "Call me one?"

"You got fingers?" asked the man.

James pulled his hands from his pockets. At the tips of his arms grew two hands, ten fingers. He seemed somehow surprised by this.

"Call em yourself," said the man, dropping the phone down on the table. "Leave a dime on the counter."

Twenty minutes later James sat shivering in the backseat of a cab while the driver eased along SC 123 toward Anderson.

"You sure you awright, partner?" asked the man.

James nodded.

"It ain't nothing catching, is it?"

He shook his head no. "Just State Street, please," he managed to say. "I'm fine."

"Where's that?"

"State Street. I don't know where it is. Downtown, maybe."

"You sure about the downtown part, partner? What you need over there?"

James made no answer.

"Awright then," said the driver. "Your dime."

They pulled through a neighborhood of falling clapboard houses peeling yellow and pink and bright blue paint. A few girls skipped rope along the street. Old black men sat on porch steps, and everywhere people seemed to loiter: beside the block walls of an abandoned Exxon, in an empty lot sown with weeds and the remains of a backstop.

"Nothing but niggertown out here," said the driver, as much to himself as to James. "Nothing but the wrong side of the tracks."

James sat shivering, clutching his coat and hugging his arms to his body, afraid the man might hear his teeth clattering. They passed an elementary school and a liquor store.

"Awright," said the man. "State Street. This good?"

James nodded at the eyes in the rearview mirror.

"How much?"

"Nineteen dollars. Tip's up to you."

He passed over a twenty then stepped out just as the man muttered something about getting the fuck out before he lost his hubcaps. The air was cold and sharp and hustling trash down the open street. In the shadows sat patches of brittle snow. James could feel every eye on him, eyes behind curtains that parted behind the slats of metal bars, unseen. He walked up the street past a dilapidated, hatless snowman, yellow grass at his feet.

Two blocks up he found the place, a brownstone marked GROVE ARMS APTS. on the sign out front, NEXT TIME BY FIRE stenciled in bulging letters beside an ebony Jesus on the wall behind. He climbed the stairs to the third floor, then walked down the hall counting off doors. He could hear a baby crying, cars in the street, the heavy bass thudding of music barely muted by paper-thin walls. A door slammed. Near the end of the hall he found 9C, the lettering gone, marked now by its pale outline. He knocked, waited, knocked a second time before he heard someone coughing, then footsteps, then a bolt sliding. The door opened perhaps three inches, catching on the chain, and within the gloomy half-light he met the haggard face of a white woman, her stringy hair down in her face, a pink housecoat cinched with a purple belt.

"Who are you?" she asked.

"My name's James. I'm looking for somebody named Banger Jones."

"You a friend of his?"

"Not exactly."

"What'd you say your name was?"

"James Burden."

"Well, tough shit, James Burden. He ain't home."

She slammed the door shut, and James stood listening to the sound of the sliding bolt. He knocked again. The woman opened the door with a sigh.

"What do you want? I just told you he's not here."

She leaned forward, her bathrobe loose so that James could see one pale breast, the nipple flaccid.

"I wanted to buy something."

"Well, you got the wrong place."

"This is 9C."

"You got the wrong place, buddy. Now get lost."

She slammed the door before James could edge the toe of his boot there. He listened to at least three bolts sliding, clacking, sounds he had missed before. The hall was empty but for a tricycle that sat rusty and abandoned in a pool of yellow light. He looked at the frayed carpet, the thin door, and then knocked again, solidly this time, not stopping until the door swung open and he stood facing a black man wearing a brown turtleneck and leveling the barrel of a .32 at his chest.

"What the fuck," said the man. "Somebody done told your white ass to come up here bothering me? Girl done told you to get on."

"Look. I got your name from somebody. They said you might be able to help me."

"I'm about to help you by sending your white ass up to visit with Jesus."

Through the door he could see the girl sitting down-faced on a dark red loveseat. The windows were covered in sheets of opaque plastic, and except for the chair, the room was empty. The girl looked up at him then back down between her feet.

"I just wanted to buy something," said James, slower, trying to feign a measure of calmness. "I've got money."

"I'm gonna give you to three before I part your motherfucking head like a canoe," said the man.

"Please."

"You at two right now."

James turned back up the hall, looking back once to see the man standing in the hall watching him go. When he reached the stairwell, he heard the door slam shut. He walked back up State Street, finally flagging down another cab.

"The hospital," he told the driver.

"Something wrong with you?"

He said nothing.

"Well, don't you dare puke in my car, you hear me? You tell me in time so I can pull over."

Ten minutes later they pulled into the hospital's drive.

"You need the emergency room or something?" asked the man.

He paid the driver and walked around behind the building, where several dumpsters sat behind a slatted fence, one marked MEDICAL WASTE in large yellow letters. He had never felt so desperate, so close to the edge. He clutched his jacket and sat on the curb until it was clear, then slipped behind the fence and into the dumpster, but could find nothing to stick into himself. He climbed out and sat leaning against the cool of the metal until it grew dark then walked downtown to the Gospel mission that sat across from the mirrored façade of the branch library.

A young Catholic priest sat behind a collapsible metal desk just inside the door. James was shaking, clawing at his body, his eyes an unnatural, gummy white. "My son," said the priest, but nothing else, leading him by the arm to a cot in a small room. He returned a few minutes later with a towel, a blanket, and a small pitcher of water, leaving all three on the floor. James slept and woke to the whine of a passing ambulance. The pea-green walls of the room seemed to breathe, inhaling and exhaling, moving toward him then away. A long water spot ran across the ceiling from sight, turning, evolving into new shapes, figures, and faces. He touched the cool metal tubing of the bed and thought about Eleanor then couldn't. They had him again: faces, voices. He felt something driving up through his liver and lodging itself into his breastbone, a shard of heated rubber. He felt his organs swelling and then rending themselves, no different in the end than overcooked sausages. I'm dying, he thought. He wanted to die. Let it come, he prayed. Crucify me. I've already asked You once. For Christ's sake, kill me or let me be in peace. But there came an answer: What will be will be. And he saw a long road unfolding before him, a path to righteousness, a window onto his life. But the road was slick, and he could find no foothold, no purchase, and went sliding into the blinding sunlight of memory, that ineffable quietude, the aloneness without God: where there is language there will be silence; where there is love, indifference. Where are You hiding? he begged.

Then he found himself washed completely back into memory. He remembered a great-grandfather who had lived to the age of 102, a large tumor growing like a fruit from the side of his head; remembered the night Enis was born and he and Roy had tried to sleep on the cold floor of his father's study, listening to their mother cry out to God in the front room, listening to the scrape of the dogs as they came clacking onto the porch, howling; saw the face of a girl dragged with hooks from a still pool of the Chattooga River, so bloated her body strained outward against the buttons of her shirt. Birth. Death. Was there not something else? He couldn't remember. He doubted it. If there was a secret, no one was telling. His father's God was silent. Then he slept again and woke with sun streaming through the dusty, curtainless panes, and he thought—he thought of Eleanor.

He hitched a ride back to Seneca and walked up the street to the house. Despite the cold, he had soaked through his shirt, his socks. His throat had closed as abruptly and as finally as a caved mine shaft. He stopped on the walk. A sign on the front lawn read FOR SALE. He thought this impossible. He looked at the sun: it was no later than three o'clock.

He unlocked the door. The front room was just as he had left it, the couch, the TV, the empty bookshelves. The kitchen he did not enter, not caring about the money. His clothes still lay spilled across the bed. Everything was the same. Except the closet. Her clothes were gone, only a tangle of metal hangers. There was no note.

Marlon was behind the counter staring into nothingness.

"Don't come in here."

James stumbled up to the counter.

"I said for you not to damn come in here."

"Please, Marlon."

"She's not here, James."

"Please."

Marlon looked at him. "Are you sick?"

He nodded his head. "Yes, I'm sick. I'm real sick. Please, Marlon. Please help me."

Marlon licked his lips, sighed. "I think you're a son of a bitch, James, sick or not," he said.

"I know."

"I think you are a low-down good-for-nothing piece-of-shit son of a bitch, and I don't care what you done for any damn country or what any damn war did to you."

"I know. Please." Sweat dropped off his forehead to bead along the counter.

"All these years she's loved you, waited for you. Now you come in here dirtying up my place of business. I'll be dogged if I'll abide it."

"Please."

Marlon sighed. "She's at the hotel. I don't know whether she wants you to know or not. Don't know whether I've done her a favor or not."

James nodded. "I got to ask one more thing of you, Marlon."

Marlon looked at him.

"I got to ask to borrow your truck. Two hours, Marlon. I'm dying, Marlon. I've got to ask that of you. This is the last thing for me."

Marlon laid the keys on the table.

"You bring it back to me," he said. "You bring it back and don't ever darken my doorway again, you son of a bitch."

James took the keys and hobbled out.

"I'm not drunk," she said. Faith was sitting in a rocking chair on the front porch, two empty wine bottles at her feet. "I'm not drunk—I haven't had a drop—if that's what you're thinking, Millie."

"I didn't say anything."

Faith looked at her. Her sister stood in the doorway, one hand on each side of the jamb.

"Well, maybe I can read your mind tonight," Faith said. She stared down between her feet then over the edge of the porch at the hedges and gleaming blacktop.

"Sit down," she said. "You're making me nervous."

"It's too cold out here to sit."

"Then go inside where it's warm."

"Why are you sitting out here, Faith? You're not even dressed."

Faith looked at her wrist. She wore no watch. She made a motion of dismissal, of surrender, willing to test the fire. "What the fuck," she said. "Doesn't matter anyway."

"I thought you said you weren't drunk."

"I'm not," she said with some finality. "I'm thinking."

An hour later Roy's Fastback was bucking across an open field toward the large white tent. Enis and Millie sat in the back, hand in hand, Roy and Faith in the front, silent. The ground outside the tent was pure mud, red and gutted with tire tracks, faint ripples wrinkling otherwise still pools of water.

"Give us one minute here," said Roy. He forced a smile and squeezed Faith's knee. He and Enis stepped out beneath the shadow of the Ferris wheel then disappeared through a flap in the tent. The women sat watching them.

Faith found Millie's eyes in the rearview mirror.

"All right?"

Millie nodded.

A moment later Enis came skipping across the field, almost slipping in the mud. He jerked open the back door.

"Hot dog," he said. "Come on. Come on, the man said. He said there's a room over to the side with a mirror and sink and all that, if you need to get fixed up."

"I'm fixed up as is," said Faith.

"Just as well." Enis jerked there, bouncing with one hand on the car door, as if caught by some rogue current. "Well, we're waiting," he said, and went bouncing back across the field into the tent.

"Idiot," said Faith when he was gone.

"I happen to love him," Millie pointed out.

Faith found her eyes again. "I would hope so."

Eddie Gathers had spent much of the last half hour digging the wicks from the melted candles he had found in a crate in the back of the reverend's trailer and arranging them about the stage before lighting them. Now the dim tent was soft-lit, appearing for the first time, he realized, like an actual place of worship. He was just lighting the last of the candles when he heard a car driving up. Before he could go find the reverend, two men were slipping inside the tent.

"Beautiful," said one of the men.

"Real nice," agreed the other. "Classy."

"Can I help y'all with something?" asked Eddie.

"Yeah," said the second voice. "We've got an appointment with the—oh, shit. Is that you, young Gathers?"

"Roy?"

"Shit, it is. Where you been, boy?"

"Around and about, you might say."

"Well, I'll be damned. I went by Bobby's and he was all sulled up and I wondered what was wrong. I'll be damned indeed."

"I'll thank you to mind the foul talk, Roy." Eddie motioned toward the lit altar. "House of the Lord and all."

"Oh, yeah. Sorry," said Roy. "Well, you know my brother Enis, right?"

"Acquainted," said Eddie.

"This the old drinking buddy?" asked Enis.

Eddie shook his head. "Not no more it ain't. Religion done went and put a hold on me."

"You fondling serpents now, young Gathers?"

"Hell no I ain't, and you good and well know it, Roy, and I'll thank you kindly not to make light of it either. Many a good man's handled a snake."

"You ever met one?"

"What's that got to do with anything I want to know."

Roy wasn't listening. He walked around the altar. "This is nice," he said. "Real classy work with this, Gathers. Now where's that reverend at?"

"He's coming. Reviewing vows, I reckon. How's Bobby? You say he's sulled up."

"He was. But he's managing. Got married, I heard, but I can't confirm that."

"Married. Who married him?"

"The reverend here did."

"Hellfire, rev sends me to visit my mamma for one day and I miss everything."

"Now, Eddie."

"Yessir?"

Roy winked. "Do mind the foul talk."

The reverend emerged from the back, wearing a long white cassock, clean-shaven, bald but for a tonsure of gray hair hung above his ears. Both Roy and Enis removed their hats.

"Gentlemen," said the reverend, spreading his arms.

"Reverend."

"How do, Reverend."

He explained the ceremony, remarkably simple, he said, and then pointed out the facilities behind the tent. "Courtesy the good people over at the Anderson County Chamber of Commerce," he said.

"Can I get the girls, then?" asked Roy.

The reverend bowed, the pleats of his robe billowing before him.

"At your convenience, good sir."

"Why are you doing this?" Roy had her by one arm, standing outside the tent beneath a portable streetlight. Somewhere beyond sight, a Honda generator hummed. "You've never explained a thing to me."

Faith pulled her arm free of his. "Don't ask me that," she said. "Just let it be enough that I am, all right? Just let that be enough."

Roy nodded his head. "Well, you look beautiful."

"Don't start that shit." She looked away then back at him. "Just let doing it be enough, Roy."

They pulled apart at the sound of someone approaching. It was Enis, panting and trying to undo his belt.

"Well, a shit storm's done blown in with the rain," he panted.

"How eloquent," said Faith. "Tuck your shirttail in."

"I'm trying. Sorry."

"Elaborate," said Roy.

"It's Millie," he said, desperate to catch his breath. "Millie. She says she ain't gonna do it. Says she won't get out of the car."

"Did you try to sweet-talk her with words like 'shit storm'?"

"Please, Faith, you got to talk to her. Please?"

Faith walked around front toward the car. It was dark, the sky bright with stars. The wind picked up through the distant trees that rimmed the field then swept unencumbered to meet her. Faith leaned against the car and knocked

on the back window, studying her reflection in the glass. She wore a sleeve-
less gown, and the hair along her upper arms was prickled. She knocked again.

"I'm freezing here, Millie."

The window came down a few inches.

"What's the problem?"

"I'm not going in there, Faith."

"Are the doors locked?"

Millie shrugged.

"Let me in, why don't you. I'm freezing."

The door opened and Faith sat.

"I want a church wedding, Faith. I just saw what it would be like, sitting
here. I want a dress and I want flowers and I want Mamma there and I want
Daddy in a suit. I always thought just being married would be enough, you
know? Just being with Enis would be enough. . . ." She trailed off.

Faith nodded. "I see," she said.

"You do? You don't mind?"

"Just tell me this one thing, Millie. Tell me why you came out here."

"To marry him," said Millie.

"Right. Right. But why?"

Millie shook her head. "I don't know why."

"Because deep down you know being with Enis *is* enough, that the rest
is just show. You know that because you love him."

"Oh, please."

"If you think about it, it's the truth."

Millie nodded, seeming to consider this. "Nice speech," she said, "but you
can save it."

"Oh, come on, Millie. Hasn't he waited long enough for you?"

Millie snorted. "I've never made that boy wait for a thing. That was the
first mistake I made."

They were quiet for a moment.

"So why did *you* come?" asked Millie.

Faith shrugged. "You can't put it in words. Sometimes words are no good."

Millie looked at her.

"You know that little snow globe Daddy brought back for me years ago
from Chicago?" said Faith. "You know the one."

Millie nodded.

"Well, the funny thing about it is, well, I always thought it could tell the
future. Or show it, I guess is really more what I thought. That I could look
in the little windup hole in the back and ask about something and then see

it like it was a movie or something. I always thought that." Faith was nodding, staring at the seat back, staring beyond it. Millie studied her. "So last night I took it out and asked to see the future, to see this"—she motioned around her—"all this. And you know what? You know what, Millie?"

"What?"

"It was bad. All of it. For me, I mean. I saw the way it turned out, and it turned out bad. So I smashed the little thing. I smashed it to bits down on the sidewalk and the water ran into the cracks and the little fake snow blew away and all the Chicago skyscrapers broke. All because it said things would come out bad. I could see it and I just knew, I just knew. But I also knew it didn't have to come out that way, or I thought that maybe. I don't know. But I damned that little globe, Millie. I damned the future, I . . . I knew it could come out the way I wanted. Christ, I just . . . This is stupid." She opened the door, the key buzzing in the ignition. "So that's why I'm here. We'll wait a little in case you decide to come in. But it's up to you. Whatever you decide, it's up to you. I'm going in there to get married."

No music, no accompaniment, only a ring of flickering candlelight. Faith stepped toward Roy and took his hands in hers, smiled, and she felt a certain lightness, a sense of worry falling away, and for a brief moment her bottom lip quivered before she caught it. She was no crier, more given to making fun of those who cried than anything else, but now she felt moved almost to tears. Her mouth felt large and ungainly but beautiful, and she slid her tongue over her even teeth, opened and closed her mouth. As light and clean and beautiful as candlelight. Roy's hands closed about hers.

Millie's faced was tracked with mascara-tears she made no effort to wipe away. Enis was crying too, his eyes running, an oversized plastic smile on his face.

"Are we ready now?" asked the reverend.

Eddie Gathers sat in the wings and cried himself. This is just so damn beautiful, I cain't bear it, he thought. Just so damn pretty.

Roy and Faith nodded yes. Enis and Millie did not move, eyes locked, bringing to the reverend's mind something he had read once in Plato, something about the locking of eyes, something about soul mates and mending circles broken at birth. It almost moved him but, in the end, did not.

He shook his hands free from the sleeves of his cassock, a Bible held before him. Eddie choked and sputtered.

"Dearly beloved," began the preacher.

Oh, that beats it, thought Eddie, crying. That just does me in ever damn time.

Ten minutes later the reverend and Eddie stood outside the tent passing a joint between them and watching Roy's car roll and pitch its way across the field toward the highway.

"They're in some hurry," said the reverend, still waving.

"That was just something beautiful, Rev. Just something else. What I wish, is we could get us a TV show. You and me. Tell the whole wide world, Rev. It just beats it all."

The reverend nodded. They watched the car ease onto the highway, honk once, then disappear pushing a cone of light.

"I wish Stump could have seen it."

"Indeed," said the reverend. He blew a ring of smoke. "But I'm afraid Mr. Stump has found greener fields, my friend."

"How's that?"

"He's left us."

"Hellfire."

"Exactly." The reverend patted Eddie's shoulder. "Looks like it's you and me now, my friend. Come hell or high water."

"Well, if that's the Lord's will, I reckon that's the way it'll be," agreed Eddie.

The reverend snorted. "Oh, ye of little faith, in the grave there is no remembrance of either sorrow or joy," he said, then laughed.

"Meaning?"

"Meaning," said the reverend. "Meaning the Lord hasn't a thing to do with it."

He was smiling on them, God was. Eleanor took the rest of the day off from the café after James left, then walked home to find his note saying he had went to see Bobby, and it was perfect. She had a little time. From a cookie tin hidden behind a piece of loose molding in the bathroom she took a small roll of bills, $589 in twenties, fives, and ones, and walked up the street first to the Billings Insurance and Real Estate office to make the arrangements on the house, and then to the jewelers.

Turner's Jewelers smelled of lavender, a soft, cradling smell, the smell of a child, of hope. In the glass cases sat diamonds resting on velvet, and when she walked, shifting the light, the room seemed unmoored, moving with her, a shimmering kaleidoscope. A woman stood from behind the display case and asked, "May I help you with something?"

Eleanor smiled. "Just looking for now," she said.

"Well, let me know."

She nodded. A few minutes later she motioned the woman over.

"These?"

"Please."

"Beautiful, aren't they?"

"They sure are."

"A little Christmas shopping?"

The woman unlocked the case and set on the counter a tray of six men's wedding bands. "White gold," she said, fingering the ring and passing it over. "See the scrollwork?"

"Just beautiful."

"That's all handcrafted."

"How much is it?" asked Eleanor.

"One second." The woman referred to a small spiral bound notebook attached to the register by a chain. "One hundred and eighty nine dollars," she said. "It's a real bargain, actually. What do you think?"

"I think I'll take it."

"Wonderful. I'll wrap it up for you."

"One other thing, ma'am. Might I use that phone?"

"Of course. Please."

"Do you have a phone book?"

"Here, darling."

Eleanor thumbed the yellow pages. Halfway down the left column she found the listing for the Clemson Trailways Bus Station. Things were changing for them. Oh, she thought, how God is smiling.

She had been working in the Five and Dime on Main Street back in '48 when she had met James. What he came in to buy, she had never discovered, but he came back two or three times a week all summer before he ever spoke to her. Finally, reluctantly, he asked what time they closed. "Five," she had told him. "It's on the sign out front." He tipped his filthy hat, a felt hat, crumpled and soft, his pants and white work shirt streaked with red clay and ovals of sweat.

Eleanor had been living at the time with two other girls in a room over the store. The previous spring she had graduated from the women's D.A.R. school, a school for orphans, having been sent there after her mother had died and her father had been sent down to CCI in Columbia for eight to ten, barring good behavior. "I had a hammer in my hand and they calling me a safecracker. Sending my ass to the pen. You believe that, sugar?" she remembered his asking. So she wound up at the D.A.R. school, and she had loved it there. All the buildings were named for the thirteen original colonies. She'd lived in Georgia, across the street from Virginia and down the way from Maryland. She had run track, setting a school record for the half and quarter miles, and felt certain she could have beat most boys at either distance or at the mile had she been allowed to race that far, but it was feared anything past 880 yards would overwhelm a woman, given their reputed lack of endurance. So instead of expending energy running longer distances, she spent it on rising every morning at five to help clean the dormitory by the six AM inspection, then helped cook breakfast, then class until noon, lunch, chapel, class until three, chores until five, repeats run on the cinder track until six, dinner, then homework. The rest of the time until the nine thirty curfew was hers to spend as she pleased—which was something of a joke to the girls.

In the spring of her senior year she had began to work as a cashier at the Five and Dime with Amy Boyles and Harriet Wood. The job was considered something of a reward for her hard work. She was sixteen. I was so damn naïve, she thought. Thinking ringing up nylons and Icees was the be-all and end-all of the world. The three of them listening to the radio, staying up late drinking Cokes, giggling behind the backs of overweight men buying tube after tube of hemorrhoid cream. When James Burden started coming in on his twice or thrice weekly non-buying trips, Amy and Harriet kept telling her he was after her. She would blush but otherwise not respond. Then, as the summer progressed, she grew bolder, impatient—so much so that in the end she had cornered him in the hair ointments aisle and demanded his intentions. He had pulled off his hat as if it were afire.

"Ma'am," he said.

"Don't ma'am me. I said I want to know right now, James Burden—you think I don't know your name?—I want to know right now why you keep coming in without ever buying anything. I know you're not that interested in the ever-changing price of deodorant. Now are you?"

"Well—"

After that it had been a short walk to courtship, then engagement, marriage in the summer of '49 and a weekend honeymoon in Gatlinburg, the house on Oak Avenue. She had wanted a child, he had wanted a child, then another war came, Korea this time, and one day she woke to find him in the bathroom shaving, the light off, a single candle burning along the ledge of the sink.

"Jimmy?"

"I didn't mean to wake you."

He took a long swatch of shaving cream off one cheek and tapped the straight razor in the basin of warm water.

"It's four AM, honey."

"I know it. I couldn't sleep."

"You're getting up?"

That day, with no explanation, no apology, he had joined the marines and was gone two weeks later, headed for basic at Parris Island and Camp Lejeune, then shipped west to Camp Pendleton, then San Francisco and after that, Korea. She grieved herself over his absence, over her solitude. Desperately, she had tried to get pregnant just before he left, but it hadn't taken, and because of this she had felt a deep guilt. But whether it was guilt over the unarticulated possibility that he wouldn't come back or whether it was guilt because she could not give him even this, could not give him a reason to stay, she could not say.

She had kept working at the Five and Dime, taking on an extra shift, writing fevered four- and five-page letters at night that she would destroy in the morning and replace with a few lines of news and her hopes that he was safe. He wrote regretfully, as if he had blundered in leaving her but didn't know how to undo the mistake. At night she would wake, thinking she heard the footsteps of the child they'd never had, the child they were cheated. A girl whose long blonde hair she would roll and curl, a girl in a red and white fur-trimmed dress at Christmas. A boy with a spray of freckles across his nose. She watched the stomachs and feet of her friends swell. She held their hands during the cramps, wiped their foreheads with cool cloths, and kept working fifty hours a week.

When news came first that James was dead, and then that he was only missing and believed captured, she had wept, then slept a sleep more sound than any she had ever known. Only the uncertainty bothered her, the not knowing. Which was not to say that she was happy—she was miserable, sad, she felt cast adrift—but her previous life had faded so completely, so quickly, that like waves rippling out over a pond leaving behind only still water, there was nothing there to mourn, nothing to remember. Had there been a ghost here she called her husband? Maybe. A man who held her hand in hand, woke beside her? Perhaps, but who could say with any certainty? The only certainty was that something had changed, but Eleanor was hard pressed to say exactly what.

Then a telegram came from the Red Cross saying he was alive, and dormant memories suddenly burst like star-shells. He was alive, coming home. Except the letter didn't say he was coming home. Months later, the war unwinding itself, stubborn to reach its ugly stalemate, she received a letter from James in which he detailed the way in which he intended to kill himself. At first she had thought it wasn't real—it was propaganda, of course. The godless, bastard Communists. Then she thought perhaps he was disfigured, shamed. Then that too had passed. The letter was real. She recognized the writer of the letter as the man hiding among the toothpastes and foot powders, different, but the same. She burned the letter in the sink and fixed a drink, sat at their kitchen table to toast him, Fuck you very much, James Burden. She quit showing up at the Five and Dime, was fired, got waitressing jobs here and there. For a week her wedding ring sat at the bottom of the porcelain toilet, but she lacked the courage to flush it. Finally, it came out, was back on her finger—why, she couldn't say. Then the first check came, waiting there in her mailbox as if it meant to strike her. That was the fiercest blow, the most difficult thing. She carried it gingerly, finger and thumb, into the house and there set it flat on the counter, where she studied it from all angles, as if its meaning might somehow depend on her physical relationship to it. DISABILITY AND COMPENSATION. So what was it she was to be compensated for? She sent away for the necessary paperwork then drove up the mountain, transferring everything to Madison Burden. Then satisfying emptiness, a great yawning void. Years of nothing passed, years filled with waiting for something she thought she no longer cared about, years of waking in anticipation that this would be the day—but the day for what? She kept forgetting. It was all emptiness. So this was life, she thought. This is what they call living. Then the rumors, talk at first, that he was back in town, and at first she had prayed fervently that he would stay away. When he had, a depression as black as night fell over her.

Then the odd sensation of waiting, of feeling grains were running not from an hourglass but into it, toward their inevitable encounter. When he had shown up, it had been anticlimax. He was just a man, a thin, sallow man who looked tired and old beyond his years. Now, God was finally smiling.

She waited for James in the kitchen. On the table was a bottle of wine and two bus tickets marked LOS ANGELES, CA. She studied her reflection in the head of a spoon, wound up falling asleep in the kitchen, then woke and dragged herself to bed, numb to whatever circumstances his absence might entail. He'll be here in the morning, she thought. It's the only thing he's ever promised me. I'll wake beside him.

She woke alone. Marlon was waiting for her when she arrived at the café.

"Well, well," he said, "if it ain't Miss Lazybones. Decide to come to work did you?"

"Don't, Marlon."

He looked at her, looked through her.

"He didn't come home."

"Who?"

She shook her head. "Who do you think?"

"That son of a bitch," he said.

"So I come by to tell you I'm leaving. For good. And to say thanks." She touched the flat of one hand to his cheek, and then let it fall. "Thanks for everything."

She walked back home because there was something she had to leave for him, then decided she couldn't stay, packed, and walked up the street to the hotel. She had the operator ring Marlon just in case anyone was looking for her, just in case James was looking for her.

That night the rain turned to snow, and again she slept alone. I'm already used to it, she thought. That quick. The splinter of memory that hardens, grows over, callused. That quick, and I remember what this being alone is like. That quick, she thought.

They took two rooms at the Chief Downtown Motor Court in Seneca, Roy registering under the name William Westmoreland. "In case any of the Fowles's goons are chasing us," he explained. On the way over Enis had popped the corks on two bottles of Brut champagne, and he and Millie were beyond happy by the time they stood wobbling in the lobby.

"I don't even care what Mamma says," Millie kept repeating. "I don't care cause I love him." She kissed Enis's mouth, and her face slid across his like a car on black ice. "I just don't," she said. "I don't care."

Roy parked the car around back and carried in the bags. Faith had her arm hooked through his. Enis and Millie were kissing.

"This is where we part ways for a little, brother."

"Damn right it is," said Enis.

Millie hung from his shoulders like a puppet. "Oh, how about in a half hour we meet back down here and go eat something," she said. "I'm just about starved. We can get some fried chicken or something."

"Better make it an hour," said Roy. He winked at Enis. "I don't want to rush the boy."

"Better believe that shit," whooped Enis. "Come on, baby."

Millie squealed as he lifted her into his arms. She kissed his mouth before he could speak again. Roy and Faith watched them disappear up the stairs.

"One hour," called Roy. They watched them go. "Ain't they a match."

"Happily ever after," said Faith. "I see it in the cards."

Roy too thought this, but said nothing.

Faith stood by the door, an unlit cigarette in one hand.

"I told you this didn't have to be complicated," said Roy.

"You did, didn't you."

He nodded. "Come here," he said, but she stood fast, a bedsheet draped about her like a robe. "It looks slim sometimes, don't it, babe. Faith?"

Out the window a siren whined, vanished.

"They're out there, just waiting," she said. "Aren't they?"

"Who?"

"Them. Everybody. People."

"You mean Peyton Fowles and his idiot frat brothers? I ain't worried about them."

She waved him off. "Please. Not them, no. I don't mean anybody," she said. "Or at least, I mean everybody. The whole world. It doesn't matter."

"That's a sad thing to say."

She nodded agreement. "It's a sad world."

"Doesn't have to be."

"But it is."

"Come to bed. I want to feel you."

She laughed. "You've been feeling me for years."

She stubbed out her cigarette and slid beneath the sheets, and he held her from behind. The insect movements of his fingers, sliding one hand beneath the elastic band of her panties, the other cupped her loose breast. Around the nipple his thumb and forefinger touched, making the sign for okay. He nuzzled his mouth and nose against her neck and her ears.

"Tickles," she said. "What are you doing?"

"Same thing I've been doing for years, trying to find your smell."

They lay like that, the room dark but for the glare from the neon Chief's sign out the window that flashed on and off, him feeling her with his hips.

"Do you think we'll make it?" he asked after some time. "Is the suspense not just killing you?"

She almost laughed.

"My heart feels heavy," he said. "Heavy and drugged. It feels like a clock that's winding down."

"Please."

"I'm being serious here. Even clocks die, baby."

"Christ, don't be so damn dramatic. You can always wind a clock back up, start over fresh."

"No," he said. "It doesn't seem to work that way."

"Maybe. I don't know. Maybe not."

They lay on, listening to a car pass in the street. Faintly, they heard piano music.

"What time is it?" he asked. "Should we meet them yet?"

She rolled to face him. "Forget them. Let's get drunk, Roy."

"All right."

"No, I mean *drunk* drunk. Bombed. Plastered. Let's lay up here and drink and have sex and drink and just lay here in bed passed out until someone comes up and throws us out and we're freezing to death in the street." She wrapped her fingers around his limp cock. "Get hard for me," she said.

He sat up in bed.

"Let's do it, Roy," she said, but whatever edge of desperation there had been was gone now, replaced by resignation. She sat there, profiled, her face gone fuzzy in the near dark. She put out her open hand. "I've seen—"

"What?"

"Nothing." She waved him off. "Here's a story for you, you being a preacher's son and all. You might like this. A Bible story. You know the crowd that cheered for Jesus, waved the palms for him?"

"Yeah."

"Same ones that nailed him to the cross three days later. Think about it."

He looked at her.

"Now come on, Roy. Get hard for me."

But before she could finish, he was out of bed, pulling on his pants, a look clouding his face.

"Get dressed," he said.

"Why?"

She lay there, reaching out into empty space.

"Because I said so," he told her. "Because I won't let it happen this way."

"Come here," Millie said, and ran Enis's zipper down its track, hooked both hands in his loose jeans, and pulled him onto her on the bed. "Now get them mean old pants off." He folded over her, rolled, and she spread across him, and he felt as if he'd been swallowed, and they made love, first awkwardly, in the drunken clumsiness of unpracticed love, their clothes hanging from them like useless flags, then lay in the quiet of the room listening to heat rumble and gut the building's ductwork.

Millie was not the only woman Enis had ever been with. There had been two others. The first had been ashore in the Philippines, where he had paid three dollars for a sagging forty-year-old. Drunk on foreign beer and shots of potato vodka, he had regretted it later, considered how useless it had been, and sworn himself chaste, then gave in again just as quickly once they were ashore in Japan. A geisha girl of perhaps fifteen. Soft and delicate, she had smelled of citrus, and he had smelled of sweat and machine oil and cigarette smoke, the smells of shipboard life, the smells of a Butterstinker. After that a combination of regret and nightly masturbation into a tube sock had lasted him until returning to the States and finally back to Oconee. Whether or not she had been with other men before or during his absence he didn't know and wasn't about to ask. When he'd returned, there had been a week of bliss, of constant touching, that had ended as quickly as it had begun: she'd cut him off. "Nothing below the belt. If I can wait, so can you." That was her explanation. Enis thought he'd go blind, insane, wind up tearing through the house with an axe.

The second time was slower, measured. Finding the tendon that flared from her neck, the slope of her shoulder, the hollow where he would rest his head, the dream-flutter of her eyelids. Words unformed on her lips. First, him atop her moving slowly, deeply. Then moving onto their sides with one of her legs thrown about his hips to rest on a blade of pelvic bone. Then her astride him and they had stayed this way, riding into some frontier land they had only imagined existed. She pressed her hands down against his chest, his stomach. He was lean and wiry from work, his chest hairless, a light down along his arms. She felt electric. Her fingers pressed bloodless down against him, first leaning forward then arching her back swelling her small breasts up toward the ceiling. The Oh, God, Oh, God, Enis. . . . Don't. . . . No. . . . Don't stop. God. Don't. . . . No Oh. . . . Him moaning, his voice strangled in his throat. The country they invaded was one of brilliant strobing light flashing behind walls of paper and collapsing as soon as they entered it, folding about them like a poorly constructed tent. She crashed into him, both panting, lying there in the empty spaces between breaths, her mouth against his shoulder, hands pressed deep into his skin.

"Oh, God," she said.

He stroked her hair, found a single bead of sweat and touched it.

"God. That was the best we ever."

"I know," he said.

"Is that being married?"

"Lord God, I hope so."

They separated into a silky tangle of bedsheets and limbs then lay still until she rose and walked into the bathroom and shut the door. He could hear her use the toilet then brush her teeth, the suck of footsteps on the tile floor. When she came back out, she was wearing panties and his discarded shirt, fingering her cheap dime-store ring, twisting it with her right hand.

"It's been almost two hours," she said.

He smiled.

"You think they're waiting on us?"

"I doubt it," he said. "Come here."

"Maybe we should walk down and check? I still need to eat something."

He sat up. "Me too, actually. But let's come right back."

"Right back," she agreed.

They dressed and walked into the lobby, which was empty but for the night clerk listening to the Beatles on the radio.

"Excuse me, sir?" said Enis. "You see a man and woman down here? Actually we came in with them just a couple of hours ago."

"Sorry, slick," said the man. "Just came on a little while ago." He looked at Millie's tousled hair while John and Paul sang *Love, love me do.* "Looks for sure like I missed the fun, though."

They crossed the street and walked down to an all-night diner and ordered.

"I hate to eat without them," said Millie, after their food had arrived.

"I promise they're not suffering for anything. Just got tired of waiting. They understand."

"I guess so."

But the next morning the car was gone. The original desk clerk was back on duty.

"The tall fellow," he said, raising a hand. "Let me check here." He thumbed through the register. "Would that be the good General William Westmoreland?"

"That's the one."

"Checked out last night, friend. Got a half-refund, left within an hour."

"Gone?" said Enis.

"Gone. What can I say, friend? Poof. Gone."

There is a way a mother senses a child, a way without need of language, much as a swimmer senses a current threading past without need of sight. And though her sense was acute, Maddy could never separate thoughts of her children from thoughts of her childhood. They tangled, they wore the same smell. She thought of Christmases as a little girl, of bringing down boxes from the attic, foam balls decorated with trinkets, the threadbare angel hunched in the ceiling corner like a distant cousin, awkward, yet invited. Then she realized it was not her childhood she was remembering, rather it was her sons'. It was Will, and not her father, reading from the second chapter of Luke, Will, and not her father, lighting the Advent candles.

Then her father's face floated up out of the predawn darkness of childhood, her mother's hands hard and sharp, pulling at Maddy, shoving her arm into an overcoat, shushing her, suffering her sleep.

"I always wished it another way." Her daddy speaking, his face hanging and seemingly disembodied.

"Get up, child," said her mother. "Come on, hon, get up."

"I always wished it."

The little red fingerprints that would be left along her arms and stomach. Years later, she was so careful with her sons, careful not to leave the same careless marks. Then she recanted: they were not marks of indifference, they were marks of survival.

She cast out for her father's face, and what she found was a quiet thin man turning to Peter: "Who is it they say I am?" Rubbing away the little red prints, the hints of a crime, while they rolled silently down the slope out to the highway where only then would her father start the car. He'd pull back the blankets covering her. *I always wished it.* Here was his cross: pulling his daughter from a warm bed, fleeing to another life, another sharecropper's cabin. Her mother's voice would cut the air, that fierce whisper the only thing that kept them alive.

"Get up here. Come on, now."

Then Will again, his face. How she had absented from her life one man only to replace him with another, then with three, and what after this? What is security when you're trying to sleep along the back roads of the Piedmont in December? Or crossing the mosquito-choked Pee Dee in July, the corn all pulled and shucked and still you owe the store forty dollars? Where is faith when your husband turns inward like the hills and locks away not only his heart but his physical self? When your sons are gone or going, sailing out naked into the bloodshed—where then is comfort? There was only a sense, like she felt now, of something else.

She'd almost drowned at baptism. She hadn't understood it. In the clear cold of the Chattahoochee, they had waded out, clouding the water with sediment until the preacher covered her nose and mouth and dipped her backward. Beneath the surface, she'd opened her eyes and there were gauzy blue-green shapes, legs, a rock, maybe the sudden flip of a trout, nothing certain, but it was a new world, a still place where the constant churning fell away, replaced by a thick silence. She'd opened her mouth then too, and breathed deeply, washed now in the Blood of the Lamb. Then they'd beaten the water from her lungs. Facedown on the sandbar and wearing her clothes like bandages.

Little girl. Mother. It was right she confused the two, because the same sensing of a child was the sensing of comfort, of faith. It was the same giving over to God. It wasn't the fellowships or Bible School nights or prayer circles, or anything else marked by occasion. It was the heavy quiet, the thick skin of a silence measured by absence. It was the breathing deeply. It was the water being beaten from your lungs.

Maddy was alone now with Will. She hadn't seen Roy in weeks. When she saw Enis, it was only in and out, headed to or from work or to meet Millie. James was fog that curled over the morning fields, some whimsy that burnt away with sunlight, a single moment in a hospital room, a broken man between them. Still, she sensed her sons, at least she sensed Enis and Roy. Their physical needs—hunger, pain—their spiritual needs—the pains that wouldn't surface for years, or had risen already only to settle to bone—they passed over her now and then and she would feel everything fall away. The world would hush.

The day Will had whipped Roy for his fishing disaster—Will's single act of violence—that day, she had felt it. She had sat on a chair on the back porch and shifted, unable to get comfortable, a burning coming up through her that had less to do with the whipping and more to do with the searing away of pride. She'd sat there looking out at her garden. All summer she'd worked in it, and she was brown from the sun, her arms and shoulders muscled as they hadn't been in years. Row to row, she'd named her crops: *Pole beans. Tomatoes. Zucchini—can't nothing kill zucchini,* trying not to feel what she felt. Then a single tear was rolling down one eye, and a moment later she heard Roy cry out for the first time. Right then she'd known she was feeling him, she was beneath his skin. A child is more me than this, she thought looking down at herself. This body, this—shaking out her hands, crying now—this . . . this what?

It was the same with Enis. Black eyes, puppy-love breakups—when her son hurt, she hurt. When he rejoiced, she rejoiced. One Saturday morning,

Enis and Roy were hunting with Bobby Thorton and a sudden cold had settled over her. She'd been canning and had kept on canning, keeping her hands busy, telling herself *now ain't you silly, Madison Burden. Don't you think you are just something else. Getting all worked up like this.* She'd forced herself to sit when she heard the truck pull up, and when Enis burst into the room smiling, she had thought her feelings had betrayed her, Enis jumping up and down, his face lit like a bright window. He had just killed his first deer.

She felt certain then: her feeling had betrayed her. *Once,* she thought. *Just this once.* But that night, Enis had come to her, teary-eyed and regretful.

"Just to see it laying there, Mamma, trying to breathe through the hole in its neck."

"It's OK, baby."

"The way it kept bubbling, Mamma."

"It's OK. Don't let your brother see you like this, baby."

For whatever else in their lives, she could always measure the hearts of Enis and Roy. James was different. It was strange. They had always been the closest. Her firstborn, the closest—*God forgive me this,* she thought—the closest to her heart. But she could never feel him the way she felt her others. Once, watching him play outside the church, July it must have been, after the Wednesday night service, watching him play, touching the moss at the base of an oak tree, how gentle he had been, while the other children ran screaming, playing tag, you're it, no, you're it, silly, freed from an hour of quiet on hard-backed pews, seeing him there she had thought: *I am too close to you. You are me. We are one.*

What she had lacked in sense, she'd made up for in comfort. She saw those early years in James's life as rose-colored, painted golden by memory. They had seemed special then, just her and her James, and no need of anyone else, the Lord setting down a little acre for just the two of them, a little space they could grow in.

Who is it, Lord, they say we are?

Now she knew, as only a mother can know, there had been no such thing. They had only orbited each other, passing like distant planets seemingly bound to collide, yet slipping past, separate and tailing to opposite ends. Two thieves let loose. *I always wished it.* Her eldest son, her father, the man she had married. *We are strangers in this life. Lord,* she prayed, watching Will in his dreamless seam. *They will beat the water from my lungs, these strangers. But please Lord, let it not be so in the next. Let us not be strangers there.*

Part Three

Loss

They drove south, first along the winding back roads of South Carolina and Georgia, where a deputy with a gut like a swollen tick pulled them over to ask where the fire was, then Highway 1 along the Atlantic coast of Florida. Near Jacksonville they found a motor court and sat idling beneath the covered walkway, Roy looking out at the flashing sign, Faith with her knees pulled up to her chest, a half-eaten bag of popcorn on the floorboard.

"They got one just like that up in Cherokee, North Carolina." Roy motioned toward the sign. "Except it's called the Pink Lady up there. But the same little Tinkerbell on it."

The green and blue outline of a tiny fairy hung on translucent wings and pulsed with the words OCEAN COURT, below that: VACANCY.

"You see it, baby?"

She didn't look. He started to reach for her, but she seemed so distant, pressed against the door, and for the first time in his life he tried to turn a cold eye on her but couldn't.

"Well, hell," he said. "I'll go in and see about a room."

He left the car idling and came back after a moment with a key attached to a green triangle.

"Number nine. Supposed to be around back." He looked at her. She could just stay shut the hell up for all he cared, let her sulk. As far as he was concerned . . . then it all dissolved. He reached out to touch her elbow. "You all right?"

She nodded. "You think you could find us something to drink?"

"Sure I could. Let's just find the room first."

They pulled around behind. The sun was down, but it was still light out, and through a chain-link fence they could see the silvery figures of children swimming, their voices carrying out across the parking lot.

"Tar and chlorine," said Roy. "Smells nice, don't it, Faith?"

"Please don't."

She followed him into the room and lay back on the bed, her feet on the floor.

"Think you could find us that drink, Roy?"

He walked around the room touching things, the clock radio, the TV bolted to the floor.

"I told you already I could, baby." He walked into the bathroom and emerged stuffing a plastic bag into a small bucket. "Tell you what, why don't you find the ice machine while I'm gone."

He bent forward to touch her, but she rolled away, and he was left searching the pillow for her smell.

The boy at the desk said there was a liquor store just up the street but it closed at dark so he might want to hurry. Roy hustled out, his hands in his pockets, the air finally free of humidity and smelling now of gasoline and tar and the ocean. Clean and light. Gas—the smell of gas would always remind him of flying, of vapors rising from the warm desk of the *Forrestal*.

He hurried.

There was no sidewalk, only a series of parking lots that adjoined the road, motor courts and souvenir shops, the Honey-Do Lodge, the Roadside Inn, everything glittering like cheap jewelry. The evening grew darker, lit with neon pulses, the slow-waking headlights of cars, plastic outsized candy canes that glowed beneath the streetlights. Horns honking, heads slinking out from windows. Everyone seemed young. Everyone seemed to be going somewhere, though no one seemed in any hurry.

He found the liquor store two blocks up.

"Told you I would," he muttered, then noticed an old woman was locking up. He started to jog.

"Hey! Excuse me! Excuse me, ma'am!"

She turned, took a pull on her cigarette then sent a jet of white smoke directly over her head.

"Sorry." He was almost out of breath. "I. . . ."

She arched one eyebrow, her face a geographic wonder with its twisting crannies and crevices. Too much sun, too much time. Then he realized she was waiting for him to speak.

"I'm sorry," he said. "I just wanted to get something for my wife and I before you closed. We're newlyweds."

"Couldn't open it if it was life or death, friend." Her voice hoarse, coming reluctantly, eyes crow-footing at the corners. "Life or death," she said.

He smiled. "Well, it just might be."

Then he smiled wider, feeling her break.

He took the fifth of Jack behind the building and tore off the plastic, sat down on an old cross-tie and took a drink. Things would be all right. They just needed time, a drink. A few miles would make things better, a few miles and a little something to drink. He capped the bottle, slipped it back into the paper bag, and started back up the street. The traffic had thinned. The street-lamps burned lonely but for the haze of moths and bats. Time. A few miles. Maybe a drink here and there. They could keep a fifth with them the whole way down, dip into it for a little courage now and then. They would be all right. He wouldn't let it end like this.

When he got back to the room Faith was still on the bed, her feet still flat on the floor, the ice bucket with its opaque bag right where he had left it.

"Couldn't find it, baby?" he said. He set the Jack on the nightstand and bent over to unlace her shoes. "I'll get it then."

It was around the corner, dumping squares of ice with a great grinding sound. A vent shuddered on. When he got back to the room, Faith was sitting on the end of the bed with the fifth between her legs, rubbing the instep of one foot against the opposite ankle. She walked into the bathroom and peed with her head balanced in her hands.

Roy shut the door and they drank themselves into oblivion.

He woke the next morning to the sound of Faith vomiting behind the bathroom door. His mouth was dry and a dull pulse throbbed behind his left eye. Something in his stomach kept flipping. He listened as she heaved. "Oh, Christ," she muttered. "Oh, God."

He opened a single eye. Sunlight sallowed the curtains a faint peanut butter brown. The carpet was pea green. The mattress, broken by years and random bodies, sloped away at the edges like an umbrella. He stood and pulled on his shorts and T-shirt, eased open the bathroom door. She stood there, legs locked, doubled at the waist like a jackknife. Her hair hung straight down and was clotted at the tips with bits of yellow vomit. Through the V-neck of her shirt he could see her breasts, the nipples flaccid and pale, the wrinkled skin of her stomach an amphibious white.

"For Christ's sake," she yelled at him then dry-heaved, wiped her mouth on her wrist. She spat bile. He made to pull back her hair. "Oh, for Christ's sake, can't you see what I'm doing to myself?"

He pulled the door shut behind him then pulled on his pants and set out to find breakfast. Just down the highway was a café with the OPEN sign pulsing. He ordered two breakfast plates, two coffees, two orange juices, walked out with the four paper cups secure in a cardboard carrier, the Styrofoam plates in the bag. When he came back, she was showered and dressed and sprawled across the bed. He kicked the door shut behind him.

"If you don't get that smell out of here I'm going to start puking again, Roy."

He looked at her. "Breakfast," he said.

"I'm serious. Eat it out on the step if you don't mind."

"All right."

"Leave the coffee."

He ate sitting on the concrete curb looking out at the mirrored surface of the pool. When he walked inside, she was sitting on the end of the bed wearing one of his shirts, bags packed at her feet.

"How are you?"

"Better," she said. "Sorry about all of that."

"Don't worry about it. Ready to keep moving?"

They skirted white sand beaches, bungalows tucked away among the palm trees, the occasional pink stucco hotel, then bent inland through endless fields of citrus. Trees in long geometric patterns intersected abruptly. Tractors moved silently between the rows. Faith sat sipping her orange juice. Roy drummed his thumbs on the wheel, both silent, only the glide of tires against the road. Between St. Augustine and Daytona Beach they stopped at a roadside stand where an old man sat on a plastic crate whittling. A hand-lettered sign read ORANGES—LIMES—TANGERINES. The air smelled of hibiscus flowers and the warm tar of the road. The man looked up as they approached.

"Afternoon," said Roy, pushing his glasses into his hair.

"Is it?" asked the man.

Faith was picking through bins of brightly colored fruit. The man was barefoot.

"Mind if I sit in that shade with you? It ain't supposed to be this hot in December."

"No," said the man. "I suppose it ain't."

Roy sat.

"Right nice place you got here."

The man seemed bored, studying the horizon, where row after row of citrus trees stretched from sight.

"I said, nice place."

"I heard you," said the man. He seemed to consider things, as if apprais-ing his stand with new eyes. He nodded. "It's fair. Bout the best a white man can hope for in this world, what with the colored and Cuban folk taking over everthang."

"Well. Weather's nice."

"Fair to middlin," said the man.

Faith was filling a brown paper sack marked FLORIDA GROWERS CO-OP with fruit. Roy walked back into the wan sun. It was warm, though not powerfully so—short sleeve weather so long as the breeze was still.

"Headed down to Miami. My wife and I. Our honeymoon. We just got married."

The man nodded. "Lot a Cuban folk down in Miami."

"That so?"

"Hope you like Cuban folk is all I got to say."

The man wiped the blade of his knife on his pants and went back to his stick. Along a far rise, Roy noticed two bulldozers moving not between the rows but through them, plowing dark earth, snapping the trees like matchsticks.

"What's that?" he asked the man.

"What's what?"

"The bulldozers there."

"That," said the man, looking up. His tongue darted like an eel through a gap in his teeth. He spit down between his feet. "That right there is what they call progress."

"They're bulldozing the trees."

"Ain't you a sharp one."

"What for?"

"For progress. Hell." The man sucked his teeth, swallowed something. "Tract housing is what's coming. Progress is what's coming."

"That a fact?"

"You mark it down it's a fact, young fella."

Near Melbourne they bent west, stopping for the night near the town of Frostproof, and finding a hotel just past an alligator farm and across the street from what appeared to be an abandoned air field. Night fell. The air grew cool, a bite to it. They lay on the made bed, their feet touching the floor, still dressed.

For some time neither made any motion to move. The bed was the point of a compass, steady, unmoving, while around them the earth spun regular, dizzying revolutions. A fly orbited. There was the danger of losing themselves.

"Hungry," Faith said after a while. "Hungry. Roy. Roy, wake up. I'm hungry."

They lay for a while longer. Roy propped himself onto one elbow.

"Should I go hop the fence and drag an alligator out?"

"Stop trying to be funny. It always embarrasses me."

A car passed along the highway and for a moment a lattice of light fell across them.

"Seriously then."

"Seriously, I'm hungry."

"You want to go out?"

She shook her head no. They were both watching the ceiling.

"Could you just get something? I saw a McDonald's or something back up the road."

"Yeah. Sure." He stood, tugged at his pants. "What do you want?"

"Whatever. A hamburger."

His shadow lay across the road like a dark finish line. Something scurried into the tall grass at his approach. He felt alone with the night, the highway, the bright full moon that hung like a mirror, the broad golden arches that shone like malefic oracles, like the precursors to a future that promised hope and happiness amid the surgical cleanliness of stale living. In the McDonald's he ordered two hamburgers, two fries, two Cokes, and the waitress bagged them, and he tipped her a dollar then waved her off as she explained this simply was not done. When he got back to the room, Faith wasn't on the bed. The TV played low, and the bathroom door was shut, though he could hear the water running, see a slim band of light fanning across the carpet.

"I got it," he called. "Hey."

No answer.

"Shit then," he muttered. "Take a bath, doll."

He opened the bag and began to eat, finished the burger then peeled the lid off the Coke and drank. "Hey," he called. The water kept running. "You all right in there?" He tried to eat the fries, but found himself full. "Food's getting cold," he called. "Fries soggy. Coke warm." He closed the bag, played for a moment with the rabbit ears atop the TV, then walked to the door. At his knock the door eased open. The mirror was fogged, the tub empty. Water lipped at the edge and was just beginning to trickle over onto the discolored linoleum. He turned off the water.

"Faith?" He studied the round rust-colored drain. The water lay mute. "Faith?"

The car was in the parking lot. Her bags lay on a chair in the corner of the room. He walked up toward the McDonald's then back toward the hotel office. The lights were on but the doors were locked.

"Faith?" he called across the parking lot. "Faith, baby."

Somewhere a door slammed shut.

Roy walked back up the road calling for her. Now and then a car streaked past, silvering the fence that separated the road from the abandoned air field. He changed direction, stopped across the street and studied the field by the neon of the GATOR MOTOR INN sign. A field of misshapen objects, figures without form, without outline. When another car passed, he saw them for what they were: silver B-17s sitting in long rows, their wingtips folded skyward as if in prayer. The obsolescent relics of a war fought in black and white. Sacred fathers to the Phantoms he had piloted, blood kin to the B-52s he had flown cover for. He walked along the fence line. It took three more cars passing before he found the hole in the fence.

An irrigation ditch of syrupy brown water ran toward a concrete culvert. He bent back the torn chain-link and eased into the field then called for her, sniffing the air like a dog. Overhead the moon slipped its accompanying clouds, and once again he could see.

"Faith? Faith, baby, are you out here?"

He walked on. The planes had been gutted, stripped clean of their engines and in some cases the glass of their cockpits. Grass grew from beneath the wheels. He touched a wing, warm with the day's faint heat. It all seemed somehow obscene.

He stayed parallel to the highway, letting one hand run along the rivets of the planes' nose cones, flinching at the occasional sound of a passing car. I shouldn't be in here, he thought. Then: Shit, these are part of me. He felt caught in a long unfurling river of violence that knew no end, no beginning, no sense of purpose—and he felt himself burning, flying on wings of flame toward some rumor of glory. Then he saw her, or at least thought he did, her blurred shape. She was crouched down near a wheel assembly perhaps two hundred feet away. When he called, the figure twisted, froze, ran. He ran after her, his brain flashing sudden snapshots onto the acetate of memory: the sound of his feet on the dirt path, the moon overhead, a limp orange windsock on a bamboo pole, the whirring of crickets and tree frogs, her breath when he finally caught her, the warm sweat dimpled along her skin. He was panting, too.

"Faith. Faith, God . . . stop . . . stop for a minute."

She tried to wrench free from him.

"Just let me . . . can't you see. . . . Christ, let me go."

He let go of her. She collapsed forward down an embankment onto her knees, where a drainage ditch ran foul with water, and there she sat crying, her fingertips drifting atop the water's surface.

"Faith . . . please," he panted.

She was crying, saying *Can't you see what I'm doing? Can't you see?* over and over.

"Get out of the water, Faith. Come on."

"Leave me alone, Roy."

"Please . . . all right. I'll leave you alone if you come back. Please. Get out of the water. This is crazy. Come on, Faith."

"Can't you understand this? Don't you realize anything? Christ, Roy, are you that stupid?"

"I must be. Please." He put out a hand for her. She pushed her hair back from her face. Moonlight ran along the water. A car passed.

"Faith."

"Christ, Roy. I'm pregnant. Do you not realize that? Can you not see that much? All this time. All everything, it just. . . ."

"Just what?"

"Fuck you, Roy."

He looked at her humped shoulders. She divided the water. The water seemed not to care.

"And yes. Yes, it's his. Fuck." She shook her head. "From Charleston. Christ, Roy, can't you see that much?"

"Please come out of the water, Faith."

"Leave me alone."

"Please come out."

"Say something first."

"Faith—"

"Something besides my name. Fuck. Aren't you even going to say something?" She looked at him. "Anything?"

He stretched out his hand. After a moment, she took it.

At the motel, she ate in silence then slipped into the now cool bath.

Roy felt the temperature with one finger while she sat on the toilet. He turned on the hot water.

"Just leave it be," she said.

"It's cold."

"Leave it be."

She sat in the tub, wrinkling the water like old skin. "I'm afraid of it," she said.

He sat in the other room on the edge of the bed and listened to the occasional movement of water. After she had dried and dressed, she climbed beneath the bedsheets.

"Don't you see what I'm doing to myself?" she asked, once he was beside her.

He held her from behind, his face in the slow curve of her neck. "No. I don't know," he said.

She rolled to face him.

"I'm not a good person, Roy."

"You're good, Faith. I think you're very good. As good as me, at least."

"That supposed to make me feel better here?"

"I'm serious."

"Don't you see what I'm doing here?"

"Maybe you could tell me."

She shook her head no, kissed him. They lay in silence.

"How do you know," he said sometime later, "that it's his? How can you know it's his and not mine?"

She lay still. "I just do."

"Bullshit."

They lay on in silence.

"I just know, Roy. It's something you just know."

"I want a blood test then, a paternity test. I'm serious. You can't just know. That's crazy."

"Go back to sleep. It doesn't matter."

"How can you say it doesn't matter? Why can't you just tell me what's happening, Faith? Please."

"In the morning. In the morning, all right? I'm so tired right now."

"Faith—"

"Please, Roy. In the morning."

"All right. In the morning."

In the morning she was gone. He woke slowly, stretching like a cat before realization snapped. He sat up. A shallow depression where she had been. He searched the pillow for her smell but could not find it. He wasn't surprised. He dressed and walked outside. The Fastback, its vinyl top sutured with bands of duct tape, sat in the early morning sun. Cars went zipping through the sunlight up the highway. He walked up to the hotel office, where a man pulled his feet from the desk and stood.

"Checking out?"

Roy nodded. "In a little."

This seemed to please the man. He took a pencil from behind his ear and began to speak. Roy stopped him with a hand.

"I wonder if you've seen the woman I came in with last night. Dark reddish hair. Green eyes. About yea tall."

"The redhead. Sure. Your girlfriend?"

"My wife."

"Wife? No shit."

"So she was in here?"

"Yeah, she was in here. In here looking for the bus station. Cab picked her up maybe two hours ago. Sorry, buddy. If I'd a known I could have woke you, could have let you know."

Roy nodded and turned for the door.

"One other thing," called the man.

Roy turned.

"She had a roll of bills on her. I'm not telling you what to do, but you might want to check your wallet."

When he got back to the room, he opened the top drawer of the nightstand. Where a Gideon's Bible, his wallet, and a clip of money had been, now sat a Gideon's Bible, his wallet, an empty clip, and two pieces of folded hotel stationery that read: *I'm sorry, but you were wrong. It is complicated. It can't be any other way. I took just enough to get home. I already know I'll be sorry. Just don't ever remind me of it.* The note was written in lipstick. He held it to his face. He found her smell.

Bobby sat in the driveway, a restless beagle pup squirming in his hands, the rain streaming off him. James left the truck running and ran inside. Bobby stroked the dog and watched him, watched the still house, the rain pouring off the eaves, the headlights of the truck backlighting him.

"Bobby?" James came running out into the yard. "Bobby?"

Bobby dropped his head, his eyes crinkling at the corners. James took him by the shoulder. There in the mud lay Sharon's porcelain dolphin.

"Bobby?"

Bobby whimpered, opened his mouth to show the fleshy gums where his false teeth should have been.

"You're gonna freeze out here."

"Where you been, James? Thought the whole world had done went and left me."

"Get up. You're gonna freeze."

"It don't matter."

"Bobby? Where's my—"

"She's gone, James. The lying cunt. She was the love of my life now she's gone with my truck and ever bit a anything I ever had. Sharon's good silver, the TV."

"Bobby?"

"They God Almighty, James." He was crying.

"Where's my stuff, Bobby?"

"The drugs?"

"The morphine, Bobby. I've got to have that morphine."

"Gone. Everything's gone. The lying cunt. Even took old Gus, and there ain't nothing honorable in this damned, godforsaken world but a good dog. He was the best hunting dog I ever seen, James, the damn best, the truest friend, the only true real friend. I tell you that right now."

"Bobby?"

"Gone, James. Understand me? Gone. The lying cunt took everything and split with some son of a bitch named Stump. James—" But James was already running away, headed for the orchard and the gaping forest beyond. Bobby watched him going, hearing no sound but imagining one: the long-ago full-lunged baying of Old Gus, angry and sad with his head back and showing the white fur of his newly vulnerable throat.

Two hours later, Bobby had found his spare set of teeth, dried off, and was sitting on the porch talking to a woman he thought he might know.

"He come through," he told her. She stood out in the yard wearing a yellow rain jacket, arms crossed on her chest, breath coming in little crystals of white. "Yeah, he come through looking for something but he's gone now."

"Well, if he comes back," said Eleanor. "Tell him I came looking too. But I gave up. He'll know who you're talking about."

"You're his wife, ain't you?"

"Was. A long time ago."

"I hardly recognized you. That ain't your truck there in the yard, is it? He drove it up here."

"No."

"Well, should I tell him to come find you if I see him?"

"No." She shook her head. "No, I won't be around."

"Well, what should I tell them then? If he comes around, I mean."

"Tell him," she said. "Tell him he promised. Tell him that. And I couldn't wait any longer. I wouldn't. Tell him I gave up. For good. You tell him that."

"All right," said Bobby. He had the beagle pup in his lap, warm and curled inward like a burnt leaf. "I'll tell him as much."

Eleanor turned for her car.

"You driving back down the mountain?" Bobby called.

She didn't look back.

"Well, you be careful, ma'am. That road's treacherous, iced slicker than owl shit."

He sat back down on the porch and watched her drive up the road through the dirty snow. When she had disappeared from sight, he flipped on the radio—all, he felt, that was left to him now—took out his pocketknife and began to whittle on a stick. A song came on. *Turn back before it's too late,* sang some faraway tenor. *You're drifting too far from the shore.* He laughed then, just laughed and laughed, laughed until he was crying.

That night Will Burden lay still as the snow fell, and through a troubled sleep sensed the devil coming to take what was his, coming to take his due and settle old accounts. One son fell from a great height, another disappeared into the darkness. The third, his youngest, he could not see. So Will went looking for him. He felt himself walking along a dark path, a dense arbor of leaves above him, pine shadow on gray snow, his vision fast failing. He called the name of his missing son, but there was no reply, only the cold cracking of tree limbs that sounded like gunshots or the lightning from some long-ago summer storm. Finally, he came upon a house with a light burning in the front room, a thread of smoke rising through the chimney. An abandoned car sat out front wearing a cape of snow, bits of insect carcass and twigs caught in the wipers. He trudged on through the snow among the remnants of His people, past the scattered twisted bodies, past the still-warm ovens hissing with the still-falling snow, past the piles of shoes and gold teeth and the old underpants nailed like riding tack to the walls, onto the porch.

He helloed the house. Knocked at the door. Birds pecked in the yard, and a light dusting of white lay across a pile of firewood stacked between two trees. An antenna lanced the sky.

"Who's in there?" he called. "Hello? Is somebody in there?"

He sat down to wait, drifting into a sleep within sleep then waking sometime later, having dreamed of his sons. He never should have struck Roy— that was what he understood now. Having raised his hand, he had let loose a bit of his own father, the Dark Corner's Monster, and it was because of this he had later retreated: the fear of becoming him. It was only the ugly blasphemy of Roy's act that had led to his whipping. A river is a holy place, a conduit to God, a place where one washed not in mere water but in holy water, living water, a place where one washed in the Blood of the Lamb. He'd read Eliot in seminary and remembered still *". . . the river is a strong brown god—sullen, untamed and intractable."* As a boy he'd crawled through creek beds, the sand-colored stones like ancient faces, hard and drawn, the current bending around him, so cold he sucked at his fingers. He remembered too the church socials that followed baptisms, ice cream churns grinding out ice and rock salt, watermelons resting in swift, narrow creeks, fish frying. He could have taught them something then, his sons, the simple frying of a fish, the smells, his fingers in the cornmeal. Then he would have shown them the creek bottoms of his own childhood: the egglike stones and slabs of bedrock, the speckled and rainbow trout that glimmered like oil slicks; waterbugs, spiders, glossy mountain laurel brushing the surface. He could have walked them to the edge, waded out with them. *Here is God,* he might have said. *Look around you. Believe.* For it is impossible to stand in a mountain river and not believe in God. What was it Kilmer had said? *Only God can make a tree.* Or a river, Will thought.

Then he knew it was almost time. No, he never should have struck Roy. He had been mistaken about everything—that single truth that was now true and irredeemable and in itself holy. But now the clock was nearing the hour of service, neither mechanical nor human time but the heart-time to which souls march. He had known it before, and along with his father's acts, it had driven him to the pulpit, to the grace of high steeples, the outward groping of inward hands feeling for that deep stone of sin he sought to dislodge. Sabbath morning: no hour nearer the unknowable mystery of God. Silence. Birdsong. He heard again the piano, the sonorous bellow of the organ. No moment where fallible man stretched so keenly to touch the face of God, to kiss His lips, to grab hold His hand. On Sabbath morning, he knew, there was faith enough to turn one's back on the world. There was faith enough to go on.

It is fitting and just—so went his thinking—*that I am to leave it there, my physical life, in a river, in the waters of forgiveness.*

He was shivering. He could not feel his legs, and the light was growing dim, paling above the tree line. Then, for a moment, he was child again, child enough for name: William Jennings. Will. Little Willy. He was forever seven. He was forever eight, nine. But now his father was tromping through the creeper vines again in defiance and defilement and Will was no more a boy but a dying old man. That, he knew, was the way of time.

He stomped his feet on the porch boards for warmth. Where was his son? He was inside, wasn't he? He knocked at the frosted glass. Inside was movement. He could sense a peculiar warmth emanating from the house, some warmth that burned past or through the coldness gathered in the human heart. He knocked and knocked, stomped his feet, cried hello again and again. There was warmth there, life, but it offered no sign, and eventually he gave up. He was too tired. Too numb. The time was at hand. Inside there was fire, hope—but wasn't knowing it was there enough? He pulled his coat about his thin shoulders and without sensation began to trudge away, past the firewood, past the tracks of the snowbirds, past the dead and back into the pine shadows, trudging without direction, keeping his eyes fixed on the valley below, his eyes fixed on that white, untracked casket of snow. He was moving downhill now, toward moving water. And walking again, he remembered his Eliot: he would do in death what he could not do in life, a simple promise, a prayer—make me a river—it would be enough: *like a river,* he prayed, *I will be the "reminder of what men choose to forget."*

Part Three

Madison Burden sat perched forward, holding Will's hand and listening. The room was dark but for the lampshade that burned a deep October orange. His breath was like a dying breeze, growing weak, weaker, and then catching in his throat. He would cough, sputter back to life, keep breathing. Once he had tried to speak, mumbling of the deliverance not of his flock but of his herd, and she had leaned close to hear what else he might say. There had been nothing else.

She still had his hand when she heard the car coming up the drive. She listened as the door swung shut, a voice, loud but indiscernible, steps on the front porch, but she wouldn't let go Will's hand. His breath kept rising, rasping, his eyelids faintly twitching. He was nearing something, so near. *Lord, deliver him.* She sat on, shadows folding into the room, arching from the window, the angle of the dresser, the metal tubing of the bed, the dusty rows of books stacked on the shelves. Outside, the sky heaved snow. Then the voice again, steps. A rocking chair clattered. The door opened, slapped shut, opened again. A car started. Will's breath like a prayer, so faint, so faraway. *Deliver him, Lord. You owe him as much.* She looked up at the framed Jesus. She felt alone in the room and cursed herself for feeling so. Wasn't the Lord near? Wasn't her husband by her side? But so lonely.

The car tore back up the gravel of the road and out of hearing distance. *Who is it they say we are?*

Her husband's hand twitched. He inhaled, a deep gulp of air, held it, then let it go. She waited for the next breath then very calmly sat feeling for the pulse. When she was satisfied that it was no more, she pulled on her coat and heavy shoes to start for the house just up the road, the one with a phone. Then she didn't. She just stood in the front room looking out at the patchy snow. A single shotgun shell lay on the floor like an omen and she just wanted to stand there. Not forever, but for another minute, another second, anything before the changing began. I can wait, she thought. I can. But God's will, not my own.

Old man Joseph Cory was welding a sheet of aluminum to a large metal object when he sensed the figure watching him. He cut the gas to his torch and slipped back his glasses. The figure stood hunched in the edge of the forest.

"Come on out," called Cory.

The figure did not move.

"Come on out. I see you. You ain't no haint or allow I would've done smelled you. You one a them got-damn government people, ain't you? I done told y'all you got no business up here. You let the dead rest in peace."

He flipped his visor back down and peered blindly through the rectangle of dark glass.

"To hell with you then," he called, "you got no call to be bothering me anyhow. I'm a law-abiding man and I won't stand for it. Good way to get your ass shot." He went back to welding. When he was finished, he turned to find a man sitting on an upturned crate, hugging himself, his hair strung with brambles and beggar-lice and dead bugs, boots scuffed with mud and ice. The man was skinny and pale and appeared not to have shaved in a day or so. Cory was not alarmed.

"Decide to come up did you?"

Around the yard were scattered cars in various states of disrepair: tireless, engineless, one with a poplar tree growing up through the open hood. Cory's wheeled cage sat beneath a chinaberry tree beside an antique dunking booth the color of rust. Dinosaur hulks of machinery. The toothed bucket of a backhoe splayed against the sky. Oxygen bottles were stacked as neatly as cordwood and dusted with snow.

"You lost or something?" asked Cory. "Or are you sick? You look to be sick."

The figure nodded without looking up.

"Something catching?"

He shook his head no.

"Hungry?" Cory waited. "Reckon the cat's got your tongue. Well, come on in, then. I reckon it's on about lunchtime. A little food ain't never hurt nothing. Might even find us a little taste. Fella named Hoghead didn't send you up this way, did he?"

Inside Cory's house they sat at the table eating ham and leftover biscuits that had soaked through a sheet of waxed paper. Cory's hands lay on the table, battered, gray and protuberant, like things that have lived too long beneath the earth. He had a thermos of black coffee and filled the lid for the man and sipped from the bottle. The man smelled of body odor and rank mud, his face as scratched and pockmarked as the moon.

"Eat up," said Cory. "I got work to do. I cain't sit and babysit no vagrant. Snow's coming and I got to get done here. Time's just about to run out."

The man ate the biscuit then another. The husk of a beetle fell from his hair.

"I allow you heard about my youngest, Mary Anne, ain't you?"

The man said nothing.

"She was my pumpkin. She was." Cory sipped his coffee then stared for a moment down into his wrinkled reflection. "Now most might've figured you for a haint," he said. "But that ain't so. I knowed it when I couldn't smell you. You know that? Always smell a haint before you see it. That or hear it flailing about. A haint's bad for flailing." He straightened himself in his chair. "I have tasted the Bread of Life and spat it from my lips," he said.

They finished in silence and Cory put what was left of the food in a Sunbeam Bread bag and tied the top.

"Take it on," he said. "Likely you'll need it."

Back in the yard the stranger made to speak, "Roots," he said.

"Say now?"

"Roots. You know where I can find them?"

"Roots? Oh, what, like sang or milkweed?"

"Mushrooms," the man managed.

"You say mushrooms, do you? You got to talk at my left ear."

"Mushrooms."

"Well what about em? You looking for em?"

The man nodded. Cory stared at him with the mad eyes of a prophet.

"You ailing something fierce, ain't you. You look to be for sure. Need em for medicine, I reckon."

Again, the thin figure nodded.

"Hell, I don't know, friend," said Cory. "It ain't really the right time of year after first frost. I never knowed of nobody to find anything after first frost. You bout two months too late." He picked up his welding torch, shifted it from hand to hand as if testing its weight, then let it rest in the crook of one arm. "Looks like you done dug down along the river. You might try past that creek next holler over. Once you out my pasture, it's all Forest Service land far back as the rifle range."

The man nodded. "What is that?" he asked.

"Say again?"

"That thing."

"Oh, this here? Spaceship. When Jesus comes back direct like, I don't plan on sitting still for it. I'm getting out." Cory tapped the welding torch against the iron, bell-shaped object. "He's real. I'll admit as much, like it or not. But when He comes I'm taking off and flying away right smart. The moon maybe. Got a tank a compressed air. Got some food. Water. I plan on getting out, and that's the gospel of it."

The man nodded. "Is He up there then?"

"Who?"

"Him." He lifted his eyes toward heaven. "Is He watching?"

Cory turned and again tapped the metal of the torch against the metal of the ship.

"I tell you what I believe," he said. "I tell you right now. I don't believe in no goodness. I believe He's out there just laughing like some"—he looked up to find the man halfway across the yard, trouncing through the dead stalks and headed back into the forest. "Take care now," he called.

The man raised a backward hand for reply, let it fall.

The sun fell, bleeding down through the trees a last light of luminous blue so pure James seemed to smell it, the crispness of winter air. He found himself deep in the belly of the only place he'd ever truly known. Home. The homeplace. The middle of Forest Service land, unpopulated but for the misbegotten, the wretched, the fouled or forgotten. Wherever he'd roamed, it had always been a search for here, for this place.

He was a soldier, a vagrant, a day laborer, a wanderer. He had never spoken of things; he had told no one. Now he felt the light settling on him, only to travel through him. He smelled Chosin, clean, cold. There were broken teeth in the sand. Then faces began to appear. He saw his grandfather, the monster, tramping and cursing through the brush up ahead. He saw Ellie on their honeymoon terrace, his mother and father in their Sunday best. He saw not Bobby but a dolphin diving up into a fine spray. He saw his brothers, his blood kin, and there was a certain unity to things, but there was also a certain disassociation.

He sat on a fallen log looking out into bare trees. It was almost dark now, though overhead shone the last vestiges of copper light. No birds sang. Time had all but stopped, the clock's face broken and made still, showing the teeth of mechanical gears grown useless. Then he felt himself twisting, peeling away from himself so that on the log sat two men, both James. Himself and his other.

"Time to get on," said one.

"Let me sit for another minute," he said back.

"Sit if you want but it's getting dark."

He looked around him. The naked upper-works of the trees were vanishing, blurring into a single patched canopy, maculate and breathing. Dark clouds blew overhead, crossing shadows. No stars.

"There ain't nobody waiting on us."

"I know there ain't."

"We're both gonna be lonely."

Still they sat, pants growing damp and then cold. A little fern had sprouted from within the hollow of the log, and one James touched a waxy frond. Lichen grew, tufts of it waxy and soft, and he touched these as well.

"This was our lot from the start," said the other. "Everything else was make-believe."

"I know it."

"Then why we still sitting? Look down there. Look how dark it is."

But instead of looking down into the darkness the James looked up at the face beside him and suddenly it wasn't his own face he saw but that of his grandfather. Over his shirt, the old man wore a coarse duster cut from burlap, a crinkled hat, brogans, and work pants. "Look down there," he said.

James looked down where the forest sloped away into darkness. "I hear water running," he said.

The old man shook his head, smiled showing rotten teeth, spoke in his ancient voice. "That ain't water you hear, son. Oh, damn. Look here." Blood had begun to seep from the old man, coloring his shirt and matting it against his skin. James could make out the shape of his breastbone, below it a cathedral of gaunt ribs. The blood seemed to gather strength, like a torrent now, pulsing with the final suspirations of a dying man.

"Once it gets started it's liable to never stop," said the old man. Blood dripped onto the log then onto the loam beneath their feet. "Come on," he said standing. "Let's hurry. We'll drown in it, we sit here." He was holding his shirt, one arm cradled over his stomach as if to hold something in. The blood had begun to puddle. "This has been our lot from the start, son. There's rules that govern man. Then there's rules that govern them like us."

James nodded.

"Them that turn their back on the world," said the old man. "Them's the ones that hear the voice out of the whirlwind. Them's the ones that wrestle with God."

It was growing colder, and though he heard water running below, he knew he would have to go soon. He thought of his own trips to the river. He thought of the old McCallister woman, what she had said about healing the body but not the spirit, about washing one's soul in the Blood of the Lamb. Her words had not taken. He was unclean, ruined and lost there in the temple of knowing, and he would not go back to them. He thought of that morning in the bathtub after the war, hoping his mother might find him, the way God had constructed the intricate orbit of people and events so that they might never touch but go on swinging, loose and without hope. He would not go back. *Crucify me,* he prayed. The old man turned and started walking. "Got you a fresh trail to foller," he said, then turned again and laughed and went on his way. After a moment, James stood, wished himself a new, risen soul, and then followed.

So he was gone.

"Gone looking for something, I reckon," said Bobby. He stood on the porch looking down at Roy. "Left somebody's truck in the yard. Don't even know who it belongs to. Some dope peddler, maybe. Who knows. His wife was up here looking for him, too. She's done gone and left him, I fear."

"Well, shit," said Roy. "That's James for you, coming and going however it pleases. What you got to drink in there?"

"Nothing. Not a thing. I got cleaned out, Roy."

"I know you got something in there."

Bobby shook his head. "You look like you don't need it, Roy. You look rough. I'll be honest with you, you look rough as shit."

"Don't hold out on me now, Bobby. Don't do wrong by me in my hour of need."

"If I wasn't too old for such nonsense I'd say you're just about scaring me a little, Roy. Way you talking."

"Good. You got reason to be scared."

"Talking such nonsense." Bobby sighed. "I might have a little something tucked away."

He came back out with a mason jar two-thirds full, passed it over, looked out over the yard, everything hard and absent of color, tree limbs drooping, gigantic and heavy with ice.

"Don't let the law catch you with that. I ain't got any store-bought whiskey or I'd give it to you."

"I'll pay you back for this."

"I ain't gonna hold you to that," said Bobby.

"Just the same."

Bobby nodded.

"Have you seen Enis?" asked Roy.

"No. Heard he was married was all. Married and living happily ever after. You seen the Gathers boy?"

"No."

"Well, if you see him—"

"Yeah," said Roy. "Yeah, I'll tell him you send your best."

He drove to his parents' house, the fast-emptying jar clenched between his thighs, swallow after swallow burning into his stomach. No one answered inside, not his mother, not his father, even the dogs seemed uninterested in his presence, raising their heads from the dry ground beneath the porch eave then settling them again, as if overcome with fatigue or boredom.

"Fine then," said Roy. "Lay in your damn cold yard and freeze to death. I hope you do."

The dogs slept. Pom-pom-headed tulips his mother had planted in the fall rose through the snow, a shock of color against the bone-gray ice.

He sat in a rocking chair on the porch and finished the moonshine. The air was cold but he was sweating beneath his coat. The tips of his fingers were blue. He thought of nothing, or tried to clear his head at least, looking blankly up the drive where twin bands of dirty snow ran from sight. He laughed, blew hot air into his hands and wiped snot along his sleeve and laughed again. A black terror had seeped into his brain, but nothing changed. The terror was nothing. The space it was filling was nothing.

He waited, rocked, fingers curled and knotted.

Then an idea flared, flashing color over the yard, and he felt pinned beneath a sudden halo of pain; the sweat ran and he carried an awareness of his heart and its leaden beating, no faster, but fuller it seemed. Then it passed, though the sweat still ran, and he thought clearly. His whole life, he realized, had built to this very moment: who was he? What couldn't he do? What couldn't he have? It was his child, he knew it. When he stood, the rocking chair toppled behind him, but Roy didn't notice. He was remembering a conversation he'd once had with some old salt, a master chief who'd seen three wars and thirty years at sea. "What if," Roy had asked him, "you knew exactly what you wanted in the world, the only thing, and it was right out in front of you just waiting for you to grab it."

"Easy. You'd grab it. You'd do anything in the world to get it. Whatever it took."

"All right then," he'd told the master chief. "But suppose by getting it you might also destroy what it was about it that you loved most. By getting it, you'd ruin it. I'm asking a different question here."

"But I'm giving the same answer: you'd do anything in the world to get it."

Salvation—you either believe in it or you don't.

He staggered into the house and dug James's .410 from where it lay buried in a chest in the back room. Their mother had hid it from their father years ago, unwilling to allow him to do away with another link to James's past. Roy clutched the gun under his arm and dumped shells from the box, stuffed three in his pocket, a trinity of shells, one for each of them, and walked out. He clapped his numb hands and started for the car.

Halfway down the steps he found himself on all fours, his face inches from the dirty snow. A single band of grass rose tenderly through the ice. He stood and dusted the wet knees of his pants, picked up the shotgun and brushed water and snow from the stock. Never so much as a scratch. Not a broken fingernail. Not a scratch, he thought. Eighty-one sorties and not so much as a broken nail. He walked out into the yard, looking up at the sky.

"Do You think You're the only one to lose a child?" he cried. "Do You think I haven't seen? That I don't know? Answer me, why don't You?"

The sky overcast and mute.

"Answer me, damn you. It's mine, isn't it? Answer me. You think You're the only one?"

Then, somehow, he was behind the wheel, joyous at his luck, at his fate, considering flaps, wind speed, radar position, while around him the snow turned to sleet and the useless sun slid down an indifferent sky. He started the car and tried to warm his hands. When he shifted it into the reverse, the dogs' heads rose briefly then disappeared again. Roy laughed at them, then turned up the road and headed down the mountain on 28.

Then it was like flying all over again. The giving over to instinct, the defiance of gravity, the defiance of death—that message scripted across his heart: I cannot die. He passed the Isaqueena Restaurant and continued on, releasing the steering wheel over to its whims, then finally letting go, reaching out to touch the heater vents. The car streaked left, and he smiled. He had a child. He was so far past panic, so far past fear. He was flying again, tearing through the wooden guardrail. Never so much as a scratch. He was born again and here it was—you either believe in salvation or you don't. Eternal life. Heaven or Hell. Eighty-one sorties. Eighty-fucking-one. And it was like taking a trainer up to eight thousand feet then killing the engine: a controlled stall, then the dive, feathering the engine again, pulling nimbly away from the on-coming earth. Except there was no engine to feather, only a broad sea of green, as green as—as what?—as green as the high-spined mountains of North Vietnam, as green as any dream he had ever dreamt. Eighty-one. I'm not so different, he thought. I want common things. But he would be a father and here was the world for the taking, for his own, for his child's. He would never die now. There were things he was willing to visit upon the self, but he would never die. He started to laugh, pressed back against the seat, laughing again, flying, still holding his hands against the heater vents—never, never would he die—laughing with his hands against the vents while the car plummeted the two hundred feet toward trees as dark as the sea floor.

The dead yellow eye of a flashlight waved them forward, and Enis eased off the brake, slush crunching beneath the tires. The blue light off one of the deputy's cars pulsed over pockets of dirty snow so that they appeared as deep bruises in the soft land. There was a wrecker, the deputy's car, a state highway patrolman, a couple of first responders in pickups. He looked around but couldn't find the high sheriff.

He shifted the car into first, set the parking brake.

"Wait here."

Millie opened her door. Enis looked at her.

"You sure?"

She nodded.

"All right then. All right."

She took his hand. A deputy was hustling over, his Smoky Bear hat covered in plastic.

"Hey, Enis. Millie," he said. "I'm sorry to bring y'all out in this weather. I know this ain't easy."

"Hey, Scruff. The sheriff here?"

"No. Was, though. I reckon he went when the highway patrol showed up."

"Where is it?"

"Over here. Watch your step, too. All this ice."

The deputy led them to the bank where the guardrail hung like a mangled arm. Tracked incisions, marking where the tires had left the asphalt, were skimmed now with muddy ice. The wind came gusting for a moment over the open valley then settled. They could see all of the town spread out before them like a train set, tiny and distant, but clear.

"Right there," said Scruff, pointing down.

The car was almost directly below them, a blue toy nestled in the wreckage of shattered trees. The windshield was spiderwebbed and the tires appeared bent outward. Otherwise it appeared fine. They could just make out the silver duct tape Roy had used to close the gashes in the vinyl top.

"Oh, God," said Millie.

Scruff sucked his teeth. "Reckon this curve's claimed many a Christian," he said. "It's his, ain't it?"

"It's his."

"We all figured as much. Sheriff just wanted to be sure."

Down below, two figures in bright yellow coveralls marked W.F.D. emerged from the underbrush, one carrying an axe, the other a coil of rope.

"He could go like a motherfucker. He could." Scruff looked at him. "I mean that as a compliment, Enis."

"Can we go?"

"Yeah. For sure. And I'm sorry to've had to bring y'all out to see this."

"You're just doing your job," said Enis.

"Yeah. But that don't make none of it no easier."

"No," said Enis. "I don't reckon it does."

Night and they lay in bed, blanket and quilt to their chins, huddled against the cold that came seeping into the room. It was full dark outside, only a candle burning within the bedroom, an orange sputtering light, unfaithful, dimming now and then only to rear back to life, lighting the dark spaces then not, silhouetting boxed shapes crouching like animals. Outside the wind kept howling.

"What about your mamma?" said Millie. "Enis?"

"What?"

"Your mamma?"

"What about her?"

"Will she be all right?"

"I don't know," he said. "She's strong, I reckon. I'm sure she's strong."

She rolled into him, her chest flat against his back, one hand curling over his waist to touch the armoire, its glassy surface. In the corner sat a new chest of drawers, an end table.

"What about us? Will we be all right?" He was quiet. "I want you to say it, Enis. I want to hear the words."

"We'll see it through, Millie. We'll be all right."

The wind kept churning, gusting, fingering its way through cracks in the walls, around the window jambs. They settled deeper in the sheets. Furniture shadows hunkered over them.

"I believe you," she said. "We'll be all right."

"I've got to find James. I know Mamma'll need him there."

"He's not with Eleanor?"

"I don't know. I've got to find him."

They hugged the covers around them. Millie blew out the candle, and a curl of gray smoke swirled where there had once been light. The furniture. It was the first thing he'd done after seeing the car, after hearing that Roy was dead—headed straight for the bank and took out a two-thousand-dollar loan, walked out with the money cold and flat in his palm. Went straight to the furniture store. Fingertips smudged dirty green with the bills. "You're out of your mind." He'd waited for her to say, but she hadn't. Instead she'd followed him, quickened her pace until she was beside him and they were blundering down long rows of varnished wood, man and woman, together. "We'll need a house to go with it," she'd said as they left, the delivery truck pulling out behind them.

"Whatever happens, Enis," she said now. "We're together, and we'll be fine."

"It's just not fair when you're young like us, Millie."

"Life ain't fair."

The wind again. The room quiet, still, reverent as a church.

"Your mamma pieced this quilt, didn't she?"

"I think she meant it for James. If he'd ever had a baby she was gonna give it to him. It's old as the hills. Falling apart."

He fingered the stitching. She hung like moss to his back. The pillow smelled of lavender, the air of wood polish. The dining room set was in the hall, chairs flipped atop the table.

"I hear her up," said Millie. "Should you check on her?"

"It don't matter."

"She might want to talk to you."

"I will. In a minute. Look there."

"What?"

"Look at the wood. Looks like an eye."

His mamma's muffled footsteps on the boards, quaking, tremors like a heartbeat. She must have been stepping around the divan, past the rolltop desk, a maze of hard, solid things.

"Don't make it sad like this. We're together, Enis. We'll pass every bit of this on to our children. We're gonna be all right."

"We'll see it through," he agreed. "Maybe it'll last."

"It doesn't have to be that way. Not maybe. Not sad. This can be that one sure thing you get."

"I know." They lay in silence. "I like the chest of drawers most," he said. "Big solid thing. It's not going anywhere, is it?"

"No," she said. "No, it's not."

"But it scares me some, still."

"Look me in the eye, Enis," she said. She twisted his chin to face her. "Look in me in the eye. We'll live through this. We. Us. You understand me. We will make it."

"I know we will," he said.

"Happily ever after, Enis. I want you to promise me that. Right now. Promise me, Enis."

He did.

Scared her, just for a moment he did. Jeanne Ellcott was in the kitchen when she saw the figure coming up the walk, a gun in the crook of his arm. She was latching the door by the time she realized it was her husband. The high sheriff walked in, propped the .410 in the corner, dropped three shells on the table.

"Oh, God, Bryan. You scared the fool out of me. I thought—Bryan? What's wrong?"

"Where are the girls?"

"They're in living room playing. What's wrong, honey?"

He shook his head. His cheeks were scarlet and tiny capillaries showed along his nose. He wiped at a tear. Judge not—the words running through his head like magnetic tape, like prophecy: Judge not.

"Honey?"

"Nothing. Just . . ."

They walked to the edge of the room and watched the girls playing with Barbie dolls on the floor in front of the fire. Jeanne clenched the neck of her washed-out pink housecoat.

"Honey?"

She held him by his shoulders and began to rub up and down his arms.

"It's just the cold," he said. "It's just so cold outside."

"Well, you're home now. Sit down and warm up. I'll get you something hot to drink. This whole mess going on."

"Thank you. I think the cold must have just got to me for a minute."

"Well, it's all right now. You're home now. Sit down. Forget about everything else, you hear me?"

"I just never knew it was so cold, Jeanne."

"I know, honey. Sit down."

"I'm freezing. I think I'm freezing."

"Hush now. I know. I know. Sit down. You're home now, honey. Nothing can touch you. Don't think about none of that mean old stuff. The cold can't touch you here."

"I just—"

"Hush now. You're home. It's all right."

And the words rattling through him like a prayer:

judge not judge not judge not

Three days later the snow melted and an elaborate system of pulleys raised Roy Burden's '65 Fastback from the ravine below Deadman's Curve, all of which conspired to delay the funeral of William Jennings Burden. He was buried on the Sabbath, across the road from the Mountain Rest Wesleyan Church where he had once ministered, beneath the shade of a leaning poplar, in the small fenced cemetery that sat along the crown of a cow field.

Maddy Burden sat on the front row, dressed in black, a thin veil obscuring her face. Beside her sat her son Enis and his new wife, Millie. The preacher spoke of walking with the Father, of keeping the faith, of finishing the race; he began to read the ninetieth Psalm, and there was not a flower, cut or dried, in the church, not a single one. Maddy had asked Millie to make certain.

The days of our years are three-score and ten years. . . .

Enis had spent the day before hiking up and down the banks of the Chauga looking for James but had come back near dark, hands and nose raw from the wind, having found not a soul. "He ain't in there," he told his wife. "It's all dead in there." But at least the .410 was back in the chest. Sheriff Ellcott had brought it over that morning.

"Please don't say nothing to Mamma about it," Enis had said. "I don't know what he was intending."

"You know I wouldn't," said the sheriff.

Millie took Enis's left hand in both of hers. He hadn't been able to find Eleanor or James but would be going back into the woods after the service, if only for his mother's sake. Now, he watched her. Maddy Burden sat stiff, her eyes narrow and suddenly gray, a certain clarity having seeped into them.

. . . and if by reason of strength they be fourscore years. . . .

They walked out into the December drizzle. Across the road rose the hump of gated land around which grazed cattle, dumb and staggering, oblivious to the rain, oblivious to the cycle of seasons, to the ebb and flow of life, chewing cud among the faceless headstones. They walked through wet, brittle grass that folded beneath their step, up to the grave that was a deep clay wound in the soft earth, steaming beneath a green tarp strung over four metal poles. Twin backhoe tracks angled from it toward the road. Near it was a second hole, where tomorrow Roy would be laid. Someone from the VFW would give Maddy a flag with a field of stars, stripes of unfathomable white, red redder than any blood shed by man or God. They would pass over the flag and lay him there.

They will beat the water from our lungs, but let us know You still. Remember us, dear Lord.

Beside Will's grave was untrammeled grass, where someday she would lie. The tasseled fringes of the tarp whipped, then settled, whipped again. The grass bent. In the bare arms of a locust tree three crows sat silent, indifferent, with heads low and wings wound tight as secrets. She thought of absence, the weight of steps untaken, of empty shadows. I'll never find a colder place, thought Maddy. I'll never find a colder place than here. But when the first shovel of dirt sounded dully against the metal of the coffin, she felt better. She looked at Enis and Millie hand in hand, Enis crying, clinging to his wife. She felt better. The dirt fell, and she felt settled in an odd way. She touched a tear from one eye, looked up from the grave to the grass that shimmered like a promise. And though she couldn't see the distant shore, she knew it was there. *Remember us*—the words falling off her tongue, for she knew the truth: what will be will be. Pray, she thought, and remembered then words from long ago, Will it was, surely it was Will: On Sabbath morning—Oh! she remembered it now, she remembered and knew—on Sabbath morning, he had told her, there is faith enough to turn one's back on the world. There is faith enough to go on.

Acknowledgments

I would like to thank the following for their support and encouragement: Craig Brandhorst, who once, because I asked him, read a draft of this book in a day; Michael Collier, Jay Parini, and everyone at the Breadloaf Writers' Conference; Pete Duval, for the friendship, advice, and support; Brian Griffin, and everyone at the Knoxville Writers' Guild; Tracy Haisley, for the friendship and trips to the lake; Perry Horton, and everyone at *Ellipsis*; Silas House, and everyone at the Appalachian Writers' Workshop, for the hospitality and understanding; Bill Koon, and Peter Mailloux, for the unfailing support, professional and otherwise; Ron Rash, for the example, to say nothing of the friendship; Evelyn Rogers, for reading this book when it was unreadable; the SC Arts Council and the *Post & Courier*, and Kit Ward, who never gave up on me.

Enis's memories of Vietnam are indebted to Michael Herr's *Dispatches*.

Thanks to my wife, Denise, always my first reader, and to all my family. Everything I write is the result of growing up on porch time.

This book could not have been written without the generous support of the National Endowment for the Arts.

Blood Kin was designed and typeset on a Macintosh computer system using QuarkXPress software.
The body text is set in 10/13.5 Bembo and display type is set in Bembo Bold. This book was designed
and typeset by Kelly Gray and manufactured by Thomson-Shore, Inc.